Angel's fall

JA Huss
Johnathan McClain

Julie & Johnathan

HussMcClain.com

ISBN: 978-1-944475-42-0

This is a work of fiction. Names, characters, businesses, places, events and incidents are either the products of the authors' imaginations or used in a fictitious manner. Any resemblance to actual persons, living or dead, or actual events is purely coincidental.

Edited by RJ Locksley
Cover Design by JA Huss

ANGELS FALL

CHAPTER ONE

NINE YEARS AGO

The call ends and I just stare at the phone for a few seconds, lost in the news. The party going on around me disappears as I retreat into my thoughts, seeking solitude to process.

"Hey," Scotty says, coming into the kitchen with a few empty plates. He stacks them in the sink while I remain quiet, then looks at me with a funny grin. "Why so down, Red?"

I smile back. Because he's so… Scotty. Smiling is his default setting. "I had a birthday present for you," I say. "But looks like it's not gonna happen."

He comes over, pulls me into one of his warm big-brother hugs, and kisses me on the head. "I got everything I need from you today, Maddie."

I let out a small laugh. "I didn't even give you anything."

He leans back, but doesn't release me from his hug. "*You're* here, right?"

I roll my eyes.

"That's all I need."

"Yeah." I sigh. Because I feel the same way about him when it's my birthday. As long as he's there that day, I don't need a present. "But… it was Tyler."

"Oh," he says. Then he pokes me in the ribs, which is my most sensitive tickle spot, and that makes me double over laughing. "Sneaky Pete. Good one, though. What happened?"

I wriggle out of his grip. "Flight got messed up. He just called," I say, waving my phone at him.

"Well, that's how it goes in the military, right? They tell you what to do and where to go. Maybe next time, eh?"

"Sure," I say, not feeling it. "Yeah. Maybe next time."

"Jeez, sis. You look like someone killed your kitten. We'll see him again."

I nod, inhaling a deep breath of air, then letting it out, saying, "I know."

Scotty leans down into my face to get a better look at me. "Yeah. So… Is something else going on?"

"Like what?" I ask. Probably too quickly.

"I dunno. You tell me. But you look pretty upset."

I feel pretty upset too. But I'm not sure why, exactly. I was really looking forward to this surprise. And not just because of Scotty. I mean, I want to make him happy and seeing Tyler again would turn his twenty-first birthday into something really spectacular. But… *I* was looking forward to Tyler. He's been gone for three years. And I just… miss him.

He was a fixture at our house ever since his mom died. Practically one of the family. I hated him when I was smaller. He was forever teasing me about my hair. Or making comments about how much I liked to read. Or playing jokes on me in front of my friends.

He was a jerk.

And then that last day, right before he went off to basic, he came over from next door to say goodbye, and I stayed in my room and refused to come out. I was so sad that day. It made no sense, but every time I thought of him leaving to join the military, tears would well up in my eyes and my throat would get all tight and…

He opened my door and said, "Yo. Gotta go now, Mads." A nickname he called me for as long as I could remember because I have the proverbial fiery redhead temperament. A nickname I hated. Until I didn't. "You planning on saying goodbye?"

I just shrugged.

"Okay, firecracker. I'll see you when I see you then." And he shot me one of those lopsided grins and then gave me a salute as he closed the door.

"Tyler!" I called.

He opened it back up again. "Yeeesss?" he said, still smiling. Like he knew I wouldn't let him go off to war without saying goodbye.

But I had no intention of saying goodbye. I whispered, "Please come back."

His face went serious. Instantly. And then he pressed his lips together, swallowed hard, and nodded his head. "Promise, Mads. I'll always come back. And if you ever need me, I'm there, OK? You just call and I'll be there. K?"

I nodded, reluctantly. He gave me a kiss on my forehead, winked at me, and then… he was just gone.

Evan comes into the kitchen, bringing me back into the present with him. "Yo," he says, making Scotty forget we're in the middle of a conversation. "Are we gonna hit the strip club or what? If we have to do this, let's get it over with. Maybe I can meet some confused and lonely traveling salesman or something." He claps Scotty on the arm, and Scotty turns to me.

"We're gonna go," he says. "Hey, look at me. I love you. Don't worry about Tyler. He's an idiot." And he smiles that smile that always disarms me. Except this time.

I give him my best non-forced/forced smile and nod. And he gives me a hug and takes off.

"Tyler shouldn't make promises he can't keep," I whisper as Scotty goes.

But Scotty misses it. He's already over by Evan with his back to me. Already thinking about the night ahead of him.

Already gone. I just didn't realize it yet.

PRESENT DAY

"Do you know what I do with girls like you, Madison?"

I roll my eyes at Carlos' rhetorical question. We've been driving forever. I'm getting the feeling he's not gonna kill me. He's got other things in mind.

He can't see my reaction. I've had my forehead pressed up against the rear passenger window ever since we left Vegas.

"People who cheat me out of money, promise to pay me back, and then go back on their promises?"

I never promised him anything. I've told him all along that it's not my fault. And besides, I'm not the one who breaks promises. I'm not the one who leaves for basic training and never comes back. I'm not the one who fucking refuses to pick up the goddamned phone when someone dies. Or come home for the funeral. Or fucking... *give a goddamn shit.*

"It's not a rhetorical question," Carlos snaps.

Oh. "Well." I sigh. "I assume you probably kill us."

"Usually," he says. "But I like you, Madison. And that is why you're here. I believe we can come to an... understanding."

Great. So it's probably gonna be torture or rape. Or something equally cool, like sex slavery. I can't wait.

The car slows and we turn into a long driveway that leads up to a sprawling Mediterranean-style mansion. I try not to look interested, but I can't help it. I'm at Carlos Castillo's compound. And even though I should be more afraid than curious, I just can't muster up the proper level of fear.

Not after what happened last night. After... *Tyler.*

Why did it have to be him?

I mean... I liked the guy. Ford the lumberjack, that is. Not Tyler the abandoner. I liked that Ford persona. I liked that he never asked too many questions, and he knew just how to fuck me, and he didn't judge me for being a stripper.

I told my *mom* about him. Jesus Christ.

"Madison?" Carlos says.

It's only then that I realize we've stopped and everyone is out of the car except me. The guy who was riding in the passenger seat, that other guy who came with Logan the last time they tried to get me—

When Tyler saved you, my angel says.

When Tyler knocked the guy the fuck out and made everything exponentially worse, my devil corrects.

—is holding my door open and Carlos is extending his hand, like I'm his fucking date or something, and he's gonna help me out of the car.

I don't take it. Just slide out, still wearing my stupid *Reservoir Dogs* t-shirt—Tyler's t-shirt, it even fucking smells like him—and yellow yoga pants that most definitely belong to some long-forgotten slut he once fucked.

"After you, Miss Clayton," Carlos says.

As if, right? As if I have any other option.

I start off, Carlos too close to my ass if you ask me, Logan and Other Guy bringing up the rear. I don't think anyone has a gun out anymore. But we are—literally— in the middle of nowhere. Hell, we might actually be in damn Mexico for all I know. Took us long enough to get here.

When we get to the door it opens from the inside. Servants are all lined up in the grand foyer to greet their master in some bizarre modern-day drug-lord rendition of an English manor house. It occurs to me that I might not've taken him seriously enough. The whole thing feels very Pablo Escobar.

Carlos waves a hand in the servants' general direction, which must be the signal for them to scatter and disappear, because that's exactly what they do. And then he says, "Show Miss Clayton to her room," and walks off with Logan.

Other Guy looks at me, like he's just as unsure about this shit as I am, and then shrugs and says, "*Venga.*"

I follow dutifully, excited about the fact that my destination is a room and not a cell. And we end up in a modest bedroom with an interior door opening to a small en suite bath.

Other Guy says, "*Vuelve más tarde,*" and leaves, locking the door behind him on the outside.

I walk over to the window—which has bars on it, so I guess it's a cell after all—and decide, with a long, tired, sad exhale, that this is not good.

No fucking shit, dummy, my devil says.

It's going to be okay, the angel counters. *If he was going to kill you, he'd have done it already. He wants something.*

Yeah. He wants you to suck his big, fat tamale.

No, Angel counters. *Stay positive, Maddie.*

The power of positive thinking is a myth, Devil says. Y*ou need a plan, bitch.*

Yes, Angel says. *Get to a phone and call Tyler.*

Tyler? Devil snorts. *Fuck that twatbasket. Guy is just a long list of disappointments and no-shows. You play along, Scar. Tell El Chapo what he wants to hear, get the fuck out of Dodge, and then we can devise a plan that doesn't involve Tyler no-show Morgan. Because he's just another mistake waiting to happen.*

I kinda like this devil. He's so goddamned practical. And right. Every single time.

I'm ten paces past exhausted from last night's revelation and the long drive. Not to mention the situation I'm currently in. Whatever the hell that is. So I flop down on the bed and just... rest my eyes.

"Wake up."

I force my eyes open to find Logan peering down at me. For a second I wonder where the hell I am. But only for a second. The whole mess comes rushing back like a brick to the chest. My heart feels heavy and empty at the same time.

Tyler. Morgan.

"Shower, get dressed, and be ready for dinner in an hour. I'll be back to get you." Logan, apparently satisfied that his sentence makes perfect sense to me, leaves, locking the cell door from the outside.

I prop myself up on my elbows and wonder if it's normal for prisoners to fall asleep like I did.

Who cares, Devil says. *Just play along and see where that gets you.*

I*t's gonna get her a ticket straight to the place you come from*, Angel says.

Like chick isn't already on that train, he retorts.

"Fuck you both. And get the hell off my shoulders."

There's a dress on the bed. It's white, low-cut, and looks like it'll barely hit me high-thigh when it's on. And there's a pair of red stilettos that would look right at home on stage at Pete's. "Are you fucking kidding me?"

No way I'm putting this shit on.

But… I feel gross from all the (fabulous) sex last night. Not to mention I'm wearing another woman's pants. So yeah. There's worse things than cleaning up and changing for dinner.

I roll my eyes at myself. Because this is a serious situation right now. I've basically been kidnapped. But the devil's right. I should just play along and see what happens, because I can't see any way around all that's happening, so I decide to just put my head down and drive straight through.

By the time Logan comes to collect me I'm showered, changed, and feeling optimistic. I mean, none of this looks much like any Lifetime movie drug-lord kidnapping I've ever seen.

I follow him down the hallway, back to the foyer and then outside onto an expansive patio. The sun went down hours ago, so the night air is cool and breezy.

"Madison. Please. Sit," Carlos says, motioning to the only empty seat at a small, intimate, patio table. There's a bottle of champagne and bread already waiting "We've got a lot to talk about. And you've got decisions to make, Miss Clayton."

"Just call me Maddie," I say, placing my napkin in my lap and reaching for the bread. I'm fucking starving.

Carlos makes a "very well" gesture with his hands, and pours us each a glass of champagne. Then he sits back, smiles, and says, "So. You owe me—"

"I do not owe you," I say, my take-it-all-in-stride attitude disappearing as I become fed up with this whole stupid situation. "You *hired* me, for fuck's sake. And then I hired people to get you what you wanted. Which was a wedding for your daughter. It's not my fault you guys called off the wedding. In fact, it's completely unreasonable for you to expect me to return that money. I don't have it. Go ask the fucking caterers for it back. Or the goddamned reception hall. Or the fucking florists! They're the ones who have your money."

Carlos cocks his head at me. Sits there silent for a second. "Are you done?"

I snort and drop my bread onto my plate. "Sure. Whatever."

"None of that is the point."

"What the fuck do you mean it's not the point? That's all the fucking points!"

He points his finger at me and says, "Shut up." I recoil. Slightly. But enough to make him smile at my reaction. "You have two options. Are you ready to hear them?"

I blow out a long breath of air. I want to choke this asshole. Reach across the table, wrap my hands around his throat, and choke him until he gasps. But the devil is whispering in my ear. *Play along. Tell him what he wants to hear.* So I dial it back, take a deep breath, and say, "Yes. I'd like to hear my options."

"One," Carlos says. "You can repay what you owe me. Today." He points his finger again, just as I'm opening my mouth to protest, and says, "Shut. Up."

I sit back in my seat, my leg bouncing a mile a minute as my stripper shoe taps out my anxiety on the stone pavers beneath my feet. "What's the other option?"

He smiles. It's not a friendly smile. Not a fatherly smile, either. It's a creepy-as-fuck drug-lord grin that sends chills up my spine. "Stay here with me."

"Stay—" I have to shake my head to try to wrap it around that statement. "Why the hell would I do that?"

"Because… I like you. *Maddie.*"

Uggghh. The way he says my name. I regret telling him to call me that. But Miss Clayton just sounds worse. And Madison sounds like my mom. So I deal.

He stares off into the unknown distance like he's looking at something. "My last wife attempted to leave me five years ago." He stops to frown.

My eyebrows go up. I want to ask what he means by "last wife," I also want to ask what he means by "attempted," but I'm a little sick at the notion that I already know the answer.

"It was a terrible thing what happened to her after she tried to go, and I miss her. I truly do." Yep. I knew it was going to be something like that. He continues, "And since then I haven't found another woman who intrigues me quite the way she did."

Oh, God. Please don't tell me…

"Until you," he finishes. "You must understand… Maddie… people are talking about the stripper who stole one hundred and eighty-five thousand dollars from me. My reputation is being compromised by the notion that I would just allow this to go unaddressed. But they will understand if they see that there is something between us. They will say, 'Ah, Carlos loves this girl. And that's why he let her keep that money.'"

Oh, Christ. He's nuts. Fucking nuts. This argument isn't even lucid.

He's moving his head around in a way that looks like he's trying to seduce me. Either that or he's having a stroke.

I do a quick check-in with the devil on my shoulder, who says, *Shit, kid. I dunno. This is fucking weird.*

"Thanks," I apparently say aloud, because Carlos says, "Thanks? You're agreeing to these terms?"

"No," I say, standing up, realizing now that the only way out of this is by gambling that if he really, really has some kind of fucked-up hallucinogenic feelings for me, I might have one card to play. So I lay it all on the line.

"No. I'm not staying here with you. I don't care if I have to sell my fucking soul to Satan himself. I will pay you back. Because I'm *not* staying here!"

CHAPTER TWO

TYLER

I sort of recognize this place and sort of don't. It looks like the heaven from my DREAM, but it's no longer clean and white. It looks charred, and sooty, and black. I walk along carefully, because I'm not sure what I'm stepping on. I know how it feels to step on the incinerated flesh and bones of the previously living, and the sensation I'm experiencing is very much like that. I don't look down.

No one is around. All the helpful, wingless angels dressed like Apple Store employees are gone. Everyone is gone.

"Angel?" I call out. Nothing.

"Scarlett??" I shout. Silence.

"Maddie!?" I yell. Not even the whistle of wind.

And then… from behind me… I hear her voice.

"Tyler?"

I spin around, tingling with hope and fear, but instead of my angel, Maddie, I find standing in front of me…

James Franco.

A dude who looks EXACTLY like James Franco.

I remember when I was having THE DREAM, I kind of sarcastically mused over the notion that if there was a God inhabiting this particular version of heaven, he would probably look like James Franco. Well, shit.

"'Sup, bro?" he says. "Hey, why so slack-jawed, Ty-Bo?"

"I—" I begin stammering. "I didn't—I—Who are you?"

"Bro," he says, "I'm God. Who the fuck you think?"

I feel very confused. "But," I start, "I heard Maddie."

"Oh, yeah," he says, "Nah, bro, that was me. Here, check it. I'll do it again." And then he says, sounding exactly like Maddie, "Tyler? Is that you?" I stare at him, mouth definitely agape. He laughs. "Ha! Look at your face. Oh, man. Classic. Hey, sorry. I was just fucking with you, homey. All good."

He sticks his hand in the air. Palm out.

"What's up, my dude? You gonna leave me hanging?" he says.

I raise my hand slowly and he slaps me five.

"My man!" he says. Then, "Yo, come chill on this, um, I think this used to be a chair or a desk or something. Can't tell. It's all burned the fuck up, but come sit on it with me for a sec, will ya? Need to rap with you about some shit."

He steps over to the burned-up whatever-it-used-to-be and I don't follow right away. I just continue staring. Profoundly disoriented.

"Dude," he says, "Cop a squat. No fuckin' around. Need to chat."

I eye him and amble over carefully. Then I cautiously take a seat on a smoldering lump of ash a few feet away from him.

"OK," he says, "you wanna keep your dist. I get it. If I had managed to burn down fucking HEAVEN, I'd be pretty worried about incurring My wrath too. All good."

"What?" I manage. "What are you talking about? What's going on?"

"Duuude," he sighs out, "you know exactly what's going on. I hooked you up. Like, HOOKED you up. Gave you your dream angel, the salvation to ALL your sins, the key to your redemption, and you just torched that shit like you was making Baked Alaska. You fucked me, bro."

I shake my head trying to make any sense out of what's happening right now. "I don't understand," I say. "Am I dead?"

"You're in *heaven,* Charlie Brown. Albeit a fucked-up heaven that you jacked yourself, but, uh, yeah. Obviously, you're dead, dummy. Duh."

Wow. God's kind of a dick.

"But so look here, cat-daddy. Here's the skinny: You is one stone-cold sinner, my man. You should probably be in hell right now having big dudes dressed like milkmaids shoving cattle prods up your butt—

"Is that what hell is?"

"Maybe? Not sure. Haven't been in a while, but they do some freaky shit down there. But anyway," He continues, "the only reason you're not there is because I've always kind of liked you for some reason. Not sure why. But I have. And so instead of letting you suffer down there for eternity… um, I'm gonna let you suffer here."

"What?" I ask, understandably. "What does that mean?"

"It MEANS, Mocha-Choca-Latte, that you broke it, you bought it. You took all that was good and you fucked it up. So you're gonna help me rebuild it. Plate by plate. Cloud by cloud. Whatever. You have to fix what you fucked." He's now eating an apple. I have no idea where he got the apple. It just kind of appeared. Which should not even enter my consciousness as the weirdest thing about what's happening right now, but it does.

"So— I start.

"OR," He interrupts.

"Or what?"

"OR… you can do something MUCH harder."

Harder than spending eternity in hard labor trying to rebuild heaven? I'm afraid to ask. But I do. "Harder? What's that?"

"Same thing, only you probably gotta confront a less forgiving soul than yours truly. I'm saying there's another way to restore this joint to its previous glory. I can send you back down to earth and you can make right what you did wrong down **there**."

I pause, considering what he's saying.

"You mean with Maddie?"

"No, dude, with Celine Dion. YES, of course with Maddie, you fucktard!"

Seriously. A real dick.

"But… How would I even start? I fucked up so badly that I can't even—"

"Oh, boo-hoo. Shit, man. You are not living up to my expectations at all. Damn, I didn't save you from that explosion and then dump all that fucking money in your lap for nothing. I expected you to do some good shit with it! You really fucked that one up, though, didn't you?"

"You—"

"Of course it was me! You think an asshole like you has something like that happen to them by accident? Wake up, Little Susie!"

He takes a bite of his apple.

I sit there for a beat, dumbfounded and unsure how to respond. So I just say, "Why me?"

"Why you? I dunno. Maybe because with that scraggly hair and beard you're rocking, you ... you know, you ... remind me of someone."

"Jesus?" I ask.

"No, no, don't be stupid. Oh! I know! Brad Pitt in *Legends of the Fall!* That's who it is! Ugh, been driving me crazy. But also… no real reason. Not one you could ever understand, anyway. Sorry, man. I know you probably want a better answer than that, but… Humans are funny, dude. I give you a cerebral cortex and now you're always trying to find the MEANING behind shit. Well, sometimes I just do stuff for no comprehensible rationale at all. But what can I tell you? I work in mysterious ways."

"But—" I start.

"Okay, okay," He cuts me off. "You want a reason, you want a reason, why you? Of all the seven billion dipshits on earth, why you? Well, honestly, dude… it's because despite your best efforts to be an asshole all the time, deep down, you're one of the best people I ever created. You just can't see it."

Even with all the stunning things happening to me right now, this particular comment takes the cake. And then I remember that Evan said the same thing to me just hours before when I was with him before I set paradise on fire.

"That's…" I mumble. "My friend Evan said the same thing earlier."

"Yeah, no shit, Sherlock. Who do you think put it in his head to say it? Fuck, bro, I'm starting to wonder if being dead has fucked with your think-box too much."

He sits there, shaking his head, half smiling at me. There's so much about what's happening that I can't get my brain around that I don't know where to start. So instead, I just say, "Y'know, you swear a lot more than I thought you would."

"Whatever, bro," he says back, "they're just words. I didn't invent 'em. You assholes did. They don't *mean* anything. Unless. You *give* them meaning."

And as I stop to ponder this, he slaps me across the face.

"Yo! Wake up, bitch! There's decisions to be made."

Seriously! A dick!

"So, whatcha say, man? You got two choices. Head back to earth, do right by Maddie Clayton, get her to forgive you for all the fucked-up shit you've done, remind her why she fell in love with you in the first place before you turned into no-show Johnson, and basically Adam-and-Eve paradise back into being—"

"Wait. Whatayou mean Adam-and-Eve paradise back into—?"

"I'm using it as a verb, bro! Like how Adam and Eve ruined the Garden of Eden with their Original Sin and all that shit? YOU and MADDIE can reverse that through the power of your eternal connection. You can make a heaven-on-earth for yourselves. Or whatever. I dunno. The whole Adam and Eve story is actually bullshit. If they had really been around back then, dinosaurs woulda eaten 'em for fuckin' lunch, but I'm trying to employ a myth that will make sense to your tiny human brain. Look. Stop complicating the simple. I'm just sayin'… fix what you broke with Maddie, NO MATTER THE COST. Hell, you can fuck like a couple of incarcerated rabbits on conjugal visit day if you want, I don't care—just **make it right**. OR be a huge fuckin' pussy and stay here for eternity helping rebuild this Me-forsaken mess." He gestures to the rubble around us. "Choice seems pretty clear to me."

I shake my head. "This isn't happening. This can't be real."

"What's real, homes? Reality is a construct. It's only real if it feels real to *you*. And what you've done to Maddie sure as shit feels real to her. So… ball's in your court."

I hang my head, ashamed. "I don't know if I can face her again. After what I did. I… I'm not sure I can…"

I sigh. He takes a breath and lifts my bearded chin with his hand.

"Hey. Look at me." I meet his eyes, reluctantly. They're kind. He smiles a tiny smile and says, "Not everything is always about you, bro."

I take a beat. I breathe in deeply. Then I nod.

"That's my boy!" He shouts. "Cool. Alright, G, so I'll go ahead and dump you back in your body, and when you wake up, you'll be good as new. Oh. Word of advice: Forget all this has happened and REALLY don't tell people about this. They'll just lock you up in the fuckin' nut house and then you'll just be stuck making baskets and shit all day."

"Don't worry," I tell him, "I'm not saying shit about fuck. I don't need anyone thinking I'm any crazier than they already do."

"My man." He slaps me five, winks, and starts walking off. And as he's heading away into the great expansiveness of forever, I realize I have one last question.

"Hey," I call after him. He stops. Turns. "...Why do you look like James Franco?"

He gets a small little smile and says, "...Dunno. That's you, man. People see me how they wanna. Honestly? I've got no idea what I look like. No mirrors at my place."

And then he's gone.

"Clear!" Evan's voice shouts. And then it feels as though a bolt of electricity is being shot through my body. Because it is.

"Clear!" he shouts again. Again, another shot of current surges through me and I startle into alertness.

Lights. Flashing, spinning lights. The lights of Vegas. The spinning, pulsing lights of the Strip. And also police cars, and ambulances, and a fire engine decked out like a hearse. I considered earlier tonight when I was at the Halloween charity thing at the firehouse that if they had to go on a call with the engine looking that way it would be disconcerting to whoever it was coming for. Now that it's come for me, I actually find it pretty funny. So I start laughing.

"Oh, Jesus," Evan says, "Jesus Christ. He's back!" he shouts.

"Hey, dude," I manage to mutter. He leans down close to me so I can hear him over the din and commotion around me. As I look up, I see smoke billowing out into the sky from my swanky penthouse apartment. Oh. That's right. I set my apartment on fire. Wow. You don't hear someone say that every day.

"Dude," Evan whispers. He's traded his *Great Gatsby* Halloween tuxedo for his fireman's gear. I'm glad. If he came to save me while wearing a tuxedo, that'd be weird.

"Dude," he continues, "are you okay? What the fuck happened up there?"

"What did it look like?" I croak out.

"Bro, it looked like you started a bonfire with all your shit in the middle of the living room and it got out of control, like real fast."

"Yeah," I muster up, "that's about right."

"Dude—" he begins.

"Maddie," I interrupt.

"What?"

"Maddie," I say again.

"Maddie?" he asks. "What're you—? Maddie… Maddie ... Maddie ... Clayton?"

I nod. I can't see all that clearly just at present, but I can see enough to note the worried expression that lights his face.

"What about her?" he asks.

"The stripper. The angel. Scarlett," I say.

"Yeah?" he half-says, half-asks.

I don't say anything. Just letting him work it out. The realization washes over him like watching the sun rise. It creeps up slowly and then it's just there, all at once.

"Oh, my fucking shit," he says. "Did you guys…?"

I nod.

"Oh, my shitting fuck," comes bumbling out. "I—" he says, "I don't even—"

Just then, Rod, the South Boston transplant who works in Evan's station house, comes over. "Jesus, Tyler," he says, "you're one strong son of a bitch. Bear was sure we lost you up there, but I said, 'It'll take a lot more than a little smoke inhalation to kill Tyler fuckin' Morgan!'"

Bear, the company officer, approaches next. "Nice, Rod, that's a solid bedside manner you got there."

"Fuck did I say?" grouses Rod.

Bear leans into Evan and says something, but I can't hear what. Evan nods. He looks back down to me. "Okay, brother," he says. "We're gonna get you to Sunrise and get you checked in."

"I'm fine," I say, as I start to get up. "I gotta find Maddie, she—"

Evan gently pushes me back down. Whispers down to me. "You flat-lined for almost three minutes, T. We need to check you in. Please, brother. Come on. There's time."

I look into Evan's eyes and see something there. Normally his darkened gaze prevents any insight into his emotions, but what I see now is fear. And love.

Fuck, man. Damn.

So I nod, and lie back again. Which is probably for the best because I feel like I've been run over by a rhino stampede. Not that I ever have been, but I imagine it feels shitty and surreal. And so does this.

The only thing I know for sure is that Maddie Clayton left my apartment earlier tonight and went off into the streets with a fuck-ton of unfinished business between us. And what I have to do now is correct my mistakes. Be absolved of my sins. By her.

I owe Maddie Clayton. And whatever I have to do to, whatever price I have to pay, mountain I have to climb, or dragon I have to slay to show her that I am worthy of having this chance to make it right between us, bet your fucking ass that I will do all that it takes and then some.

Swear to fucking James Franco.

CHAPTER THREE

Carlos just stares at me with an expression that says, *I'm being very patient right now, but don't push it, bitch.* "Maddie—"

"Listen, I'm sorry. I didn't mean to—Look, I'll pay you back. Every fucking cent. I just—I can't stay here and—"

He looks like he might just choke me right now.

Beg for your life, says the devil.

What? Angel says. *That doesn't sound like you.*

Fuck it, says the devil. *Alive and embarrassed or dead and dead.*

Devil's a pragmatist.

"Please," I say. And then I get on my knees and look up at him. Ugh. This fucking sucks. "Please, Carlos. I'm sorry. Please just give me the chance to pay you back and make it right."

I should see if any of the shows in Vegas need a bitch who can cry on cue because right now, I'm Meryl fucking Streep.

He looks at me dubiously, but clearly it's working a little, and finally he says, "You've got two weeks."

"Two weeks?" I stand back up. "You know I can't come up with a hundred and eighty-five thousand dollars in two weeks! That's not even reasonable!" Oops. Oh, well. It was an honest reaction.

He smiles at me. A nauseating, sick smile that turns my stomach. "Your parents could get that money together."

How the fuck does he know anything about my parents? Shit.

"I—I can't. They don't have any money."

"Maddie," he drawls, slowly, "I'm being more gracious than you have any right for me to be. Do not insult me."

"I can't," I say. "I can't ask my parents to pay off a debt I don't even—" The look he shoots me stops my sentence there.

I start pacing back and forth in front of the table. My red stripper shoe gets stuck in a crack between the pavers and I have this stupid, embarrassing moment when I almost fall. But then Other Guy catches me with a hard grip on my arm.

Carlos is still looking annoyingly patient when I shrug off his thug and finally get myself together. "Fine. Don't ask them. I will get what I want one way or another. But I cannot even imagine the pain they would feel at losing another child. The way they lost poor Scotty was terrible enough. The things that could happen to you…"

He sucks in air through his teeth and I almost pass out thinking about everything that's wrapped up in those four sentences.

Focus, Devil says. *Calm down, tell him what he wants to hear, and focus on negotiating.*

Fuck. What the hell would I ever do without the devil to guide me?

I sit. I take deep breaths. I study Carlos as he sits there and looks smug and satisfied. I cross my legs, fold my hands in my lap, and say, "Look. I'll pay you back, OK? I promise. But I can't do it in two weeks. Just give me time."

"How much time?" Carlos asks.

Start high, Devil says. *You can always go down.*

"Six months?" I say.

Carlos laughs. "Three weeks."

Don't panic, Devil says in my ear. *Just renegotiate.*

"Three months," I say.

"One month."

"Two months," I say. "Come on, Carlos! Please! You know that's fair!"

It's never gonna happen, but two months is enough time to come up with a plan. Like hire a hit man to take him out, or something.

Now you're thinking like a sinner! I mean a winner! Devil says. Smartass.

"Six weeks," Carlos says. And then he pounds his fist on the table and makes all the silverware jump. "That's it! Six weeks. And if you don't have it…" He stands, comes over to me, takes my hand, lifts me up from my chair, presses himself close to me, placing his hand on the inside of my thigh, shoving his fucking face into my hair and smelling it, whispering into my ear, "Well, you should just feel very lucky that I have a soft spot for you, Madison Clayton." Then he takes my hand and shoves it onto his crotch. He has an erection. "But that soft spot is not here." He presses my hand hard into the fabric of his trousers so I can feel the outline of his dirty fucking dick and I grimace.

Then he pushes me away, snaps his fingers and says, "Take her home."

And then Other Guy grabs me by my arm, this time not being careful with me, and drags me back into the house and straight out the other side into the courtyard where the car is parked.

"*Vamonos. Entra,*" he says, pointing to the passenger seat.

I get in. And in doing so, I just… give up. What's the fucking point?

"*Ponte el cinturón,*" he says.

I put the stupid seat belt on while he closes my door and walks around to the driver's side to get in. "My life would get exponentially better if you killed me in a car crash on the way home, ya know."

Other Guy laughs and says, "*Te rindes demasiado fácil,*" as he starts the car.

"Fuck you!" I answer back. "I try harder than anyone!"

"*No,*" he says. "*Solo prueba hasta que falles. Entonces te rindes.*"

"Dude, you don't even know me. And you're one to talk, anyway. You work for that asshole."

"*Sí, pero… tengo planes.*"

Hmmm. "What kind of plans?" I ask as we pull through the gate that surrounds the Castillo compound.

"*Solo soy un tipo que tuvo la oportunidad una vez. Vendiendo tequilla…*" He goes on in Spanish like that for a while.

I wait 'til he's done and then say, "Tequila sales, huh? Where was that?"

"*Acapulco.*"

"Is that where your family is?" I ask.

"*Sí. Y volveré pronto para conseguirlos.*"

"Get them and go where?"

He shrugs. "*No lo se.*"

"Well, that's kind of a stupid plan if you ask me."

"*No lo hice.*"

I don't respond right away. This guy is hallucinating if he thinks he's just gonna hang out with Carlos Castillo as his henchman for a while, make some money, and then take off and go back to his family. "Sorry, buddy, but you're in the same spot as me. Stuck."

Other Guy shrugs, then turns his head to look at me and says, "Maybe. But at least I keep my cool and do what I'm told until I have better options. You just lose your temper every chance you get."

His perfect American English surprises me. And his opinion pisses me off. "Like I said," I say, crossing my arms. "You don't even know me."

"You're wearing a sexy white dress and red stripper shoes, Maddie Clayton. I know *everything* about you."

I laugh. Hell, he laughs too. Because that's the line Tyler used on Logan right before he clocked Other Guy in the jaw and knocked him out.

"Did you know that guy?" he asks. "The one who hit me?"

"Yeah." I sigh. "I know him."

"He's your boyfriend?"

"No." I huff. "Fuck no. If there's one person I hate more than Carlos, it's that douchebag."

"Hmmm."

"What's that mean?" I ask.

"I dunno. He seemed to like you a lot. Seems like a good guy to have on your side. I don't remember the last time anyone was able to knock me out like that. Just saying."

"Fuck that. I don't need him. He's not dependable, anyway. Fucker comes and goes. Never shows up when I need him."

"He showed that night."

"Yeah, but he didn't know it was me."

Other Guy gives me a weird look. "What?"

"He was my brother's best friend." And then I let out another sigh, but this time it's sad. "Back when I had a brother, that is. And when he died, Tyler couldn't even bother to show for the funeral."

"Oh, well, that sucks. Was he out of town?"

"Well, yeah. Sorta. He was deployed somewhere. In the military."

"...Okay. So, he couldn't come. But you hold it against him?"

"I already have a therapist, man," I snap. Which is a lie. Because Plumeria Brown can kiss my ass. "I don't need your armchair psychology bullshit. OK? The fact is, he never showed. And I called him, and sent him letters, and the last letter was like… a desperate plea for help. And he just fucking sent it back!"

I kinda yell that last part. Other Guy actually jumps in his seat, sorta surprised at my anger. Then he points to me and says, "*Ese es tu problema. Tienes mal genio.*"

"I do not have a fucking temper!"

He's quiet for a long time after that. So I just curl up against the door, press my head against the window, and close my eyes.

"Where do you want to be dropped off?"

I pull myself fully awake at his question. The fucking Nevada sun is coming up and I'm all sweaty as I squint out the window and try to figure out where I am.

Vegas. We're back in Vegas.

"Why the fuck didn't we just fly? Doesn't Carlos Castillo own a plane?" I ask.

"He's afraid of flying," my new driver/counselor/bff says.

"Classic," I mutter under my breath. Carlos is actually crazy. Fab.

"Where to?" he asks again. "*Tu casa*?"

"No," I say. "I need to get my car. If it's still there at all. And I gotta figure this shit out. I don't fucking—Shit. Just drop me off at Pete's."

We fight the morning traffic near the Strip and then Other Guy pulls into the alley behind Pete's and stops the car. Pretty much exactly where they picked me up… two days ago? Jesus. Christ. My roommates are gonna be wild with worry.

I look over at my driver and say, "You got a name? So I can stop calling you 'Other Guy' in my head?"

He smiles. He's a couple years older than me, I decide. Nice-looking guy if you like that thug look. And then he reaches for his wallet in his back pocket, pulls out a business card, and hands it to me.

It says, *Ricardo Ramirez. Vendedor, Castillo Tequila, Acapulco División.* With a Mexican phone number underneath his title.

"That's me," he says. "Call me Ricky."

"OK. *Ricky*." I smile, because that's how you be friendly, and then say, "Thank you," because that's how you be nice.

He says, "*De nada*. Now go show your tits and make lots of money. Because you only have six weeks to figure this out. And if I have to kill you when your time's up, it'll bum me out. You remind me of a girl I used to date." He winks.

I get out of the car and slam the door. Asshole.

I'm walking to the back door of Pete's, just about to pull it open, when the horn honks and makes me jump. I look over my shoulder and see Ricky leaning over into the passenger seat with the window down. "Don't let pride get you killed, Maddie," he yells.

"Fuck off," I mutter. then go inside.

I decide pretty much immediately that Pete's is even more depressing in the daytime than it is at night. There's like five customers, two waitresses who look bored out of their minds, a bartender who's sitting on a stool drinking coffee as he watches the morning news, and a girl on stage who swings around the pole like she's planning her grocery list.

Pete's. My last resort. Shit. But I can make money here. I know I can. I was doing so well a few weeks ago.

Before Tyler came into your life, Devil says.

"Please stop talking." I sigh, exhausted.

Anyway, I'm never seeing him again, so my luck should get better immediately.

I take a deep breath and resign myself to doing what needs to be done as I walk up the stairs to Pete's office and knock on the door.

"Come," he calls.

I open the door and find him hunched over his desk, furiously typing on his computer. "What?" he says. Like I'm annoying him.

"Um, Pete?" I say. "It's me, Scarlett. I need to ask—" But he whirls around in his chair and lowers his glasses so quickly, I stop.

"Scarlett," he says.

Pete isn't scary. Like at all. He's more like your favorite grandfather with a little weird uncle mixed in. He's got a white beard and bushy white eyebrows and I bet he'd make an awesome Santa. If that wasn't creepy as fuck, which it is.

He lets out a long sigh when I stay quiet and fidget under his intense gaze. "I already know."

"Know what?" I ask, looking down at my feet, suddenly aware that I'm dressed up like a whore.

"Carlos Castillo?" Off my surprised expression he says, "Raven told me. I'm amazed to see you standing and walking and breathing. What are you into, kid?"

"I'm just… I'm a little strapped for money these days and—"

"You owe Carlos Castillo money?" Pete asks.

I shrug. I mean, the answer of course is no. But… "Yeah," I say instead. "It's a long, stupid story. So I just wanted to know if I could work here during the week too. To try to get back on track."

He crosses his arms over his barrel chest and looks down, apparently thinking about this. "You ever think of doing some multi-level marketing?"

"What?"

"You know, sell leggings. Or that stupid lipstick everyone talks about online. The plumper kind?"

I squint my eyes at him. How does he know about that stuff? I guess he owns a strip club though, so I shouldn't be that shocked. "Um… no," I tell him. Which is a lie. I did that already and it was a giant waste of time and money. According to my pyramid-scheme boss, I'm not "friendly enough" to sell makeup. "Please, Pete. I just need a few more nights, ya know? I've got a little following here." Another lie. Tyler was my only fan. Tyler. Who I fucked. Tyler. Who thinks he's fallen in love with me, even though that's insane. Tyler. Who I've known my whole life. And who is evidently richer than Croesus now. No. No. Fuck that. I'll work here twenty-four seven before I take that asshole's money.

Pete sighs long and loud. "Well, the nights are pretty full. We've got some celebrity porn stars doing sets through the holidays and I can't screw with that. You can do mornings."

I unconsciously look over my shoulder, thinking about how dead it is out there.

"No," Pete says. "It doesn't get any better. You won't make much, but girls are always coming and going. And I like you. You're smart. And you don't come in wasted from the night before. So tell ya what. Do mornings for now. I'm tossing Charlotte," he says, nodding toward the door, "she's lost her enthusiasm. And then I'll see what I can do about juggling some things around to get you some evening work. Okay?"

Mornings. Stripping at Pete's.

I have turned into a Las Vegas cliché.

"Sure," I say, feeling sick, but swallowing it down. "I can do that. Thanks, Pete."

"Tomorrow then," he says. "Be here at seven."

"Seven? AM?"

He shrugs. "We got a breakfast crowd. It's only like a dozen people, tops. But this city never sleeps, remember. And neither do we. Well, we do, from five to seven for cleaning, but then we're back at it. Remember, seven in the morning is some guy's seven at night."

"Okay," I say, resigned to my fate. "I'll be here."

He nods, and I take that as my cue to leave. But just as I turn to walk out, he says, "Hey, Maddie?"

Just hearing my actual name in this place makes it all real. "What?" I answer, my focus on getting the hell out of this office as quick as possible.

"Be careful."

No shit. "Yeah," I say. "I'll figure it out." And then I leave and pull his door closed behind me so he can't say anything else.

It hits me then—I have no car. And I mean that literally because I'm pretty sure it got stolen the other night along with my purse.

So I go to the bartender—I've met him a few times when the regular weekend guy had the night off—and say, "Can you call me a cab?"

"Sure," he says.

"And can I borrow a hundred bucks to pay for it?"

He laughs. "What the fuck?"

"My purse got stolen," I say, confident that's not a lie, but not really caring much. "I'll pay you back tomorrow. I'm the new morning girl," I say, nodding up at Charlotte, who is just kinda leaning against the pole on stage, like she forgot where she was.

It takes a few more promises to get that money, but I do get it. And then I go outside and wait in the glaring sun for the cab. Feeling dirty. Like I lost my soul this morning. Like I might never find it again, even if I do manage to drag myself up out of this hole I'm still digging.

And then… everything hits me. Tyler. Halloween. Scotty. That last letter I sent, practically begging him to answer me. And how he broke my heart when he sent it back unopened with that message.

"Please stop sending me letters." I say it out loud, just to keep it fresh. Just to keep the memory of us the other night where it's supposed to be. Tucked away in a mental box that says do not open.

Do not talk to him. Do not trust him. Do not fall for him. Do not ever let that man back into your life.

But the tears come anyway. Because there was a time when I loved Tyler Morgan. When I thought he was the only person who could ever make things right again.

And that last night we were together… I felt that again. I felt that connection I once had with him. Before Scotty died. Before he took off and never came back. Before he started making promises he never intended to keep.

And yeah, it was a stupid childhood crush on my brother's best friend. But… I loved him once.

I won't make that mistake again.

When I get home the girls are all awake, looking red-eyed and beat. Annie spends ten minutes asking me, "What the fuck? Just what the fuck?" because apparently I've been gone for almost three days.

But I'm too sad, and defeated, and ashamed of what I've become to even bother listening.

So I offer them a teary shrug and walk away. Lock myself in my room. Fall onto my bed. And cry myself to sleep.

CHAPTER FOUR

TYLER

"No, I feel great! Why?" That's me, answering Dr. Eldridge, my shrink, who just asked, "Are you nervous?"

We're sitting by the pool at Evan and Robert's house. Normally I go see Dr. Eldridge at her place, but Evan's been hovering over me like a watchful mother hen since I got out of the hospital a couple of nights ago. He's making me stay with him and Robert for now. Making me. That sounds so... Nobody makes Tyler Morgan do shit Tyler Morgan don't wanna do!

But... I do need a place to stay while they repair my apartment, which is gonna take a while, and Evan's all worried that I'm gonna do something else "bat-the-fuck-shit-crazy," as he called it. So...

(I'm still not a hundred percent sure that the Mandarin Oriental isn't going to try to bring arson charges against me. Evan kinda managed to... tweak... the fire inspector's official report, and I did offer to pay for the damages out of pocket so we don't have to fuck around with the insurance company, but the management people at the corporate office I talked with were real bitches about it. People can be such fucking babies.)

So anyway. Dr. Eldridge agreed to come see me here at Evan and Robert's because Robert asked her to, and he's super-charming and shit. But right now, I just want to get this little session with the good doctor over with. I've got some serious amends-making to get to. So when she asks, "Are you nervous?" I do my best to put on a face that lets her know I'm not.

"No, I feel great! Why?"

"Because," she says, "your knee has been bouncing for the whole session and I'm worried that you're going to start biting your fingertip off. The nail seems just about gone."

I take my hand with its now-bloody fingertip from where I've been chewing and place it on my jackhammering knee to make it stop jouncing.

"Nope. I'm gooood," I say, super smooth and convincing.

"Are you still feeling suicidal?"

"What?" I'm honestly shocked by this. "I've never felt suicidal. What makes you think I feel suicidal?"

"You told me that you set your home on fire so that everyone on the Strip could watch you burn, you told me that you pressed your head into the barrel of a gun in a back alley and told the gunman to shoot you, and you told me that you've been having a recurring dream that you're dead and that it gives you pleasure. So. Y'know. I'm just spitballing."

She's so cool. She's like the coolest sixty-year-old lady I've ever met. But I still need to get this fucking "talk session" over with so I can make moves.

"Okay, first of all," I start, "the fire thing… like I told you, that was a thought I had, yes, but I didn't think I was gonna *DO* it. I don't even remember starting it. I looked down and it was just going. I might have blacked out or something."

"Oh. Okay. Well then, no problem." She says it with a smile.

"That didn't come out… Look." I try again. "Yes, I can't deny that things have been a little, uh, out of balance with me. I admit that. But I'm fine. I really am. I think I've just been feeling a little purposeless, but that's all changed."

"What exactly has changed?"

"I told you. The woman that I've fallen in love with is Scotty's little sister. It's Maddie. That's… I mean, what are the odds? And it's incredible because we need each other. We're what the other needs to get whole. I don't know if that makes sense, but I know I'm right."

I'm smiling. She's not. Which bums me out.

"I'm not certain that needing another person to make you whole is the sentiment that gives me the greatest sense of assurance," she says.

"I know, I know. We have to find our whatever within ourselves and blah, blah, blah. I get it. But that's not… Look, all I know is that we have come into each other's lives for a reason."

"Yeah?" she says. "What reason is that?"

"Well… I mean…" I start. But I realize I haven't yet developed a completely cogent rationale for why Maddie and I have tumbled back into each other's lives in such a fucked-up and dramatic way. But then, in a flash, it comes to me.

"Okay! Okay! So… haven't you been telling me, as much as anyone, maybe more than anyone, that there are unresolved wounds I need to heal!?"

"Well, I—" she begins, but I'm on a roll, so I keep going.

"Okay! So then, don't you think that making things right with Maddie goes a long way toward healing some of those wounds? For me AND now for HER?" Bam! Drop the mic! Fuck with that logic, Doc! I'm clever as balls when I need to be. Everybody says so.

She's quiet for a second. The waterfall that cascades into Robert and Evan's pool is the only sound in the desert right now. I'll be honest. I don't hate staying here. It's a sick fucking house. It's actually got me thinking I should buy one like this instead of moving back into the apartment. Might be good to get away from the chaos of the Strip. Quiet in the desert. Too quiet? Would my mind wander? Nah. If I lived in the desert and stuff, I'd probably be inspired to take up meditation and shit. It'd actually probably be the best thing for me. Yeah! This is a great idea! I'm gonna buy a house in the desert! I'll bet Robert can find me a sweet deal. Dude's probably the most powerful land baron in Vegas. Evan totally married the right guy. And—

"Well…"

Oh, shit. That's right. I'm still sitting here with Dr. Eldridge. All good. I bet I'll be super focused after I start meditating.

"I think," she continues, "that… yeah. Finding some way to connect and repair with Maddie Clayton would probably be a very good thing as far as helping you both heal goes."

Oh, snap! I was right!

"I would only caution you to remember that it's a two-way street."

"I know."

"I mean, she has to be ready to let you in."

She was sure as fuck ready to let me in the other night, I joke in my head. Not out loud. Because, you know... inappropriate.

"I know," is the version of the answer I offer aloud.

"Okay," she says, "well, good. And I'm glad to see you seeming physically well."

"Tip-top, Doc. Although I think I may be done with fucking hospitals for the rest of my life. For a thirty-year-old dude, I feel like I've had more than my quota of near-death experiences. See? Not suicidal at all!" I beam at her and tap my head. I just need her to believe me and take off. Because I'm clearly not crazy! It's SO obvious!

"Good enough," she says after a brief pause. "You'll call me if you need anything." She does not offer that as a question.

"Abso-tively," I say. Charming as hell.

She stands, gives me a hug—which is something she's never done before and kind of catches me off guard—and heads in through the open wall (it's like a glass wall that folds out like an accordion, making the pool and living room a total indoor/outdoor space. When I buy my dope new desert house, I want it to have one of those too) where Evan is standing to talk with her. Presumably to get a debrief on the mental health status of one Tyler Hudson Morgan.

I watch them as they talk, Evan nodding and looking over at me, when I hear, "How ARE you feeling?"

Robert Vanderbilt (Nope, not those Vanderbilts. Total coincidence. Even though Robert does look a little like Anderson Cooper. Go figure), Evan's husband and probably the most sophisticated, erudite, smooth-ass, James Bond motherfucker I've ever met is standing behind me, wearing light blue trousers and a white cashmere sweater (again, these are things I would never notice or appreciate without Evan—and even though I notice them, I'm still not sure I appreciate them). He's holding two beers. He hands one to me.

"I'm okay," I say, taking *la cerveza*. I can speak Spanish like a motherfucker. Multitalented. "*Gracias.*" I nod to him and take a swig. Makes me feel like a cowboy.

He sits on one of the pool chairs. He glances in to see Evan. Evan glances back, sees Robert looking at him, and smiles.

"It makes me happy to see Evan so happy," I say to him. I've only known Robert since I moved back to Vegas. They met while I was still out of the country and got married about a year and a half ago while I was traveling in… I wanna say… Thailand? Musta been. Only something as important as Thai prostitutes could've made me miss one of my best friends' weddings.

"Yeah," Robert says, trying to hide a shy smile. "I don't hate him either."

Fuck, I love seeing people who genuinely want to be around each other. Evan jokes all the time about how high-brow Robert is. He likes fine wine and opera and all that shit and Evan is much more a "hang out with the fellas" kind of a guy, but they work. I never really believed much in marriage until I spent some time with (as Evan refers to themselves) Siegfried and Roy. (I don't think Robert likes it much, but it cracks me up.)

"So," I start, trying to make small talk, which I'm shitty at, but feel obligated to make since Robert is letting me stay in his mansion, "how's the real estate game?"

"Not bad," he says. "Okay."

"Just okay?"

"It's fine. I've just got a huge project I'm developing out on the Arizona border, near the Hoover Dam, and—"

"I love the Hoover Dam," I interrupt. "When I was a kid, I used to think that if you ever wanted to kill yourself in a really spectacular way, jumping off the dam would be an amazing way to go."

There is now a, to say the least, awkward silence. It was just a silly thought I had once or twice as a kid after my mom died and shit got really bad with my dad. But I wrote it off to adolescent-drama-brain. Really.

For real.

Anyway.

After a moment, Robert says, "Sure. Yeah, so anyway I've got this massive project out there but it's a huge pain in the ass to survey because of the terrain and coordinating the boots on the ground part of it and… whatever. It'll work itself out. Hey, if it was easy everybody would do it, right?" He winks and takes a sip of his beer. Guy is capital 'b' Businessman to the bone.

I look over and see that Evan is closing the door behind Dr. Eldridge, and that's my cue to take my leave. "OK, man, um, I gotta run out for a bit, so—"

As I'm heading into the indoor portion of the indoor/outdoor space, Evan intercepts.

"Where are you running?" he asks.

"Nowhere, MOM. Jesus."

"Dude," he says, "you flatlined three nights ago. You were DEAD. Three nights ago. You're not just bounding back out into the world to… get into whatever fucking trouble you're planning on getting into."

"I'm not going to go get into trouble," I say with slight indignation.

"You're going to go find Maddie."

"So?" I shoot back. "What's troubling about that? That's not trouble. In fact, Dr. Eldridge says it's a good idea."

"Mm-hmm… Does she, though?" Evan asks with squinty-eyed skepticism, his voice getting weirdly high as he poses the question.

"Evan," Robert chimes in, "he's a grown-up. If he wants to go find Maddie, let him go find Maddie. Stay out of it."

"Easy there, Siegfried," says Evan.

"Don't call me that, please," retorts Robert.

"Roy is the one who got attacked by the tiger. Be glad you're Siegfried," Evan fires back and Robert gives up. Evan turns to me again.

"Okay, fine," he says. "Go. Do whatever you want. But just… just make sure you're taking care. Okay? This is… you're in the middle of an incredibly intense situation. Just take it slow. K?"

"I will," I say. "I will take it slow."

He eyes me with skepticism.

"Promise," I promise.

The speedometer in the Defender says I'm going a hundred and fifty. I could probably push it another thirty miles per hour or so, but I don't wanna be reckless.

I'm racing through the desert to the only place I can think to go. The strip club. The place where I met my angel. My angel who turned out to be called Scarlett. Scarlett who turned out to be Maddie. Maddie who I fucked and when I did caused me to feel safe and happy like I was finally coming home. Because she is. My home. In every way that can be understood.

I know there's like no chance at all that she's at Pete's. Why would she be? Why in the world would she ever go back to that place? It's like returning to the scene of a crime for her, I'll bet. But still. Maybe. Just maybe. And besides, I don't know where else to go.

I push down on the accelerator. I can't get there soon enough. My heart is beating. Fast. Like it's going to pop right out of my body. Like maybe Evan was right and that I should take it easy considering I was just recently dead and all. But I don't give a shit. I'm on a mission.

A mission to heal her. A mission to heal myself. And this time, I'm going to show the fuck up.

CHAPTER FIVE

MADDIE

I come out of sleep feeling like I'm drowning. Like I'm underwater, looking up at bright light, legs and arms flailing, desperate to reach the surface.

Nothing makes sense. Where am I? What's going on? A voice. I hear a voice. A man's voice. Carlos? Logan? Ricky? Are they here to kill me?

I open my eyes, gulping air, and sit straight up.

But it only takes moments—long, weirdly stretched-out moments—for me to understand that I'm at home, in my own bed, and the booming male voice coming from the other side of the house is not Carlos, or Ricky Other Guy, or Logan.

Who the fuck?

Is that—

No.

No, it can't be. He would not do that. He couldn't do that. He has no idea where I live. Unless…

It's getting dark outside. What time is it? What day is it?

I swing my legs over the bed, stand up, trip over the red stripper shoes I kicked off… whenever it was. I manage to catch my fall by grabbing onto the edge of the bed, and then straighten up, walk towards my door, throw it open and stomp down the hall towards the living room ready to find—

"And so I said, 'No! It was the *dog*!'" And three prostitutes bust out laughing.

But this is no fucking joke.

Tyler Morgan is sitting in my goddamn living room, on Annie's goddamn couch, one arm stretched across the back, one foot propped up on a knee, holding a beer in the other hand, yucking it up like he belongs here.

"What the fuck is going on?" That's me. I'm pissed. No, I'm goddamned livid.

"Maddie," Tyler says, setting his beer down, getting to his feet, and kind of opening his arms like he's gonna… what? Hug me? He looks unsure, but steps toward me.

I put up both hands, palms out, and say, as impolitely as I can, "Get the fuck out."

"Um, Maddie?" Annie says. "Your friend Tyler is here."

"Yeah, no fucking shit. And he's not my friend." I can't believe this is happening.

"Oh, well," Caroline starts, "he's, uh, been catching us up on some really funny stories about when you guys were kids." She's holding an empty wine glass, a dopey expression on her face that lets me know she thinks Tyler Morgan is just dreamy.

How long was I asleep? How long has he been here?

"The dog." Annie titters. "Oh, my God. The fucking dog!" I shoot her a look that lets her know none of this is adorable and she wrestles back her smile.

"Who the fuck invited you?" I snarl at Tyler. "And how the hell did you even find out where I live?"

"I stopped by Pete's. Met Pete. Sweet guy, by the way. I would've imagined a strip club owner as being kinda—"

"Pete told you where I live?" Jesus. Thanks, Pete. Fuck.

"No, no, not exactly." Tyler's standing way too close to me now. The girls are pretending not to be able to hear him, but it's clear they're eavesdropping. I hope they're better at fucking guys for money than they are at spying.

Tyler leans in closer still, and I really, really wish he would not do that. Because I hate him and don't want him anywhere near me. Or maybe because I can feel the heat of his body and he kinda smells delicious. Which just pisses me off more because I *hate* him.

He lowers his voice and continues explaining how he found me. "Don't be mad at Pete. He didn't want to tell me where you live. Seems like a really ethical guy."

"Except he *did* tell you where I live."

"Well, yeah, but it cost me five grand." My eyes go wide. "I mean, he's ethical for, y'know, a guy who runs a strip joint."

Nope. This is not going down like this. "Get. Out." I'm pointing at the door now.

"No!" Diane whines. "No, no, no. We're just getting to know him, Maddie! Oh, my God. This guy. Where the hell have you been hiding him all these months?"

"Where have I been *hiding him*?" I see red as I go to him, hands out, and slam them into his chest. The force of my push makes him step back… half a step. Maybe. "I wasn't hiding him anywhere, you traitors! This asshole ducked out on me years ago. And when I needed him, when I was begging him to—" I shake my head to clear my mind. "And then he shows back up and thinks everything's gonna be *fine* just because we fucked a couple of times when I didn't know it was him!"

There's a beat before Annie says, "You fucked him?" with, like, way more excitement in her voice than she should.

"Not the point!" I shout as I slam my hands into his chest again.

But this time, he grabs my wrist and stops me, saying, "Can we please talk?"

I struggle in his grip, but he holds tight. I clench my teeth and spit, "Let *go* of me."

He does. Immediately. Both hands up as if in surrender.

I decide to change my strategy. Because clearly Tyler Morgan is being *Tyler Morgan.* He attracts people to him like a siren song calling sailors to the rocks. He knows how to play up the act he perfected long ago. Seemingly genuine, charismatic, and fascinating as he leads the rest of us to our destruction.

So I pull the friend card out and whirl around to face Annie, Diane, and Caroline. Taking a deep breath, I say, "He's not what you think," in the calmest tone I can muster. My voice is shaky. My hands are trembling with anger. But I hold it together. "He ruined me," I say. "He broke me into tiny pieces, dropped me to the ground, and walked all over me."

Annie just stares at me, confused.

"What do you mean?" Diane asks.

"He left me, Diane. After Scotty died. He left me alone. He never came back. He never even showed up for his funeral. I begged him," I say, starting to cry. "I begged him and he told me to stop. He just went on with his life like nothing happened. Like my brother didn't just die the most horrific death possible. Like what we all meant to each other was meaningless. So I hope one of those stories he told you about our childhood included *that* little fact. And then..." I continue, drawing in a deep breath, willing the strength it takes to get this last part in so I can twist that knife in his chest the way he did mine. "And then he went off and made millions of dollars. Been living it up in a goddamned penthouse, no cares at all. No worries at all. While I've been back here..."

But I lose it there. I can't say the words *selling myself*. Because I'll die right now if I have to say that. I'll die.

There's a filled beat while everyone stares at Tyler, who never breaks eye contact with me. And I really wish he would. Because his eyes are sad and hurt-looking and no fucking way will I fall for that shit. No. Fucking. Way.

Caroline mutters, "He's a millionaire?"

Jesus Christ.

I turn to face Tyler for this last part. Because I'm just about done here. "I was high, Tyler." He squints his eyes at me, puzzled. "High up on Mount fucking Everest. On the tippy top of life. And you were supposed to be there next to me. You promised to be there next to me. And you let me fall down that fucking mountain. You never looked back, you just kept going."

"Maddie—" he says.

But I hush him with a hand as I shake my head so that my tears fall down my cheeks. "No. Just go away. Just go back where you came from and never come back."

I take one more look at my roommates, find them all frowning, and then walk to my room and slam the door.

TYLER

The problem with what Maddie just requested is that I already *am* back where I came from. The whole reason I'm here is so I can try to live out the rest of my probably short life just kind of anonymous and doing as little damage as possible.

Shit.

I turn to face the three women who are staring at me with trapped-in-between-knowing-what-to-do looks on their faces.

"We used to be friends," I smile and say.

"So," the one with the empty wine glass—Caroline, I think—says. "A millionaire?"

"OK!" intervenes the apparent leader of this bunch, whose name I caught earlier as Annie. "So, uh, we've gotta get to work. We'll leave you guys to talk. Or whatever."

I nod. "Yeah. Thanks. Where do you guys work?"

They don't answer right away. They just sort of all look at each other like maybe they forgot what they do for a living.

"On the Strip/WE'RE CALL GIRLS," Annie and Wine Glass Caroline say at the same time.

"Oh," I say, "Well, that's, uh… I've known quite a few call girls in my day. You guys… um"—wow, this is awkward—"look like you're very… good? At your job?"

The looks have now traversed over into a very precise direction. It's the visual equivalent of someone saying, 'Bitch, is you stupid?' (I am, is the answer.)

"OK, well, it was… nice to meet you," says Annie.

"Yeah, and listen, if you ever feel like you just need to talk, or…" begins Wine Glass Caroline before Annie and the other one push her out the door, her going, "What?"

After they're gone, I stand there for a moment, suddenly unsure how to proceed. I know what to do in the abstract, I'm just not sure *how* to go about it. What I need to do is to prostrate myself. Lie at Maddie's feet and beg for her forgiveness. The way she begged for me to come help her when she needed it.

That's what I need to do. But at the same time, I can't. I can't do that. Because I am not all in the wrong. I just can't let myself believe that. I don't have a bunch of ego about apologizing when I know I'm at fault. I'm a super-vulnerable and sensitive motherfucker. Everybody says so.

So I'm not wary of asking for forgiveness to protect my image or any moronic shit like that. I'm wary because an additional truth of this matter is that I was staying away from her to *protect* her. To protect her *from* me. To avoid exactly the kind of something that's happening between us right now.

And, y'know, oh, well, that didn't work out, so now we just kinda have to deal with it. So I think we both have to just sack up and admit that while the way things went was shitty, the past is the past, and living in the past is no fucking good for anybody, and the best thing for us now is to give in to the reality of the present and move forward.

What did James Franco say when I was dead or dreaming or whatever the hell that was? I can make a heaven on earth with Maddie? That seems pretty fucking far away at the moment, but I think there is a shot that I can make her tolerate being next to me for five minutes. And if I can start there, then at least it's something to build on.

I stand in front of the door to her bedroom knowing she's on the other side, hurt, shocked, and pissed. It's just a regular, normal-sized wood door, but right now it might as well be a steel gate that reaches to the sky protecting some forbidden city. So, I calculate what I'm going to do to charm her and win her confidence long enough to get her to listen to me. I can't just barge in like a bull in a china shop, as is my usual wont. I have to be very, very tactical about how I infiltrate the precious lands on the other side of that gate if I hope to have any chance of the queen letting me stake my claim and till the soil so that I can plant my seed.

Hm. I didn't really intend for that imagery to wind up taking me there, but it sure did.

Ha.

That's funny.

MADDIE

I don't know how long I lie there in bed, face buried in my pillow to mop up the tears, but it feels like eternity. It feels like I'm stuck in purgatory. Neither here nor there, just waiting for my sentence to be handed down.

Just go away. Please. Now.

And stay away. Forever.

But no one stuck in purgatory receives peace as a punishment. So the knock on my door and the soft "Maddie?" that comes with it isn't a huge surprise.

I don't answer. I refuse to engage with the devil.

Which makes me huff an ironic breath into my pillow, because I've been engaging with the devil for a while now.

"Mads," he says, the word muffled, like he's pressing his face to my door. "Please? Let me in?"

I say no in my head.

He twists the handle and the door opens.

"Oh, it was unlocked. Look at that. Hi," he says as he enters my space.

Normally, this would be my cue to rage at him. To set him straight. To scream and demand he leave. But that's what he wants. And I'll be damned if Tyler Morgan gets one more thing he wants, just because he thinks he *deserves* it.

Footsteps as he enters. Soft click as the door closes behind him.

"Um... what's up?" he says.

I shake my head. Face still buried. New tears in my eyes as my cheeks press into the wetness of the ones not yet dry.

After a few seconds he says, "Wow. Uh, can we talk about your room for a second?"

"What?" I snap, turning my head so I can open one eye and get a peek at what he's doing.

"It's a mess. Do you need a good housekeeper? Because mine's gonna need a new place to clean while—"

"Get. The fuck. Out."

He lists back and forth like he's unsure which leg he should stand on. Which he should be. Because he doesn't have one. Finally, "Why do you have this?" he asks, picking up the controller for my drone.

"Don't touch that," I say. "It's fucking expensive."

"Yeah, no shit it's expensive," he says. "This is the Raven 900XZ. Military grade. Why the hell do you have a military-grade drone in your bedroom?"

I jump up off the bed, trip over that goddamned stripper shoe—again!—and stumble towards him to rip the controller from his hands. "It's my real-estate drone, asshole. To make property videos. Go away."

"What's this?" he asks. Now he's bending down to pick through a pile of dirty clothes on the floor. And I see that he has found—

"Give me that!" I snatch it from him before he can get a good look and hide it behind my back.

"What is that? Is that a loom?" He laughs a little. Which pisses me off even more.

"Yes. It's a fucking loom. I know how to fly a drone *and* use a loom. Do you? Asshole."

He clamps down on his smile, but it's clear he thinks he's charming me. Which he is not. Not at. All. Not one little bit. OK. Maybe a *little* bit, but not enough to make me forget that he's the source of all my misery.

"It's kinda tiny," he says. "Just, y'know, as looms go. Like, what kind of things do you weave with a minuscule, plastic loom?" The smile is back.

"I make potholders, OK? It's a mindless task that relaxes me."

"Potholders…" He chuckles a little bit. "Yeah. You used to make those when you were a kid too. I feel like I got one every Christmas."

"Yeah, and you laughed at me then, too. Asshole."

"That's not true," he says, walking over to my bathroom. "I was charmed beyond belief." He disappears inside.

I follow. "What the fuck are you doing? Get the hell out of my bathroom!" Christ. He's like a bull in a china shop. I follow after him, and find him opening my medicine cabinet.

"The fuck are you doing?" I ask, infuriated.

"I dunno. Just, y'know, looking. But it occurs to me now that I probably should've asked about this"—he's holding up my birth control pills—"y'know, before."

"Yeah, well there's a lot of things we *probably* should've fucking talked about before I let you stick your dick inside me."

"I didn't… come in you, though. Right? I mean, I came on your ass, but the second time we—"

"Get. The fuck. Out." I grab the pills out of his hand.

"I'm clean, by the way. Promise. I would never have done anything if I wasn't tested and a total 'A' student. Scout's honor." He holds up four fingers. Which, of course, isn't the Scout salute, but who gives a shit?

He's now back in my bedroom. "Tyler, I swear to God, I'm not in the mood for this charming bullshit act. I know you, remember? It's not working."

He looks on my nightstand. "*How To Make Friends and Influence People*. Ah, c'mon, you don't need this. You could write it, Mads!"

"Would you stop calling me that!" I grab the book, throw it across the room, and point my finger at his face. "What the fuck do you want?"

He stares at me for a second. Then, without warning, he grabs my cheeks and forces his tongue in my mouth.

'Forces' probably isn't accurate. 'Works it in' is more like it. Tenderly. Softly. I melt a little. And then every ounce of resistance I had just kinda melts too, because his kiss is just what I need right now. Just a little kindness. Just a little affection. Just a little…

That is until I come to my senses, and retreat backwards. "Nope. Un-unh. This isn't gonna work," I snap.

"What?" he asks, coming toward me. "What's not gonna work? Why? Why can't it?"

"Why can't it? Are you fucking insane?"

"Maybe. It's been suggested before." he says, stepping close to me so that I back up and bump into my dresser, which causes some shit to fall off onto the floor.

Including my bright purple vibrator.

He bends down and picks it up. He holds it between us, again not breaking eye contact with me. The he asks, "Where would you like me to put this?"

I shake my head. "I'm not playing this game with you."

"I'm not playing a game. Honestly, Maddie, I'm just… I'm just trying to make you smile." He turns on the vibrator and waggles his eyebrows. The buzzing starts low, but gets louder and louder as he fumbles with the controls.

"Wow, man. You really don't get it at all. I don't know how I ever fell for your bullshit in the first place. I guess it's because I was a kid, and I looked up to you, and I believed in you, and"—the vibrator continues to buzz—"and all that fake *we're in-this-togetherness* bullshit you used to spout back when we were young. Well, it won't work on me now. Because you and I both know who you really are."

The sound of the humming vibrator is the only noise. That and what I imagine is my galloping heartbeat, which is way too fast right now.

And finally, the Tyler Morgan façade drops. His smile falls and his blue eyes seem to darken. He says, "Yeah? Who am I?"

And for a second I see the old Tyler. Underneath the beard. Underneath the lines at the corners of his eyes that beg me to ask where he's been, what he's been doing. Underneath the years of separation and sadness.

But fuck it. And fuck him. I don't need to ask where he's been. I only need to remember where he *wasn't.* So I press in close and I whisper, "You're just another very bad guy." I squint at him and nod my head tightly. "That's who you are."

My chest is heaving up and down now, my breaths shallow. Somehow, this feels like some kind of moment of truth.

And then, "I'm sorry," he says. "I'd fuckin' make it up to you if I knew how. I swear I would. It was just… I was just… my life, Mads. I—It's not what you think."

"Yeah? OK. Well, I'm not thinking about *your* life," I say. "In fact, I'm not thinking about you at all. I'm only thinking about me." It sounds very selfish. And it is. But I don't care. I want him to go away. And if I have to say nasty things to get what I want, I will.

He reaches up to my face again, but before I can pull away, he's tucking a stray strand of red hair behind my ear.

The vibrator is still on high. The buzzing fills the otherwise silent room as I now hold my breath to keep from damn near hyperventilating.

"I'm trying my best to not think about my life too."

"So what am I supposed to be? Just another familiar distraction?"

"No," he says, shaking his head. "No. I don't have a ton of regrets in life. I really don't. Not to say there aren't a ton of things I should regret, it's just not my gig."

"Wrong answer," I whisper. My words are soft now. Low, and sad, and pitiful. "So not what I wanted to hear."

He swallows. I swallow. He strokes the strand of hair he just pushed away. I let him. I don't want to let him, but the fight inside me has died a little.

"Except, y'know, the way I handled everything with you, and the way I just failed. Yeah, I regret that a whole fucking lot. So…"

He looks like he's choking up a little bit. *Don't. Shit. Just don't.*

"Because I loved Scotty. I *love* Scotty. It's hard to think of him in the past tense. And I loved you too. Always loved you. I used to tell Evan and Scotty that you were gonna grow up to be a fucking heartbreaker. And Scotty used to always tell me to shut up and watch myself." He smiles, absently, remembering some long-ago moment with him and my brother. "And when I saw you, up there dancing… I saw *you.* I think. That's the only way I can explain it. Remember I told you I dreamed about you?"

I think I nod. I'm not really sure.

"I did. I dreamed of an angel who was kind to me even though I didn't deserve it. An angel who I was trying to help. In my dream, I realized that it wouldn't be possible for me to save everyone, but this angel… this kind angel with the beautiful green eyes and the red hair… I could save her. And I didn't know it was you, because I hadn't seen you in so long, but…"

He bows his head. I can feel the tears welling up in me. Which I fight.

"Did you?" I ask.

"Did I what?" he says.

"Save me. In your dream. Did you save me?"

He closes his eyes and shakes his head. "No. No. But I never stopped trying. And that's why I can't stop now."

He opens his eyes and looks deep into me. And then he closes the already narrow space between us and kisses me gently on my cheek. And I puff out a breath and the tears just pour out.

I close my eyes and let him place his mouth against my ear, powerless to move. Caught in a web of memories, and laughter, and shared happiness that I want back so badly my chest aches with the loss of it all. And when he says, "So you're not a distraction. You're the only hope I have left," I cry. Hard.

He kisses the sobs coming out of my mouth. He covers them, captures them, and holds them between us like he's desperate to make them stop and this is the only way he knows how.

And the next thing I know, the fucking vibrator is between my legs, pushing up against my pussy through the thin cotton of the boy shorts I have on.

His other hand squeezes my hip, pressing into my flesh until it burns, and even when I twist and squirm, he refuses to let me go.

I don't even have the energy to resist. I can't do anything but submit. Because I'm just too tired of losing to lose again. And there's no way I'm not gonna do this. When all you have left in the world is this one bad thing, you keep it. You hold on to it for as long as you can because it's all you've got left. It doesn't even matter that it's bad for you. It doesn't even matter that it's the worst possible decision. It doesn't even matter if it's killing you.

Hell, maybe that's why all this is happening? Maybe we're both back on top of Mount Everest, looking down at that fucking fall, thinking... it ain't so bad when you've already done it and lived.

The devil you know is the one you keep.

"What can I do? Tell me what it is you need and I'll give it to you. Anything," he says.

My mind races. There are so many things I need that Tyler could provide. And right at the top of that list is money. Tyler could pay off my debt to Carlos. Tyler could probably fund my whole real estate business endeavor. Tyler could...

What the hell am I even saying to myself? Even if this weren't Tyler Morgan, I could never ask for that. I would never ask for that. It's one thing if you've built something together with someone else, it's another thing entirely to take what someone else has. But... there is one other thing I feel I need right now. And it is something I can ask for.

"Fuck me," I say into his kiss, reaching for his cock beneath his jeans.

He doesn't wait for another invitation. He just pulls me backwards, his mouth still on mine, refusing to let my sobs escape. Until the back of his legs bump into the mattress and he sits down.

He doesn't wait then either. Our eyes don't even have time to meet. He just pulls me down with one hand until I flop next to him onto the mess of covers, and he rolls me over onto my back, pulling my shorts off as I rip the t-shirt off over my head, and then he lifts my legs up as I feel the vibrator pressing against my clit.

Warm wetness pools as he plays, and I moan. I can't help myself. I want him.

He slides the vibrator down, all coated and slick with my desire, and pushes it into my pussy. I close my eyes, my fingertips picking up where the vibrator left off, rubbing myself in small, quick circles as he fucks me with the toy.

His chest covers my breasts now, his hand still pumping in and out as he continues to kiss me, his hard cock pressing against my outer thigh, practically begging me to touch him.

I undo his belt one-handed, enjoying the sound of the jingling buckle, and then my hand slides inside and takes hold with such force, it's like a promise to never let go.

It's a lie, but aren't all promises lies anyway?

"Tell me to stop," he says, breath heavy and coming out ragged.

"Keep going," I say. Meaning it as I unzip his jeans, slide them over his hips, and start furiously pumping his cock.

I'm gonna take what I want for once. And right now, I want *this.* So I squirm underneath him and flip over, pushing my ass in the air like an invitation. "Take me from behind," I moan. "Right now."

He slaps my ass as he backs off the bed and stands up. Two seconds later he's got his boots, pants and shirt off. Scarred and naked, he locks his eyes with mine as I watch over my shoulder.

We hold our stare as both hands grip my ass and he slides his cock inside me.

TYLER

I did a shitty job at following my plan about how I would approach her delicately when I entered her room.

So, I plan to make up for it by doing an excellent job of not being delicate at all now that I've entered her.

I couldn't be even if I wanted to. I am drawn to her. I need her. We are destined.

I tell her this with my glare, holding her gaze with mine as I push my cock forward, grinding into her from behind, never breaking eye contact. That is until the very last push as I force her ass into my hips - trying to pull her completely through me - and her eyes close, her head and neck arch backwards, and she lets out a low, guttural moan that causes the muscles in my calves to tighten and my knees to dig into the edge of the mattress.

The vibrator is still buzzing on the bed. I take it up and reach down in front of my thigh, feeling the vibration as it rubs against my balls. I slip it forward to meet the lips of her slick, wet pussy that are gripping my shaft so tight, and then let it come to rest on her clit. I continue stroking in and out of her, all the while being sure to keep what has turned into a second dick (only far less charming and noteworthy than my own) planted on that spot that makes her whimper.

"How's that feel?" I mutter out, my mouth just above a whisper. Just loud enough for her to hear the question over the hum of the vibrator and the sound of her own moans.

"Good," she whines back.

"Just good?" I ask.

But before I let her answer the question, I slide the vibrator back to the opening I'm currently pouring myself into and work the very tip of the second dick inside of her as well, stretching her just that much more open and continuing to thrust back and forth while the vibrator massages the inside of her walls. She begins panting.

"How 'bout now?" I ask.

"Fuck yeah," she groans back.

Her hands splay out in front of her, gripping at the sheets, her arms stiffening and her lower back arching more as she continues pressing into me. I pull the vibrator away and lay it on the bed.

"What are you doing?" she pleads. "That was amazing."

"No," I whisper as I bend over to kiss her shoulder blades and bury my face in her hair. "That wasn't amazing. This is amazing."

And before she can ask 'what?' I'm up on the bed, my knees under me, her pulled back onto my dick, ass pressed into my thighs like she's sitting on my lap, her legs sticking out behind me, and I tell her, "Put your arms out in front of you. Like Supergirl. I'm gonna make you fly."

"What?" she says.

I take both of her arms, throw them out in front of her, grab her hips as tightly as I can, and pound in and out of her ferociously, bouncing her on my cock.

"Oh shit, oh shit, oh shit," she huffs with each thrust.

She keeps her arms suspended in the air that way like the sexiest goddamn super-hero ever, flying through the sky, propelled forward by the force of our fucking. I support her weight with my hands on her hips and the hard, fast motion of my thighs driving into her creamy skin, over and over again. I can feel her muscles tighten as she strains to hold herself aloft and it just makes me fuck her harder.

I keep my right hand in place and with my left, I take up a fistful of silky red. I yank her hair back, exposing her neck to the ceiling and her hands now fly up to grab at my fist, making sure to keep it locked there on her head.

Or so I think.

Because suddenly, she's pulling my hand away from her hair and bringing it around to rest on her throat.

"Here," she pants. "Squeeze."

I lean back, allow myself to land in a full sit with my heels beneath me, her legs straddled behind me, and both of us upright, my right arm reaching around her chest and pinching her left nipple, and my left hand wrapped firmly around her gorgeous neck. Her hair rising up and spilling down as we fuck makes me think of flames being blown in the wind. Flames that refuse to be extinguished. She's springing up and down on my balls, almost crushing them with every strike—and I fucking love it. I want to be crushed by her. Pulverized into ash and blown into the wind too.

Her hand is now reaching frantically for the vibrator, still singing its vibrator melody somewhere in the sheets. She finds it, forces it onto her clit again, and says, "Harder."

I'm not sure if she means pinch her harder, fuck her harder, or choke her harder, so I decide to be safe and just go with all three.

I squeeze her nipple and she shrieks. I tighten my grip on her throat and she coughs out, "yes." And I fuck her with the force of a tornado, sweat starting to form on my brow and drip down onto her already slick and sweaty flesh… and she comes.

She thrashes back into me so hard that we both collapse backwards off the bed and land in a heap on the floor. I make sure to move the hand that's around her throat so that I don't crush her goddamn windpipe and I twist to stay underneath her so that I mostly break her fall, very nearly snapping my dick free from my body in the process. But luckily it stays attached, which is a good thing, because I still have more for it to do.

"You hurt?" she asks. Which, given our current status with each other might either be a question of concern or hope.

"Yeah, I'm ok," I tell her. "By the way," I add, "I was right."

"About what?" she pants.

"You should write a book. THAT'S how you win friends and influence motherfuckers."

MADDIE

"Shut up and fuck me," I tell him back. This is not at all what I planned on doing with Tyler Morgan tonight. And that pisses me off. Because it makes me weak. I mean, am I *that* desperate and needy that a few charming words from him make everything OK?

I disgust myself.

"I will," he says. "I'm just gonna do it slow now." He repositions us so he's on top of me, his forearms resting on the floor on either side of my head, his legs straddling mine so that each rocking movement of his hips stimulates my clit in just the right way.

He winks. There's even a mischievous twinkle in his eye as he does it. Which is charming. I'm not gonna deny that. Tyler is one hundred percent charisma. He draws people to him without even trying. He should write that stupid book, not me.

I make a face at his wink.

"What?" he asks, kissing my frown away. And then he kisses my mouth, whispering, "What could I possibly be doing wrong now?" as he does it.

I have a list. Ten things on it, at least.

But I don't feel like explaining. He doesn't even deserve my explanation. So I just kiss him back and make the whole conversation go away.

Sex with Tyler Morgan is something I can handle right now. All these feelings he suddenly wants to talk about? No. I won't do it.

"Tell me," Tyler prods.

"Tell you what?" I ask, trying to distract him by sliding my fingernails up and down his back.

His spine arches in response, but it's not enough. Because he says, "Why do you look like you want to kill me when everything we're doing right now finally feels right?"

I close my eyes and concentrate on how he feels instead. Not his feelings, but how he feels inside me. "Is this how you want to come?" I ask, eyes still closed. "This boring slow fuck is how you want to remember me?"

My eyes open just in time to see him frown. And I get the feeling my dismissal is just another cue for him to keep asking questions. So I stop that shit before it starts and push him off me.

He gives in and rolls off to the side, still frowning, still looking like he's gonna keep talking, but I know just what to do.

I grab his dick, still wet with my come, and slide my palm up and down his shaft in a slow, twisting motion.

He practically growls in response.

Which, I can't deny, turns me on a little. But more importantly, it takes his mind off what's not being said.

I climb on top of him, my hand still very busy keeping him quiet as my legs settle between his knees, and then it's my turn to wink.

The smile he shoots back sums up everything I hate and love about Tyler. And the gruff chuckle has my pussy throbbing. I keep my eyes locked on his as I lower my mouth to his cock, my tongue reaching for his tip, and hike my ass up in the air just as I cover his head with my lips and slide my mouth down his shaft.

His hands go to my hair, grabbing it in fistfuls. A shiver runs through my body as I think about the way he was pulling it a few minutes ago. I take him deeper into my throat, his hands responding to the call, pushing my head down until his cock is practically in my throat. I gag, pull away, but he holds me there until saliva is pooling in my mouth. I pull back again, but he doesn't relent and the pool becomes a waterfall spilling over my lips and down my chin.

Finally, he lets up and I draw back, sucking in air, watching him watch me. His smile is gone, no frown replacing it. He's just looking at me like… like I'm his fucking salvation. Like I'm the only hope he has left.

I dive back down to try to erase that look, my eyes closed now, my mouth working him as I bob my head to the rhythm of his rocking hips.

He fists my hair again, but this time he tugs my head up until his cock falls out of my mouth. Erect, and red, and swollen, and glistening wet from my sucking and pumping.

I don't want to look. I refuse to look at him.

"Maddie," he groans, the word just a hint above silent.

I shake my head and try to suck his cock again, but he holds me by the hair, tugging it up towards him now, like it's a leash and he's leading me.

"Shut up," I say, my voice as husky and low as his. "Just shut up."

He opens his mouth as if to reply, but then he closes his eyes and sighs. Giving up or giving in, I don't really care. Because he lets me resume.

I forget everything as I suck him off. One hand reaching down to play with his balls, which makes him tense up and box me in with his knees.

For some reason that makes me want to cry. I'm not sure if it's because I like the way he's surrounding me right now, when the whole world is falling apart and every day I fight the inevitable decline, but every night I close my eyes feeling utterly alone and defeated, and being boxed in by Tyler wipes all that away. Or if it's because I'm just lonely and haven't had anyone make me feel so… protected in so long.

Either way, I can't deny the sadness of the moment. So I don't. I embrace it. I let the tears flow, my face hidden by my long, flaming-red hair. And I just suck his cock until everything goes tight. His body. His grip on my hair. The pressure of his knees against my shoulders.

He urges me to back off, probably so he can put me on top of him before he comes. But if I do that, he'll see my face. He'll see through my charade. He'll see everything and I don't want him to see anything.

So I refuse and just work harder. I suck him until he starts moaning. I flatten my tongue on his shaft and force myself to take him deeper into my throat. And when I swallow, the muscles pushing against his cock in a wave do him in.

He comes.

And I take it. Because I *can* take it. I swallow every drop. I let him fist my hair until my scalp stings. And when it's finally over I have it all back together. The unraveling of Maddie Clayton has wrapped back up into a tightly wound ball of nothing.

I say, "Take me to the shower," because I need to feel clean after everything that's happened these past few days. And he does, cracking some boyishly-charming joke that hits me hard. Because I love that part of him. The innocent Tyler. The one I could always count on. The one who I loved once.

But I don't love the one who loves me now.

I'm falling and it's a long fucking way down. And I know, if I get my hopes up that Tyler will catch me before I splat, he'll only disappoint me again.

I can take a lot, but I can't take that.

I can't fucking do it again.

I lean against the wall of the shower, water splashing against my hip as Tyler soaps me up. He fingers me, and plays with my breasts. And we kiss and it feels good. So fucking good. I even talk a little, but beg for bed because I'm exhausted.

It's not a lie, either. I am exhausted. So, *so* tired of this fight I never seem to win.

He dries me off. It's a tender gesture that once upon a time I'd have appreciated more. And then he leads me to my bed, and we climb in, and he talks, and I pretend to live this new fantasy with him. Until finally, I don't have to pretend anymore. Because he falls asleep, or I fall asleep, or who the fuck cares.

All I know is that the day finally ends.

I wake early by some miracle of fate, or punishment, or maybe it's the devil on my shoulder just calling me home to hell.

Either way, I heed the call and get up for my new shift at Pete's, quietly gather my clothes and dress in the new dawn light, grab the car keys left carelessly on the counter, write two notes, leaving one behind, then exit the house with the other note clutched tightly in my hand.

I lift his windshield wiper, slide the piece of paper under it so that it'll be the first thing he sees when he comes outside, and then go get into Annie's car and drive off.

The note inside said, *Borrowing your car. Be back around noon.*

The note on Tyler's window said, *If you love me then please, please stay away.*

I don't want to be his hope. I don't even have enough hope for myself.

CHAPTER SIX

TYLER

"'If you love me then please, please stay away.'" She reads the note aloud.

"Yeah," I say, nodding. "Found it on my car."

"Uh-huh. And when was this?" she asks.

"Like two days ago. My original instinct was to just go find her. Y'know? Because, shit, we had *just* had sex so how could she mean that? But then I was like, well… Maybe if I show her that I can give her the space she needs, she'll feel like she can trust me and then we can try again for real. But I don't know how long to wait. Fuck. This shit is frustrating. I've never actually been in a situation like this. A relationship, I guess. Usually I just fuck a chick once or twice and then move on. Not sure what the play is here. Thoughts?"

A moment passes. Two blank stares face me. Then…

"Shit, kid, I dunno what to tell you. I'm a strip club owner, not a goddamn shrink. Raven, you got anything?" Pete looks over to the stripper whose name I just learned is Raven, who is holding the note Maddie left me. The note I've been rolling around in my fingers for the last two days like a fuckin' fidget spinner.

"Babe," she says in my direction, "don't know how to break it to you, but you're not in a relationship *now*."

"But—"

"Well, *YOU* might be in one," she cuts me off, "but Scarlett ain't."

Hearing this Raven broad refer to Maddie by her stripper name makes me sad and nostalgic at the same time.

"Kid," Pete says, "what the hell are you doing here?"

"Dunno. Just felt like I needed to talk to someone about it all."

"Don't you have a family you can go to? Therapist? Anybody?" Raven asks.

"I mean, sure, I've got a friend whose house I'm staying at, but it's three in the morning and he's gotta work later and I didn't wanna wake him up and, you know…"

"So you came here?" Pete asks.

I shrug. He and Raven look at each other.

Pete stands, rounds his desk, stops in front of where I'm sitting, and puts both of his hands on my shoulders in a grandfatherly way. (I'm assuming. Both my mom's parents died before she had me and my dad's dad took off on him and his mom when he was a kid, so I can't know for sure. But I've seen movies with grandpas doing grandpa shit, and very often it's the kind of thing Pete's doing now.)

"Tyler… It's Tyler, right?" I nod. "Tyler, when you came in here the first time asking about Maddie, I was a little nervous. You look like a homeless psycho, and I've seen enough of those in this business to know what I'm talking about. Right, Raven?"

"That's for damn sure." Raven kind of snorts.

"But then you told me the whole story, which is just too goddamn bizarre not to be true, and you seemed like a genuinely good guy who was trying to do right, and I felt like helping you." (That, and I gave the guy five large. I'm crazy, not naïve.) "But kid"—he bows his head to stare in my eyes—"I think maybe I was right the first time. You might just be a psycho."

He pats me on the shoulder and walks over to the door of his office. He opens it. Heavy bass thumps up the stairs as if riding along with the reddish glow emanating from the stage lights below. Pete doesn't say anything. Just stands there with the door open. It's clear that this is my cue to leave.

I nod a little bit, give this Raven chick a polite smile, stand and walk to the office's exit, pausing there to say something to Pete.

But I don't.

I just make my way down the stairs. It feels a little like I'm descending into some kind of hell. Like the end of that movie, *Angel Heart*, with Mickey Rourke and Lisa Bonet. The movie that got her fired from *The Cosby Show* for doing a really dirty sex scene. (Which, now that we know what we know about Bill Cosby, seems pretty fucking hypocritical, but you can't know shit until you know it, right?)

I walk across the almost empty main floor. Probably fifteen or twenty sad-dicked dudes sitting around, nursing their drinks, watching some Pole Artisan on the stage spread her ass cheeks and jiggle 'em around.

The bouncer guy I almost got into it with a couple weeks back—Otis, I think—eyeballs me like he remembers me. I don't give a shit. I'm not in the mood to fight anybody tonight.

I nod to the door guy as I exit the front and make my way across the parking lot to my car. Just as I'm about to pull the handle and step inside, where I imagine myself sitting for the next hour or so, just kind of deciding where I'm gonna go next, I hear, "Hey! Guy! Tyler!" from behind me.

I turn around. Raven's coming toward me. She's thrown on some kind of kimono thing and hugs it close to herself in the chilly desert night. She's probably a few years older than me, which feels old for a stripper, and that makes me kind of sad, suddenly. But she's still pretty. Prettier than she seemed in the club. Like being away from the world inside has painted her with a gentler brush and the mask she has to wear has come off, revealing a truer version of herself.

"This is your car?" she asks, as she approaches.

"Yeah…"

She looks me up and down and nods her head a bit. "I remember you, y'know," she says.

"You remem… Whatayou mean?"

"The night you came in and spent until daybreak in the private room with Scarlett. I remember you. I also remember when I sent you off that morning you looked like someone had killed your puppy."

Wow. She remembers. Which causes me to remember. The night I saw Maddie, before I knew it was Maddie. When she was still just the angel from MY DREAM come to life. My dick's getting a little hard thinking about how she felt and smelled and tasted that night, as we talked and touched each other, and she sucked my cock. Which is now getting even harder. I decide to make a joke to distract myself.

"That's weird," I say. "I never had a puppy. Had a snake once. Used to let it slither around on the sand in the back yard. My pops would yell at me because he was worried it'd get loose and eat the neighborhood pets. But then one time it actually did get away and wound up getting killed by a neighbor's puppy. Which I always thought was ironic."

She narrows her eyes at me. "Is this the way you are all the time, or are you just fucked up right now because you're a fuckin' lovesick maniac?" she asks.

"Little from column A, little from column B," I say.

Then, "I've seen your car, too," she says. "The night that Logan asshole came looking for Scarlett."

"Can we please call her Maddie? What? Who came looking? Who's Logan?"

"I dunno his last name. Works for Carlos Castillo? I saw him follow her out into the alley a couple weeks back and then when I came looking for her to make sure she was okay, all I found in back there was this car"—she slaps the hood of the Defender—"idling, lights on, no *Maddie* in sight. Then later she showed up back inside with this rosy fuckin' glow about her. Like the way someone looks after they just got fucked real good." She tips her head in my direction, with a knowing and yet non-judgmental look. (Which is hard to pull off.)

I take a beat to let her have her Nancy Drew moment, and then I ask, "Who's Carlos Castillo?"

"Jesus, man. Seriously?"

"Should I know?"

"You live here in Vegas, right?"

"Currently. Who is he?"

"Has a tequila empire. Owns at least a piece of just about every new casino development in town. Also supplies most of the non-pharmaceutical drugs that you see flowing through. Steve Wynn meets El Chapo with a touch of John Paul DeJoria thrown in. Seriously? You've never heard of him?"

"I've never heard any of the names you're tossing around." (Not entirely true. I know who Wynn is. Mostly because I lost like a hundred grand in his dumb casino one night a few months back. Fucking Wynn. Fuck that asshole.)

"Not a big news watcher, huh?" she asks.

"The world is depressing enough without watching the fucking news. But, so, this Logan guy… Was he the one in the t-shirt or the one who didn't know how to match his belt to his shoes?"

"Fuck are you talking about?" Raven asks, fairly.

"Yes, it was me. I was there. I fucked up two guys who were chasing Maddie that night. And then she… thanked me. Nicely. Yes. I suppose I assume this Logan clown was the one holding the gun, but whatever. What do—what's his name? Castillo?—and Logan have to do with Maddie?"

"I'm not sure, but on Halloween when she got into the car with them, I—"

"Wait, what?" I interrupt. "What are you talking about?"

"Halloween night, Maddie came stumbling up here, shoeless, like she'd just been to hell and back, and got into a car with Carlos, who was waiting for her. Honestly? I thought that was gonna be the last I'd ever see of her. I was shocked when Pete told me she was back at the club, working morning shifts."

I understand all the words Raven is saying to me because she's speaking English and using proper syntax and grammar and shit, but I have no idea what the fuck she's actually talking about.

That's where Maddie went after she left my apartment? Here? And then she—? And she's working morning shifts? Here? At the strip club? Pete's strip club? In the MORNING? I'm very fucking confused. So I say, "I'm very fucking confused. What exactly are you saying to me?"

"I'm telling you everything I know, chief." (Somehow it doesn't bother me when Raven says it.) "None of what's going on with Scarlett—"

I start to correct her again, but she puts her hand up.

"—*Maddie*, is any of my business. And nothing that's going on with YOU and Maddie is my business. But… She's a smart girl. And despite being kind of an asshole, I think she's probably a pretty good girl. And what I know for sure is that she's all alone. And from how it looks, you're also all the hell alone. And you also evidently give a huge number of fucks about her—no pun intended—and I don't wanna see a smart, nice girl like that end up dead. Or maybe even worse…"

She laughs out a tiny, soundless laugh, and shakes her head.

"…managing a strip club when she's thirty-seven years old."

Shit. That's a sad fucking moment of honesty.

"So," she continues, "I'm just letting you know that even though she left you this?" She hands the note out to me. I take it. "Maybe right now isn't actually the best time for her to be without backup."

Taking life advice from a stripper with a heart of gold at three in the morning, in the parking lot of a titty-bar in Las Vegas. This is what my life is.

"So do you think I should go to her now? Her place? Find her? Get her to tell me what's going on?" I ask.

Raven sighs, seemingly exasperated. "No, you dumb-dick dummy. That's like…that's like getting what *you* want. That's *taking*. I think you need to just be there for her. Not the other way around. Seems to me, based on what I know from you, and what Pete told me, that you owe her that. Not about you right now, bud."

"Yeah." I sigh. "I've heard that before."

"Whatever she's got going on with Carlos Castillo isn't likely to end soon, or well. Trust me." She puts a little extra English on that, like she knows of what she speaks. "So I'm saying… Just keep an eye on her. She needs *someone* to. You get me?" She raises her eyebrows at me.

"Yeah. Yeah. I get you. Thanks."

She winks at me, turns to leave, then stops and turns back.

"Your car? It's a Defender, right?" she calls.

"Yeah," I say.

She nods, gets a tiny grin, then says, "OK then." And then she spins on her heel and walks back inside the strip club, kimono swaying in the night breeze.

The next couple of weeks are a blur. But not a blur like they have been for the past few months. Not the kind of blur where I don't remember what I've done or who I've done it with. Where days go by and I don't remember them. Where I take Ecstasy (which, after spending some time on the internet and discovering Raven was right, I'm realizing means I'm probably funding this Carlos Castillo character's drug empire every time I drop a tab in this town) and fuck a bunch of questionably fuck-worthy pussies. No. More like a blur of activity. Which feels amazing.

I don't know if I truly, truly realized how adrift I'd been until I had something to focus my attention on. But now, every morning, I wake up bright and early (actually, I usually just don't go to bed—Red Bull is a lifesaver) and I park just out of the way from Pete's, so that I can see who's coming and going, but so they can't see me, and I wait and watch for Maddie.

I'll have coffee and doughnuts and pretend I'm on a stakeout. It's fun! Evan caught me leaving one morning last week as he was getting back from pulling an all-nighter on third watch, and asked me what I was doing, and I must say I was pretty smooth in the way that I avoided having to get into a conversation about it.

"Where are you going so early?"

"Gym."

"Okay. See ya."

Fucking. Masterful.

I'll wait until I see Maddie go in for work, then I'll sit there for a few hours and make sure that no one shows up who looks suspicious. (I can't actually imagine if anyone is going to try anything that they'd do it at a strip club at, like, eight in the morning, but then again that's when someone would be least expecting it, so it might be the perfect time to try some shit. You gotta cover all your bases when you're attempting to guess what the next guy is gonna do. Think three moves ahead at all times. As Denzel Washington says in *Training Day,* "The shit's chess, it ain't checkers!" And Tyler Morgan is the motherfucking Grand Master. Everybody says so.)

Then when she gets off work, I'll follow her back to her place to make sure that no one comes by who seems like they're up to no good, and at that point, I'll swing back to Evan and Robert's for a couple of hours to grab some sleep, and then I start again.

She's still working at Pete's on the weekend evenings too, and that's been my favorite part of my new purposeful existence. Because it's typically pretty crowded and I can kind of sneak in the back of the club and sit there in the corner mostly unnoticed and watch her dance.

It does make me a little crazy to see her giving lap dances and shit, but the look of disgust on her face that I see when I can peek at her lets me know that she's not having a particularly good time. Which I hate for her. But I'd probably hate it more if she looked like she was getting off on it. Just being honest. Honesty is probably my second-best quality after my amazingly awesome dick.

A couple of times Raven has walked by while I've been running into the bathroom to avoid Maddie seeing me and looked at me like she was about to say something, but then I'll give her a sign to ward her off and she'll shake her head and roll her eyes, and keep walking.

The thing I've yet to figure out is what exactly this Carlos Castillo/Logan asshole drama is all about. She doesn't seem to be doing much else besides working at the strip club and going home. Occasionally she'll, like, go to dinner with her prostitute roommates or swing by a real estate office and come out looking dejected, but that's it.

I have to suspect that it has something to do with money. If for no other reason than almost everything always has something to do with money. Growing up in Vegas teaches you that, if nothing else.

Money's just never been a thing I cared all that much about. Which is, of course, probably exactly why I now have so much of it. One other thing I've learned is that the less you give a shit about a thing the easier it comes to you. The more you try to force something, the greater the likelihood it'll all go south.

I spent a little time hanging out in Nepal and I met a Tibetan monk who was cool as shit and had what we in the military (and maybe other people too) call "a thousand-yard-stare." That thing that happens when you're seeing something off in the distance that nobody else can see. It's like depth…or focus…or something. Well, my man Lobsang had a thousand-*mile* stare. (Meditating every day for like forty years'll do that for you, I guess.) And he tried to teach me a few things, but one of them was something I already knew about.

Non-attachment.

When you're defusing a bomb, you've gotta kinda have a detachment from the possibility that it's gonna blow up and kill you. You have to let go of your attachment to the hardest thing there is to dis-attach from: Your life. If you just accept that you're gonna die someday anyway, then you don't think too hard and get nervous and fuck it all up. When you start getting too precious and careful, that's when the boom happens.

Which is why I've got to handle this thing with Maddie exactly as if I was defusing the biggest, most life-threatening bomb I've ever tried to dismantle. Because it is. And If I lean into it too hard… it'll explode.

So, I'm doing what Maddie asked. Lying back. And I'm doing what Raven suggested. Being there in case she needs me. And somewhere down the line, I have faith that it's all gonna work out.

Because it fucking has to.

And this is what I'm thinking about on this Thursday morning as I sit in my car, drinking coffee and eating doughnuts, watching YouTube videos of some of my favorite movie clips, when I look up and see a vaguely familiar figure walking across the parking lot of Pete's Strip Club in Las Vegas, Nevada.

The fuck-stick I now know is called Logan.

Shit. This is it. This is what the fuck I've been waiting for. This is what Raven warned me to be on the lookout for. Whatever Maddie's into with this Carlos douchebag, this Logan cock-smoker is the fucking harbinger.

This is my chance to do right by Maddie. To be there for her when she needs me.

The problem is, now that this moment is here, I'm not sure what to do. I'm not certain what the right play is. Do I hang here and see if they come out together? Do I see if he comes out alone? If he does, do I follow him or go in and make sure she's okay? Do I let her know I'm here for her, or stay under the radar? Crap. Turns out I have been playing fucking checkers and not chess after all. And now this cocksucker is trying to capture my queen. Shit!

Logan is through the front entrance and into the club.

Damn. What do I—? I need to be cautious. I need to make sure I'm doing the right thing. I want to make sure I'm there for her, but I don't want to freak her out. I need to—

And these are the thoughts that keep cycling through my brain as I nod to the doormen at Pete's—the sunshine outside giving way to a dark and smoky cave of flesh, sex, and thudding drumbeats—and adjust the gun I took from my glove box (Logan's gun) under my t-shirt, into the back of my pants, and move forward into the shadows ahead of me.

CHAPTER SEVEN

The sigh is long and sad as I sit parked in the alley behind Pete's, just staring at the back door in the early-dawn light. It's a crappy door. Black with lots of scuff marks on it. Like it's been kicked in lots of times. Like it was old thirty years ago and no one's been paying much attention to it, so it's just getting more tired-looking. More and more ugly. Its glorious days of being a new door far behind it. Or hell, maybe it only thought it was a glorious door? Maybe it was never anything special. Never had a nice shiny doorknob, or lock, or anything. Maybe it's just been telling itself it was nice once?

My alarm goes off on my phone, letting me know that I've got five minutes to get inside or Raven'll have my ass.

Except she won't. She doesn't work mornings. I'm pretty sure there's no manager on duty in the AM. Pete's here. Pete practically lives upstairs in that office and he almost never comes down, so he doesn't even count.

Maybe I'm the manager?

"Ha!" I laugh so loud, one of the waitresses walking by to go inside looks over at my car with a scowl. Like I was laughing at her.

"I'm laughing at myself, bitch," I snarl.

But she can't hear me and she's already pulling on that tired door handle anyway. She disappears inside.

Maybe I *am* the manager? I mean, I did make the morning schedule last week. And Candy came to me with a problem the other day. One of the new girls stole her shoes, so I had to go take care of that and get them back. And then I did actually fire someone yesterday. Pete said he was doing the books, so could I just… you know, get rid of her?

So I did. I didn't like her, so I took a little pleasure in that.

Jesus fuck. I'm the goddamned morning manager at Pete's!

I sit a little longer wondering if being the manager at a strip club is better or worse if I'm only twenty-five and not thirty-seven, like Raven.

It's not.

If my mother knew what I was doing… holy shit, I can't even imagine what she'd do. Probably make my father walk inside, drag me off stage—

Don't go there, Scarlett, the angel says.

That would be fucking epic! the devil exclaims.

—and make me move to stupid France with them. My mother would cry, I'm pretty certain of it. And it's not like they're judge-y or anything. It's just… they'd be so disappointed in me. I had such potential as a teenager. My mother has actually never said that to me, but I've read the look in her eyes. Every time I start something and then fall on my ass, she frowns and gives me this look that says, *You had so much potential before…*

You know, I fell off Mount Everest after Scotty died and… yeah.

And then there's the whole Tyler thing.

I sigh again. It's even longer and sadder, if that's even possible.

My alarm dings again, letting me know I've got one minute to make it on time.

I shouldn't care so much about being on time, but I do. Because sad as it is, I need this stupid job. I've made some cash since I started working here full time. Like, almost nine thousand dollars. But I've pretty much sold my soul for that money. And I have no pennies to spare, either. I can't shop, or even try to get more video appointments with the real estate people, or fucking eat, if I'm being honest. And now I've only got a few weeks left to get the other hundred and seventy-six thousand.

It's never gonna happen, but I've always prided myself on my eternal optimism, so I just keep on truckin'.

"Ha!" I laugh again.

I grab my backpack, get out, slam the door, and walk to the building.

I am Pete's old, black door. I think I'm paraphrasing the movie *Fight Club* to myself. Which has a lead character in it called Tyler. Who is played by Brad Pitt. Who looks like the Tyler I know. Which makes me think of him. Which pisses me off. Christ.

Inside it's dark, as usual, and there's like seven people here, as usual. And Candy, the girl on stage, is bent over, holding onto the brass pole, bumping her ass up and down to the beat of *Pretty Fly (For a White Guy)*, working it hard as she looks over her shoulder at the one guy sitting up near the stage, mouthing the words, *Give it to me, baby.*

He takes a sip of his beer and throws her a single.

I walk past and head for the stairs. Because if I'm the morning manager at Pete's then I need a fucking raise.

I climb up, determined, my jaw set, my knock firm. Because I'll be goddamned if I'm gonna work my ass off like Candy down there, and take a half-heartedly thrown dollar bill as my payment.

"Yep," Pete calls.

I find him slumped over his desk, glasses perched on the bridge of his nose as he scans a spreadsheet on his computer.

"Hey," I say, all my confidence faltering.

"Madison," he says, not looking at me. "What can I do for you?"

Madison. Jesus. That's a wake-up call. I feel like I'm talking to the dean back in college and not my strip-club boss.

"Um… well," I stammer. "I just…"

He looks up at me, fluffy eyebrows raised. "Close the door."

Holy shit. "Did I—Am I in trouble?"

Pete crosses his arms across his chest. "Dunno. You tell me."

I'm not sure what that means, so I just turn, close the door, and take a deep breath. "I just… feel like I'm doing a lot of extra work." He squints his eyes at me, like that was a loaded comment. And it probably was. Because it's leading somewhere, so… "I mean, I fired someone for you. And I made the schedule last week. And I handle little problems, like with the other girls and stuff. And since, you know, you don't have a morning manager, and I seem to be filling in, and I'm pretty sure Raven gets a salary for her extra efforts, then maybe…" I run out of breath and stop, unsure if I should pull the trigger and say it.

Say it! the devil screams in my head. *You're the boss*!

"I'm kinda the boss down there, OK? And you'd be taking advantage of me if you didn't pay me for my extra work."

He stares at me. I squirm and shuffle my feet, praying that I didn't just piss him off and get myself fired. He clears his throat and says, "Yeah, I was wondering when you'd figure that out."

"Figure… what out?"

"Your worth."

"Ha!" I laugh it out for the third time this morning. But then I shut up, because I think this is going my way.

Your way? the angel says. *This is your big plan? Manage the morning shift at a strip club?*

Shut the fuck up, bitch.

That was me, not the devil.

"I am worth something here, Pete. I'm not saying I'm better than anyone, but I'm…" I swallow hard. "I'm committed. Ya know? And I'd do a good job. I swear. I'm competent."

Pete stares at me for a few seconds. "Mmmhmm. And all kinds of people are interested in you right now," he says.

My smile is tight. "Yeah, well, you know. I'm an interesting girl." I force that fucking smile to stay put.

He slides his glasses down his nose. "Guy who came here about you—"

"Shit."

"Yeah," Pete says. "Kinda crazy if you ask me."

"Look, I know it's not the best situation to be in, OK? But I'm handling it. And this job is helping me. And if you let me work harder for you… I'd be worth it, Pete. I swear. And then I could pay back my debt and Carlos Castillo would go away… and things would get better. I mean, I can't pay off the whole thing on a stripper paycheck, obviously. Or a manger paycheck, either. A hundred and seventy-six-thousand dollars is like, two years' worth of pay. I know that. But I can probably get him off my back, and things would cool down, and… and…" Pete is looking at me like I just said something *totally* wrong. "What? Why are you looking at me like that?"

"You owe Carlos Castillo a hundred and seventy-six thousand dollars?"

"Um…" This feels off. Like Carlos wasn't the guy who came looking for me. "Actually, a hundred and eighty-five thousand. But I've made nine over the past few weeks, so I deducted. Maybe it was Logan who came looking?" I say, trying to put the pieces together. "You know, that asshole henchman Carlos has doing his dirty work? Could be either of them." Pete stares at me. Not blinking. Just staring. "I guess."

"So…" He leans back in his chair, "Who exactly *is* Tyler?'

"What?" I practically choke on the word.

"Tyler? Fella who came here about you. Couple times."

"Tyler?" I say, so fucking confused. "He came in here *again*?"

"Mmmhmm," Pete hums. "Pretty crazy. If you ask me."

"Well, he's a soldier who—" I say, then roll my eyes. "This isn't about Tyler. This is about me. Remember? I want to be your morning manager?" I need to redirect this conversation back to that. Because I just admitted I owe a drug lord a lot of fucking money.

"So this Tyler. He is your friend, then?"

Jesus. He won't let it go. "Um, well, yes. We're old friends, I guess." I decide telling Pete about my sexual relationship is probably not work-appropriate. Especially when we did it out in his back alley.

"And he's *not* crazy?"

"Well, I dunno about that." I laugh. But Pete doesn't think it's funny. So I say, "No. Not really. He's just... fucking *Tyler*."

"And you left him a note to stay away?" Pete asks.

"What? How the hell—"

"He came here with that note asking me for advice. At three in the morning."

"He. Did. *What*?" I grab my hair like my head might explode and that's the only reasonable way to keep it attached to my shoulders.

"I think he's been around a lot," Pete says. "Seen him a few times since."

"When?" I actually look over my shoulder like Tyler fucking Morgan is gonna come barreling up those steps and... and... I have a very inappropriate daydream in that moment. Imagery of him fucking me in the alley weeks ago also comes to mind for the second time in like ten seconds.

"...saw him hanging around outside too."

I shake myself back to the present and say, "Outside? What the hell are you talking about? Outside here? Like... is he stalking me?"

"Do you think he's stalking you?"

I have no answer for that. I just stare at my boss, lost. I am not having this conversation.

Oh, he's back, baby! my angel says. *He's back. And you're gonna make up with him and ask him for help. Like you should've, instead of kicking him to the fucking curb*!

I laugh. My angel just said *fuck*.

"So you owe Carlos Castillo a hundred and seventy-six thousand dollars…"

"Look, honestly, I don't owe him *anything*. But that's not how he sees it."

"I'm sure."

"He hired me to plan his daughter's wedding, gave me the money for it, and then she went off and got knocked up with some other guy's kid after I paid everyone for the ceremony," I explain.

Pete sighs and nods. "Yeah. And if you can't come up with the money? He make any type of… alternative arrangement with you?"

"Um, kind of? He tried. How do—Do you *know* Carlos Castillo?"

Pete doesn't answer. Just goes back to looking at his computer.

"I'm gonna pay him back, OK? I just need a break. That's all. And you could give me a break, Pete. You could just… help me out a little by giving me this extra responsibility."

"Doesn't matter if you pay him back or not. You're in Castillo's orbit now. There's no getting out of it."

"I'll figure something out. I always do."

"Or," Pete says, looking up at me from the top of his glasses, "you could just ask your friend Tyler for help."

"No," I huff. "No. Believe me when I say this, OK? He cannot help me. He's not that kind of guy."

"Seems like he can," Pete says. "Seems like he is. He's got money. Hell, gave me five grand just to tell him where you live."

"Yeah. I know. Thanks for that, by the way."

Pete shrugs. "Point is it sounds like he really cares about you and he's in a position to make your problem go away."

Cares about me? "Pete," I start, trying to keep my temper in check, "I appreciate it, but Tyler Morgan isn't the person to help me. I'm the person to help me. I'm the only one who can. Know what I'm saying?" Pete's got kind but tired eyes that look like they've seen more than I can know, and I hold my steady gaze on them until he speaks again.

"Yeah. I respect that," he says. I breathe out a little.

"I mean, look, Pete. I didn't come up here to talk about Tyler."

"Or your Carlos problem, but you did."

"Just forget about both of those people. OK? I just need the job. Please? I'm a really good manager. I am. And I have a degree in business, so that pretty much—"

"Everyone's got a degree in business, Maddie. Even Candy has an MBA."

"Really?" Candy has an MBA? Next thing you know, he's gonna say Raven's not just some washed-up stripper. "Can I have the job, Pete? Just give me a try for a few weeks and see how it goes. And if I don't have this place running in tip-top shape, you can say forget it. How's that sound?"

"Are you working for free?"

"Free? Like... *no.* I need the money, remember?"

Pete laughs. It's a nice laugh. I kinda like Pete. He's not a bad dude as far as strip-club owners go. He runs a tight ship. Respects us. Pays us on time. Always remains calm when the girls complain, and never lets anyone harass us. Unless it's Tyler Morgan, but I can't fault Pete for falling for Tyler's charm. He's just kinda… charming like that.

And hey, if you've gotta sell your sexy for a living, you really can't ask for a better place than Pete's. I've heard stories from some of the other morning girls. They've got loads of stories about the skanky places they've worked before landing here. They're like… bottom of the barrel, if ya know what I mean.

Which doesn't say a lot about me.

"I can pay you for managing, but it's not gonna get you out from under what you owe Carlos. I'm sorry. I wish I could. But I can't."

"I know. I get it. But still… how much?"

He thinks and then he says, "Three grand more a month."

"Three…?" I ask, deflating. "I was hoping for a little more than that."

"I know, but that's the best I can do, Maddie. I don't really need a morning manager. I could just tell Otis to do shit and he would. And besides, you'll be managing a strip club in the morning, not running a hedge fund. Sorry, kid."

I can't even begin to hide the look of abject disappointment on my face. But then again, he's right. I don't know what I was expecting.

"Good enough. Thanks, Pete. I appreciate it." I force a smile and start off.

"Madison?" God, I hate it that he calls me that here. I turn back yet again. "I'm not telling you what to do. I'm really not. Just… Tyler. At first I thought he was a psycho, and then when he poured his heart out, I changed my mind. And then I changed my mind back to psycho, because, well, he is. But let's face it. Guys do dumb shit when they fall in love. And an in-love-with-you-psycho is better than a psycho who ain't on your side."

"He's not in love with me—"

Pete holds one finger up in the air. So I shut up.

"I've seen what I've seen, and I know what I know, and guys don't do crazy shit like coming up to randomly talk to a woman's boss for advice on how to win her back unless they've got it bad." He presses his lips together and suddenly looks older than I normally think of him. "So I'm just saying to ya... You don't always get a second chance to make things right. When you're young and haven't fucked your life up so bad it can't be fixed yet, you think there's always a next time. Well, there isn't always. Read me?"

He stares at me for a few uncomfortable seconds. I shift my feet and sigh. I have to force myself not to wring my hands under his steadfast gaze.

"You read me?"

I nod, feeling unexpectedly chastised, even though I did get what I wanted when I came up here.

"OK," he says. "So fine. You're the new morning manager. Go ahead and get to work."

I turn and walk to the door. This time I make it all the way out, half-hoping that I'll wake up and discover it's all a dream. But I don't. Because it isn't. Dreams are for people who still have hope.

I head downstairs, everything he said to me echoing in my head, and go into the dressing room to change.

Is it pathetic or ironic that my new costume is a devil?

I can't decide. So I just put it on. At least I don't have to wear a wig anymore. My flaming-red hair is quite perfect for this ensemble.

Candy comes into the dressing room, huffing air like she just ran a marathon. "Jesus Christ," she says. "I hustled hard out there just now, Scarlett. You saw me, right? And I made forty dollars! Forty! I can't even pay my sitter with this!"

I don't know what to say to that. It's sad. I'm sad.

So I just pull up my tacky red thigh-highs and attach them to my new black garter belt, and accept my life for what it is.

A goddamned disappointment.

There's no DJ in the mornings, just a music track, and I hear the intro music that signals the next act—which is me. So I slip my feet into the six-inch stripper shoes, force my eyes to meet my gaze in the mirror, and say, "Fuck it."

"Hey," Jerry says. He's the day bouncer until Drake gets in later.

"I'm late for the stage," I say, picking up my pitchfork as I slip past him in the doorway. I got it last week at Tractor Supply. It's real and everything. I painted it red. Usually I do this sexy little dance around it while I'm on stage. But right now I feel like stabbing someone with it.

"I just—" Jerry calls.

But I wave him off and walk towards the stage just as my song starts to play.

"He's here!" Jerry whisper-yells from behind me.

"Who?" I ask over the music. There's like, one guy in the front row, sitting near the backstage entrance. Not that guy who was halfheartedly waving singles at Candy when I walked in, but—

"Shit."

"Time to pay up, *Scarlett*," Logan says, standing up, still sipping his drink. "Three weeks is half of six. And that means you owe us half the money right now. Ninety-three thousand. Where is it?"

Logan says all this like it's reasonable to expect me, a stripper, and not a very good one at that, to actually *have* this ridiculous sum of money. On me. In a strip club. In cash.

"It's ninety-two and a half," I say, controlling my eye roll. "Not ninety-three. And when the hell did we say I had to get you half *now*?"

Logan steps in far too close for my liking, pushes a strand of hair behind my ear, which makes me cringe, and whispers. "Fair enough. I'll tell you the truth. Carlos didn't send me this time. I've been watching you." He's been watching me? What the fuck? "And I know you're here in the mornings, and as I was heading home from taking care of a few things last night, suddenly it occurred to me that you and I haven't really had a chance to… talk."

I don't like where this is going. Not at all.

"Carlos is right to feel… intrigued by you, Madison Clayton." Oh, Jesus, I think I'm going to fucking puke. "You are an absolute puzzle waiting to be solved."

My jaw tightens as he twists my hair around his fingers and says, "Remember when you showed me your pussy, Maddie? When you spread your legs and let me see that sexy snatch you've got? Shit. I'll be honest, I was so sad that you're shaved down there." He reaches one hand far too close to my thighs. "Because I imagine that fiery red cunt of yours is just as beautiful as all this." And he takes a fistful of my hair and yanks my head back just a tiny bit.

And at that instant… for whatever reason, Ricky Ramirez, tequila salesman from Acapulco, comes to my mind. *Ese es tu problema. Tienes mal genio.* And that just pisses me off.

In fact, everything right now pisses me off.

And so I decide… That's it.

I'm fucking done.

I crash my pitchfork into Logan's head, kick him in the balls so hard my stripper shoe goes flying across the room, and then give him an uppercut to his jaw just as he looks up at me with rage and pain in his eyes.

You were wrong, Ricky Ramirez.

My goddamned temper is not my problem.

My goddamned temper is all I have left.

CHAPTER EIGHT

TYLER

Well, that's some shit you don't see every day.

A devil in a strip club, at eight in the morning, beating the fuck out of the bag man for a Mexican drug lord with a pitchfork.

Huh.

One of her shoes has come off, so she's sorta limping toward him, swinging her pitchfork, as he scrambles backwards to get away. Everything else in the club has come to a dead stop, save for the song still playing. Maddie's song. The one that plays when she does her stage dance. The song I had Shazam identify for me as *Angel* by Massive Attack, and then downloaded and put on a playlist called "Maddie," which currently consists of just the one song that I play over and over, so, y'know, it's an easy track for me to recognize.

It's funny to watch a dude get his ass kicked to a soundtrack.

(And is it wrong that I think it's insanely sexy? Whatever. I do.)

Before I can take another step, she's cast off her other shoe, tossed her pitchfork down and is going full fuckin' Ronda Rousey on old boy. The daytime door guy is trying to hold her back, but she's off the chain.

Holy shit, I'm so fucking hard right now.

I'm hanging back, partially because she's got this and partially because I'm enjoying the show. The handful of other sad sacks in the joint are hanging back too, but I'm guessing that's because they're afraid of getting their dicks kicked in.

Maddie's yelling, "Fuck you, motherfucker! Fuck you, and fuck Carlos, and fuck all of you bitches!" The door guy is not small, but he's trying to hold onto an out-of-control wildfire that's scorching the earth. She shoots out of his hands and is on top of Logan again in a flash, like an escaping lick of flame.

"You tell him that his daughter is the fucking whore who's responsible for paying him his money back! And tell him that if he thinks he's gonna stick his rotten cock inside me, he's living in fantasy land! If he, or you, ever touch me again, I will feed both of you your fucking hearts!"

Jesus. I swear to God, I'm gonna come in my pants. This is the hottest shit I've ever seen.

Pete's on the scene now. One of the girls must've gone up to his office to get him because he's rumbled down the stairs with purpose in his ambling stride.

"Hey!" he shouts. "Hey! Scarlett! Maddie! Knock it off!"

He comes up from behind and as he bends over to reach for her, the short sleeves on his button-down Aloha shirt rise up his biceps enough that I can just make out a faded tattoo. It's the tip of a spear with a sword inside and three lightning bolts crisscrossing the blade. A Special

Forces tattoo. Shit, good old grandfatherly Pete was a Green Beret. I knew I liked the guy.

He wraps Maddie in a bear hug and pulls her off Logan, lifts her up, and holds her in the air, her bare feet still thrashing about untameably.

Red hair sprays across her face with the shaking of her head and Pete grips her tighter as she rips one arm free, points at Logan and bellows, "I don't give a fuck! I don't give a FUCK! Come at me, motherfucker! Let's go! Let's fucking go!"

Yep. A little bit just slipped out of the tip of my dick, I'm pretty sure.

This Logan asshole is bleeding from the nose, mouth, eye, and—I think—ear? Jesus, she covered all the bases. He stumbles to his feet and backwards, spitting blood on the floor.

"Hey!" Pete shouts. "Not on the carpet!"

(In fairness to Logan, it's a pretty dumb idea to have carpet in a fucking strip club. Like a goddamn Petri dish.)

Logan's panting in and out heavily, trying to catch his breath. An ass-kicking'll do that to you. I fade back into the far corner. I'm clearly not needed here, but I don't wanna duck out yet, just in case.

Unlucky Logan (which is what I've decided to call him) is teetering, trying to find his feet against the floor, and I'm just about to laugh when he whips out a gun from his jacket, points it at Maddie, and says, "You're dead, bitch."

If you asked me to tell you the story of how I covered the space between me and him and rammed the barrel of the pistol I'm carrying against the side of his temple before he had a chance to pull the trigger on his, there's no fucking way I could tell it. I have no idea. But it's what happens.

"Hey, Logan!" I say brightly. "I've missed you. How's things? Eating enough? You look thin."

His shoulders drop. Because of course they do. Because I don't know whose fucking nephew or cousin this jackass is, but he is *shitty* at being a bad guy.

"Tyler?" Maddie shouts, as she allows herself to go a little more still against the broad barrel of Pete's chest.

"Hey, Maddie. What's up?" I ask it as casually as I can. Given the present situation, that's not really all that fucking casual.

"What the fuck?" she yells as Pete releases his hold and lets her stand on the ground. "Why are you here right now?"

"I, um…" I'm not sure how to answer, so I just say, "Hi, Pete."

"Tyler." He nods to me.

Maddie starts after Logan again. Or it's possible she's coming after me. Either way, both of us flinch before Pete grabs her by the arm and stops her.

"Scarlett?" he says.

"What?" She spins on him and her hair kind of hits him in the face.

"Why don't you go on and head home?"

"I'm not going fu—"

"It's not a request, Maddie."

She stares at Pete. She turns and stares at Logan. Then she stares at me. Then she starts to say something to me. Then she stops. Then she turns away. Then she turns back. Then she starts to speak again. Then she stops. Then she shakes her head. Then she picks up one of her shoes. Then she looks for the other one. Then one of the other girls finds it and hands it to her. Then she picks up her pitchfork. Then she holds her pitchfork in one hand and her shoes in the other and stares at me. Then she starts to say something. Then she stops.

And then she leaves.

"Uh, Pete?" That's the bartender. "Should I call the cops?"

Pete waves him off. "Nah, nah, don't worry about it." He steps over to me and Unlucky Logan. I've still got Unlucky's old gun pressed against his unlucky head when Pete wrenches the gun Unlucky's currently holding away from his grip. Unlucky (I really like this nickname) looks like he's about to spontaneously combust.

"You work for Castillo?" Pete asks.

Unlucky doesn't answer right away so I tap him on the noggin with the barrel.

"Answer Pete. He's your elder."

Pete looks at me with a 'what the fuck are you doing' glance, but I don't care. I'm having fun. I shrug.

Logan closes his eyes and bites out, "He's my uncle."

"I fuckin' knew it!" I shout out. (Which I don't mean to do, but I really did know it.)

"Figures," says Pete, "Like uncle, like nephew, huh?"

"Fuck does that mean?" asks Unlucky. Which I would've asked too. Fuck *does* that mean?

"OK," Pete says. "Well, look, I don't really give two shits what goes on out there." He nods toward the door. "They're grownups and what they do out in the world is their responsibility. But in here… these girls are *my* responsibility. So, if you've got some kinda deal you need to sort out with Scarlett, you do it somewhere else. You get me?"

Fucking Pete, man!

Unlucky Logan must feel like pushing his luck a little bit more to see just how unlucky he is, because he squares up and gets in Pete's face. Which, if I'm being honest, I'm real impressed by. He's either even dumber than I thought or the guy really does have brass balls. (Or cojones, I guess, since it turns out he must be at least part Mexican. I wonder if it's his mom or dad that's Carlos' sibling. "Logan" is not a terribly Mexican name. I wonder if he's adopted? Whatever. Not the time. Rambling.)

Unlucky is almost nose to nose with Pete now. He leans in and he whispers, "No. I don't get you. Is this a shitty, second-rate tit-bar you're running, or a fucking day care, old man?"

Pete doesn't say shit. Just stares at him.

"So tell me… What if I decide I do need to come back here again to get what's ours? What the fuck are you gonna do about it?"

Shit. This is intense. I love it!

Pete still doesn't blink, and he doesn't look away. The only thing that might change in his expression at all is that his eyelids may droop a little, giving him a sleepy look that suggests he's kind of bored by the whole thing and would rather just be back in his office doing… accounting or whatever the fuck. And then, like he's asking someone to pick up milk at the store, he says…

"I'll fuckin' kill ya."

I bow my head slightly, entirely by accident. I have heard some cold-blooded shit in my day, spoken by some cold-blooded motherfuckers, but that shit right there was so cold it would make a rattlesnake crawl backwards into its hole.

And that's clearly how it lands on Unlucky Logan, too, because he gets like an inch shorter all of a sudden.

"Now go on," Pete says. "Get outta here."

There's a filled beat while Unlucky tries to decide how much it's worth to him to try to save face, but then he concludes wisely that today just ain't his day.

He backs away from both of us, me and Pete, who are now each holding a gun that used to be his, and I can only guess how much that has to suck for him. But what're you gonna do? Guy makes bad choices.

As he gets to the exit, he pauses and then he says, "I'll see you again," to Pete, and then to me he goes, "You too… *Tyler.*" He puts a little something extra on my name like I'm supposed to be all impressed or scared or whatever that the dummy knows my *first name.* It's like the silliest threat I've ever gotten. For less than a second, I have the same feeling I had before, when I fucked up him and his boy in the alley. Like I almost feel bad for him. But then I remember… I don't.

And with that, he pushes out of the club and into the morning sunshine.

I open my mouth to speak, but before I get any words out, Pete just says, "Go on," waving me in the direction where Maddie just left and closing his eyes and nodding his head. There's this instant where I think about asking him if he'll adopt me. But that'd be weird. As opposed to everything else that's happening which is *completely* normal.

I just nod my head in response and hand the gun I'm holding to Pete. I don't fucking want it. He takes it from me, nods at me in return, and I head towards the back of the club where I saw Maddie exit.

As I get there, just before I push through the door, I turn back to see the few customers take their seats again as some chick takes the stage. (Now HER, I do feel bad for, having to try to get dudes to think about anything other than what just happened—but then again… She has huge tits and they all have dicks, so it probably won't take long before equilibrium returns.) The song changes to some new thing, and Pete's wide back and shoulders lumber up the stairs and out of sight.

MADDIE

As I storm out the back door into the alley, the sun hits me in the eyes and I squint. I almost forgot it was daylight out. It's easy to lose time when you're inside there.

A homeless guy going through the dumpster to my left sees me, shouts, "Devil!" and runs away.

I stomp over to the car. Annie's car, which I'm still fucking borrowing. It's a candy-apple-red Audi S5 convertible. Basically, Annie's drone. Something she bought because she thought it would give her freedom but has become just another albatross.

I grabbed my bag before walking out, but I'm holding my shoes and pitch-fucking-fork and fumbling in my purse for my keys, which is when I stop paying attention to where the pitchfork is pointing and hear "screeeeeech." I don't even need to look to know that I have royally fucked up Annie's car. But I do.

"FUCK!"

I toss everything in my hands to the ground and the keys spill out. I snatch 'em up, press the button to unlock the door, and am about to jump in, peel away from here and drive into a phone pole on purpose when the scuffed-up door of Pete's opens and… he… comes running out.

"Maddie," he calls after me.

"Fuck you, dude. I asked you for one thing. One thing and you can't give me that?"

"I was trying, but—"

"Shit! I asked you to be there for me seven years ago and you couldn't do that, now I'm just asking you to stay the hell away and you can't do that either. What's it take?"

"Maddie, stop. You're in trouble and that's painfully obvious and I'm just trying to be there if you need my help."

"I don't need anything from you. Not anymore. Thanks for playing." I sit down in the driver's seat and press the starter button, but before I can get away, he yanks the door open and grabs my arm, pulling me out of the car.

"What. The. Fuck. Are you doing?" I spit the words in his face. "If you value anything about your life, you will take your hand off me right the fuck now."

He does. I bend down, grab up my pitchfork, and press the tines into his chest.

"OK, now…" he says.

"Yeah? What? That hurt?" I ask, pushing it a little harder. "Like there? Around your heart? That feel shitty? 'Cause I know what that's like."

"Maddie, stop!" He pushes it away and yanks it from my hand.

"Give it back. It's mine. I got it at Tractor Supply."

And then he does the most infuriating thing he can possibly do. He laughs.

"What? What's so funny?" I spew at him. He laughs harder. "Stop! Stop! Dick!"

I slap him on the chest, then I ball up my fist and strike him, then I ball up the other one and hit him again, and then, next thing I know, I'm wailing on him hard, pounding without restraint, and he's letting me. He takes it. Every blow I offer. And then I stop.

"What's wrong with you?" I ask. "Fight back, you pussy." I hit him again. This time across the face. A hard slap.

He twists his head back to face me. "No," he says.

So I slap him again. And again. And again. Each time his head snaps and then he turns back to me, allowing me to do it again. I pull back a step to take him in. Because I can't believe this fucking guy.

And that's when I notice the massive hard-on he's got going.

"Really?" I say with astonishment. He shrugs in that fucking way he does.

And I grab a handful of that scraggily-ass beard, pull him face to face with me, look into those stupid blue eyes, say, "Fuck," and jump up into his arms, my legs around his waist, my mouth pressed against his lips.

"I hate you," I breathe out in between kisses.

TYLER

Shit. I have so much I want to say and to ask her. I want to know what the hell is going on with this Carlos asshole exactly. I want to explain that I have been trying to stay away and that I'm only here now because I want to make sure she's okay. Because I owe her. Because I love her. Because I loved her back when she was just a kid and Scotty's little sister and now I've fallen in love with the woman she is.

But her bare ass in my hands, tongue in my mouth, and thighs wrapped around my waist convince me that I can table that shit for a later date.

I walk her back to the trunk of the car and slam her down on it. She throws her legs open and that's when I notice two things:

One: Her devil costume has a little red devil tail hanging off the back of the panties and it's dangling down on the trunk of the car between her open thighs. Which is adorable and hot as shit at the same time. And…

Two: The panties themselves have a zipper on the crotch.

And I'm done.

And then I'm undone.

Two zippers go down in quick succession.

I slide her to the edge of the trunk where my cock is waiting to receive her. The morning sunshine creates an incredibly different atmosphere than we had the last time we were back here together. It's strange. The night we fucked back here we were secret, hidden, protected, glancing furtively to make sure no one saw us.

Now, today, we couldn't be more exposed, but neither one of us seems to notice or care. And I realize suddenly that the last time we fucked in this very alley, it was also after some drama created by Unlucky Logan. The difference is last time, I kind of stepped in and saved Scarlett, and this time Maddie sure as shit saved herself. And thinking about that again pushes hot, boiling blood into my dick and I thrust myself inside her with the same kind of reckless force that she defended herself with.

"More," she grunts out, tightening the grip of her calves around my hips and dragging me into her further.

The teeth of the zippers on both her panties and my jeans rub against the skin on my shaft as I pound in and out, and the scraping, lacerating feeling makes me harder, which causes me to want to fuck her just that much more fiercely. Because I deserve to be punished. I owe her that. I can take it.

I've taken worse.

And then I pull out without warning.

"The fuck are you going?" she asks.

I bend down and when I stand back up, I'm holding the pitchfork. I hand it to her.

"Here," I say, pulling my t-shirt over my head. The look on her face lets me know that it's one thing to see the scars in the darkened seclusion of a strip club, or the black of an alley at night, or even my place or hers after the sun has taken its rest. It's an entirely other matter confronting them in the bright light of day.

I force the pitchfork into her hand as I slip my dick back inside her again.

"Use it," I say.

"Fuck are you talking about?" she says.

"Press it into me. My chest. While I'm inside you," I say as I begin pumping in and out again.

"I don't—" she starts. But I know what's right. What I want. What she needs.

"Just do it," I wheeze, as I fuck her sweet pussy. I just want to pleasure her. I want to make her feel good.

And I want her to punish me.

Now.

"Do it," I urge again.

Her eyes narrow and she gets (appropriately) a devilish grin. And then without another word, she rocks her hips back and forth with the thrusting of mine, while at the same time pressing the sharp prongs of the tool into the scarred flesh on my chest. I can feel it ripping and tearing, but I don't feel pain. Not in a conventional sense. Not even when she drags the edges down to my waist. I just know that she needs to hurt me, and this seems like a good start.

I watch her forearm tense. I can see her trying to stop herself from just fucking impaling me right here, which is what she wants to do. And if she does, she does. But as long as she doesn't, I'm going to keep sliding this big cock in and out of her until she comes.

And even though I know it's just my imagination, I could swear that from somewhere I hear a voice yelling, "Watch out, man! She's a devil!"

MADDIE

My angel is gone.

It's the devil who has a hold of me now. Complete control over me in this moment. My smile is *his* smile. The pressure of the pitchfork tines against the sensitive skin of Tyler's lower abdomen is *his* doing. The scratches I'm leaving on Tyler's scarred body—

Tyler's scarred body.

I glance up at him. He's breathing hard, his eyes fixed on mine. "Don't stop," he says, his voice urging me to resume the punishment. "Do it again."

I close my eyes for one long second, make a decision, then open them and keep the pressure constant, forcing myself to forget about the scars.

Tyler groans, but he fucks me harder, his cock crashing into my pussy like this is the last time he'll ever get this chance. And he's taking it. Embracing it, leaning down to kiss my mouth, until the tines puncture his skin and little pin-pricks of red appear on his flesh.

It's not fair, I decide. It's not fair that all his damage is visible and my tragic past is hidden inside.

"You hurt me," I growl into his kiss. He's got my knees up to my chin, spreading me open as he slams his body against mine. His cock fully inside me. His balls slapping against my ass, which feels so good. But all wrong. And it makes me sick for a second.

"Hurt me back," he whispers, still kissing me. Like he can't stop himself. Like the kiss makes what we're doing—what he wants me to do—all right. "Get even," he says. "Take whatever you need from me."

Selfishness isn't part of my true nature. I'm a giver. But right now I'm not myself. I'm the devil. I'm pissed off. So angry that I always have to fight for everything. So sick of the struggle. So tired of losing.

And right now all I want to do is take.

I want to take everything from him.

I want to wipe him off this fucking planet.

I want to make him sorry he ever came back to Vegas.

I want to make him leave me, and this city, and never fucking come back.

"Please," he says. He nips at my lip, gently first, then harder. Insistent. Unyielding. Trying to keep me on task. "Harder," he says.

I wanna hurt him the way he hurt me, only worse.

I never want to stop hurting him.

I want to lose my temper the way I did with Logan. And just… damage him. Forever. Make him stay down here in purgatory with me. Stuck in an unwinnable existence, caught in the eternal penance he owes me, trapped in the nightmare I've been living in since—

"Maddie," he says. "I said *do it!*"

I throw the pitchfork aside, dig my fingernails into the tight flesh of his shoulders, and scrape them down his arms until the scratches bleed.

"Yeah," he groans. "Just like that."

But then he's just fucking me harder. And the slap of his balls against my ass just feels better. And his tongue seeks me out, twists us together as I lift my legs a little higher, and spread my knees a little wider. Until he grits his teeth, his body stiff. Like he's about to come.

And I think—for like half a second—*Good. Let's get this over with. Just come, get off me and—*

But his fingers are between my legs. Strumming my clit the way I like it. The way I *told him* I liked it the last time we were fucking in this alley. And all that bullshit I was just spewing in my head just… floats there. Waiting. Like some ethereal mist that fuels my hate and rage. A cloud of poison that, if I let it, might just dissipate and let the engine die.

And then it does.

Leaving me alone with my self-loathing. And all my losses. The ones I've been stacking one on top of another until they became a tower so tall it reaches past heaven. And when the tower wobbles, like it's gonna fall and crash back to Earth in a pile of rubble that never gets put back together again…I come.

Lying on the trunk of Annie's car. With Tyler Morgan on top of me. Blood under my fingernails like evidence. Sun shining down on us, illuminating our filthy, sinful souls.

Or maybe… or maybe it's something else. Maybe it's our shared contrition. Maybe we're both sorry. Maybe we can let the hurt and anger go and make something new. Something better to take their place. Something beautiful. Maybe we're both looking for a way out of this fucked-up purgatory we put ourselves in since—

I close my eyes and wish it to be true, just as Tyler pulls out and comes on the front of my devil costume.

My hope dies like the manic desperation after climax.

Because nothing about what we just did was beautiful.

TYLER

As I look down to watch the vibrant red of her little devil negligee get painted with streaks of my cream-colored come, I notice the blood winding its way down my chest, along the ridges and valleys of my scarred flesh, and I feel nothing. No pain, I mean.

Unsurprising. I've never really had to endure physical pain. Which would probably sound weird to someone if they heard me say that, especially if they knew I'd been stabbed and set on fire and blown up and all that crap. But I just don't really feel pain. Not like other people do, anyway. And that's not something I'm, like, y'know, *proud* of, or think makes me cool or tough or anything. It's just true.

My threshold for corporal suffering has always been incredibly high. Ever since I was a kid. Used to drive my dad crazy when he'd smack me around and I'd just smile at him. One time, after I said, "Aw, Pops, is that the best you can do?" he went ape shit and damn near took my head off. It fucked me up, definitely, but I never really *hurt* from it. Not sure why. Maybe my nerves are wired differently than other people's.

I dunno.

Point is, I realize that this is a good start, but if Maddie's going to get satisfaction in the form of punishing me for my sins, we're gonna have to work a lot harder.

Speaking of Maddie…

"What the fuck?" she yells at me.

"What?" I ask back as the last bits of come stream from my cock onto the flowy fabric she's wearing.

"Why did you just fucking do that to my costume?"

"Wha—? I—What do you mean?"

"You coulda come fucking anywhere, dude, why there?"

"I dunno. Just… Fuck. I dunno."

My erection now does a double-time retreat and I shove my softening and still leaking dick back inside my pants.

She slides off the trunk of the car, pulling the come-covered material off, over her head, careful not to let it touch her hair. Suddenly, I feel like a fucking twat, so I look around for my t-shirt, grab it up and put it back on.

She zips up the crotch of her panties and is now standing in front of me in the morning sunshine wearing nothing but a red bra, red panties, red stockings with a fucking devil tail hanging off the back, and two little horns on her head.

And my dick catches a second wind.

She throws her little dress in my face, which I assume she intends as an act of further punishment, but when I smell her and me mixed up together like that, all it does is make me hotter.

"You coulda come over there"—she points—"or there"—she points somewhere else—"shit, you coulda just fucking come inside me, but—"

"Really?" I ask, a bit surprised at that sentence.

"Yeah, whatever. You know I'm on the pill. You saw that shit when you went rummaging through my bathroom. Jesus. But you had to fuck up my costume. And now I gotta go buy another one. Christ."

She open-hand smacks me against the chest, and when she pulls her hand away, she looks taken aback. I glance down to see that my white t-shirt is weeping with blood from where she dug into me.

And for a moment, I mean like maybe the tiniest parcel of time, I see something in her eyes that looks like… forgiveness. Which makes no sense and maybe I imagined it, but I could swear it was there.

"Fuck, I'm sorry." I say. "I'll buy you a new one."

"No. No goddamn way. I'm not taking your money."

"Yeah, OK, but speaking of," I begin as she grabs up her shit from the ground, her unbelievable ass bent to the sky, begging me to shove my tongue inside it. I try to shake off the distraction, because what I want to say feels important. "Uh, yeah, so speaking of money…what's the deal? How much do you owe those fuckholes?"

She continues scooping up her shit. "Nothing. I don't. Whatever. Don't worry 'bout it."

I'm gonna worry about it. There's no way I'm not gonna worry about it. Because if it's just money she owes these shitlickers, then I'll take care of it for her. Whatever it is. That's the easiest thing in the world. Well, when you have it, I guess. But I do, so fuck it.

"Maddie, please, just… fuckin'… let me help you! Shit! Even if you still hate me or whatever, that's no goddamn reason not to let me give you a hand."

"I got two hands of my own, and they're doing just fine, thanks." She throws her shit in the car, kind of ripping the leather seats with her pitchfork as she does. "Fuck! Me!" she shouts.

"What about your parents?" I offer up.

She spins on me, hard. "What about my parents? What do you mean, 'what about my parents?' Fuck are you trying to say, 'what about my parents'?"

I choose not to point out that she just asked the same question three different ways. "Like, OK, fine, don't take my fuckin' help, but do they know what's going on? I mean, shit, surely they can help bail you out of whatever the hell—"

"No one is bailing me out of a goddamn thing, you get that?" She's poking me now, right in the places I'm bleeding. "I don't need a fucking bailout. I can only trust one person, and that's me, and so that's who I trust, and I'm fucking fine. Get it?"

I take a breath, trying to understand and to be patient, when suddenly it occurs to me that I don't. Understand. And I'm out. Of fucking patience.

"Yeah. Yeah, I fuckin' get it." There's a little more heat in that than I actually intended, but fuck it.

Sure, I did something wrong once, but I'm trying to make up for it now.

And she *fucks* me and then tells me to take a hike like I'm… I don't even know what. And then she fucks me again, and… So, no. No. Fuck that. I'm done. I'm done sitting in the penalty box on this shit. I'll do whatever in the world I can for this chick, but if she won't let me, then fuck her. And you know what? If Scotty was here, that's exactly what he'd tell me to do too.

I know he would.

Seriously.

He would.

I know it.

She stares at me like she's surprised that I got a little terse with her.

So I do it again.

"What?" I say. "I said I get it. So… I fuckin' get it. You're fine. You're dynamite. Super. You've got a handle on fuckin' everything, so… Great. Good for you. Run with it. Do you, boo. I won't ask another time. Good luck. See ya. Bye."

She blinks a couple of times with heat behind her eyes. I keep going.

"Seriously. I'll leave you alone if that's what you want. Shit, I mean it must *really* be, because Evan told me that he tried to reach out to you back in the day, back when Scotty…" I stop short because I'm trying to make a fucking point, not be a goddamn asshole. "And he says you just ghosted on him. Wouldn't return his calls. He'd invite you out and you'd never show. Or swing by and your mom would tell him you weren't there, when you almost certainly were. And so it hit the point that when your parents moved away, he just assumed you moved with them. That's how much you fucking disappeared. I mean… ain't it?"

She looks like she wants to rip my goddamn head off. And so again, I keep going.

"So, yeah, you really must wanna be all the fuck alone. Because Evan's like the best dude on the planet, and if you were doing that shit with him to… I don't even know what. Like, make some kinda fucking statement to *me?* Well, that didn't work, but you sure as shit did wall yourself away. So brava, girlie. Bra-fucking-va."

I give her a slow, sarcastic hand clap, and ready myself for the kick to the nuts that I anticipate happening any second.

But it doesn't.

Instead, her face goes blank. Not sad. Not angry. Not…anything. Blank.

And then—"Fuck," she sighs out. "Man, you've done so much in the world, seen, I'm assuming, so much, and still… the sheer volume of what you don't know could fill an encyclopedia."

"Oh, yeah? Really? Who the fuck still reads an encyclopedia?"

I dunno why I said it. Just where my brain went.

"You're fucking impossible," she says, and gets in the car. I can hear the squeak of leather as her bare ass makes contact with the seat and I have a hard time…

No. That's it. A hard time.

She turns on the ignition and presses a button. The convertible top lowers. She puts on her sunglasses, looks over her shoulder at me standing there, bleeding through my clothes, and says, "Fuckin' dumbass. Next time just come inside me."

And then she peels off down the alley, around the corner, and out of sight.

NEXT TIME just come INSIDE ME.

Fuck, fucking yeah.

I look around to see if anyone is nearby and if we—unknown to us at the time—have been giving away a free Vegas show, and see no one. Except…

I look up and in the window above the club, looking down onto the alley, stands Pete. Coffee mug and bagel in hand.

He takes a bite of his bagel, a sip of his coffee, and then shakes his head back and forth at me, slowly, like he's not quite sure what the fuck to do with me.

I smile at him, raise both arms out to the sides, palms up, and, bloody, sleep-deprived, and still rocking a bit of an erection, I raise my left eyebrow, and shrug.

CHAPTER NINE

MADDIE

You know how it is when you're one of those hard-ass bitches? And you put on that hard-ass show for everyone? Like… you can take anything. Any. Thing. Nothing phases you. You just stare adversity in the face and deal. Climb that fuckin' mountain and get to the top no matter what. Fuck your fingertips. Fuck frostbite. Fuck everything. As long as you get to the top. That's the only thing that matters.

And everyone thinks, *Damn, that bitch is fuckin' hard.*

And you are. So goddamned hard. You handle all of it. You're even one of those women who can have an actual casual relationship, right? You want no strings, dude? Just some straight-up sex? I'm your girl.

I don't do feelings. I don't get needy. I don't expect much from people because people let you down. They don't answer your calls, or your letters, or show up for funerals. And then they go on with their lives and pretend this is just normal, everyday bad luck. Shit happens, right? Life goes on no matter what. Those seconds tick off, and time passes, and they say that heals you, but it doesn't. It didn't heal me. It made everything worse and then they come back into your life acting like they never left, and

you should just let them be there for you, and you're like…
"*FUCK*!"

I punch the steering wheel as I scream the word.

Because that's not who I am right now. Because I'm crying. Because the tears are streaming down my cheeks. Because I don't even know why I'm reacting this way.

It's not the money I don't owe Carlos, either. It's not that stupid asshole, Logan. It's not any of those major things that could actually end up killing me.

It's Scotty, but it's not Scotty. It's Tyler, but it's not Tyler. It's Pete's and it's not Pete's. It's my parents being so far away, but not.

There is no answer that satisfies me right now. God herself could float down here into the passenger seat of Annie's car and give me the fuckin' answer and it wouldn't be the answer. That's how elusive my sadness is.

And the longer I drive, and the more I search for the meaning of my unhappiness, the farther away the answer gets.

The tears are so big, my eyes so filled up with them, the world so blurry with this unexpected sadness, I pull into an abandoned strip mall parking lot and stop the car.

To cry. Over things I don't understand. Over people. Over jobs. Over failures. Over mistakes and… still, it doesn't seem right.

The next thing I know I'm holding Plumeria Brown's card in my hand. And then I'm pressing her number into my phone and she says, "Hello?"

"Plu?" I say, sobbing.

"Who—"

"It's Maddie," I say, still crying. "Maddie Clayton. Remember? I came—"

"Of course," she says. "Of course. Are you OK?"

I shake my head no, but she can't see me, obviously, so she says, "Where are you?"

I look up trying to figure it out, because I have lost all sense of time, and direction, and myself. "I don't know."

"Are you safe?"

"I don't know," I say. "Yes. I just… don't understand why people are assholes, OK? Can you please tell me why people are such assholes?"

"Who's an asshole?" she asks.

I want to say, *Tyler. And Carlos. And Logan. And maybe even my parents.* I want to blame all of them for this ugly breakdown moment I'm having right now.

But I can't.

So, I say, "Everyone. Me. I don't know. But people are assholes and I must be in that club too, otherwise why? Why would so many of them be in my life right now? Can you please just tell me that? I can take it, OK? I swear. I just need to hear the truth right now, I really just need an honest, objective opinion. And you're the only one I can trust because you give no shits, right? It's your job. I mean you have a license to practice, right? And I'm out here failing at everything. And I just need to know, OK? I just need you to tell me why the fuck this shit is happening to me. What did I do? Who did I do it to? Because I can't take it anymore, I really can't. I've had it. I'm about to drive my friend's car out into the desert and—"

"Are you having suicidal thoughts?" Plu interrupts.

"What?" I say, halting my crying. "No. Why would you even say that?"

"Well, you're leading me down a path here, Maddie."

"Of suicide?" I yell. "No. I just want a fucking answer!"

"What were you going to do in the desert?"

"Keep driving! You know, like… never come back." I snort. "Kill myself. I'm not gonna kill myself, for fuck's sake."

"Well, I'm sorry, Maddie. You just seem a little bit desperate right now."

"Yeah, desperate for some fucking meaning!"

"OK," Plu sings in that therapist voice she seems to have perfected since she became this successful adult. "Let's see here. Give me a second…" She sucks in air, lets it out, then says, "OK. People are assholes because they're people. And people aren't perfect, so they sometimes make mistakes and being an asshole is their defense mechanism. And you're an asshole because you want to blame people for things that don't deserve blame. Sometimes bad shit just happens and you happen to take it all very personally and want to punish people just for being in your general vicinity when it does. How's that?"

"Explain," I growl into the phone. "Because I'm pretty certain my blame falls squarely on the shoulders of the assholes who earned it and my reaction to them is a natural consequence that comes from the way they treated me first."

"I'm not done yet," Plu says calmly. "You're also combative. And mean. And more than a little self-righteous."

"What?"

"You wanted the truth, right? You can take it, right?"

"What kind of crackpot therapist are you?"

"A qualified one."

I snort.

"What do you want me to say, Maddie? Do you want me to find someone to blame for Scotty's death? Is that it? Should I point my finger so you can say, *Ah-ha! I knew it*? So you can feel justified for being defensive? For always having that chip on your shoulder? For all the things that go wrong that you take no responsibility for?"

"I didn't kill my brother," I growl into the phone.

"Of course not. But your parents didn't kill your brother either. And his buddies who were there when it happened didn't kill him. He was a firefighter. He fought a fire and he lost—"

"Fuck you!" I scream.

"Yes, fuck me," Plu replies, still calm. "Fuck me. That's a great answer. Just blame me now. Why not, Maddie? You blame everyone else. Even yourself. So what's one more person to stick that label on in your life? People don't mean anything to you, so who cares. I'm nobody to you. Just some person you once knew and nothing more."

"You have no idea what you're talking about," I whisper.

"No?" she says. "Then tell me where I'm going wrong."

"You weren't there when he died," I say.

"Nope. I wasn't. So why don't you fill me in?"

I say nothing. I can't say anything. Because the memories of Scotty's last moments flood into my head and I just start crying harder.

"Maddie," Plu says.

I shake my head, staring at an empty strip mall shop through eyes filled with tears.

She sighs. "Where are you going right now?"

"Home," I mutter.

"Do you want to come see me first?"

"No," I say. I have never wanted anything less.

"You need to deal with those memories eventually," she says. Her voice is still calm, but there's a softness to it that makes me even sadder. Because she gets it. She knows. She sees through me. "And you need to figure out why you want to punish people for something they're not responsible for. Because you're not doing well right now, Maddie. You're not handling things anymore. If you ever were. It's all about to catch up with you and if you don't stand your ground against the pain and deal—accept what happened, that there was no deeper meaning to it, and just let yourself move on…" She pauses. "Well, you're not gonna last very long."

I'm silent for so long she says, "Are you still there?"

"Yes."

"Do you want a prescription to cure what's wrong with you?"

"I don't want to take drugs," I whisper. "It feels like… a loss. Like a failure. And I can't fail again. I've had too many of those lately. I can't take another one right now."

"Good," Plumeria says. "Because what you need doesn't come from a pill."

"Then what is it?" I ask.

"It's very simple, really. Just forgive yourself. For not saving him. Because there was truly nothing you could've done. You know this. And then forgive the people who loved him as much as you did, because there was nothing they could've done either. It was just… it was just a very bad thing that happened. That's it. It has no meaning, Maddie. It was just a very bad thing that happened."

The station house has a bunch of guys inside. I watch them from across the street for a while. I drove straight here after running home to change and to apologize to Annie for fucking up her car. She didn't really seem to care though. She says she's gonna turn it in and take the loss. She quit her call-girl job and can't afford it anyway. Honestly, she's been acting really weird lately. But frankly, I don't have time to give two shits about what's going on with her. That probably makes me a bad friend, but I've got more than enough on my plate at present.

Looking toward the station house, I see glimpses of Evan. In there. Doing his fireman thing. I picture how Scotty would've looked now. All filled out and grown up like Evan. That boyish face I always picture on him long gone. And in its place is a scruffy beard. Maybe like Tyler's. Maybe well-groomed. Maybe no beard. Maybe Scotty was always gonna be clean-shaven. Always that all-American boy, no matter how old he got. Forever young.

That's all I ever see in my head. Scotty. Forever young. Because that's how he died.

Well, no. That's not how he died at all.

That memory is enough to make me start the car back up.

But then one of the guys in the firehouse whistles shrilly and I look over and all I see is Scotty.

"What the fuck?"

But then he smiles and… yeah, that's not Scotty. It's some kid who just reminds me of Scotty.

"What's up, Red?" he yells.

My stomach sinks at the nickname. I suddenly feel sick. But Scotty's ghost starts crossing the street to me, and I'm just putting the car into gear so I can take off before he gets over here, or Evan can see me, but—

"You've been staring at me for a while." The kid laughs, walking up to my window.

"I wasn't staring at you," I snap, then immediately feel bad when he recoils a little at my venom.

Smile. And be nice.

I do that. Sorta. "I'm… I'm just looking for Evan. I'm Scotty's sister."

Baby-face guy scratches his non-existent beard and peers over his shoulder at the other guys. Who are just now noticing that one of their own is out here talking to me. "Who's Scotty?"

God, this was a mistake.

I pull away from the curb and do a U-turn, ready to give up and maybe take that drive out to the desert after all, when I slam on my brakes.

Because Evan is standing in the street, right in front of my car.

"You like it okay, huh?" asks the older guy called Alex who apparently made the plate of rigatoni I'm devouring. Didn't know I was so hungry. But I'm wolfing it.

"Yeah. This shit is fucking delicious," I say, mouth muffled by the steaming forkful of pasta.

The firefighters sitting around the table with me laugh. "Sorry," I mumble sheepishly.

"Shit, sweetheart, I love a woman with a filthy fuckin' mouth," says a little guy with a Boston accent who slides his chair about a foot closer to me. "Say somethin' else."

"Rod. Go… coil a hose or something." That's an enormous guy they call Bear.

"Fuck did I say?" asks Rod.

"So, Maddie," says the impossibly cool and handsome African-American guy, Dean, while he pets his French Bulldog. (This is, by far, the most interesting group of first responders I've ever met.) "Was Evan always into clothes and shit when he was a kid, too? Or is that a recent development since he married up?"

I glance at Evan, who smiles and shakes his head as if to suggest that he's used to these guys busting his balls.

"Um," I say, shoving the last bit of food into my mouth. "Yeah, yeah, actually he was, I guess. He gave my brother and Tyler a makeover for senior prom, and neither one of them ever looked so good."

"Well… To be fair, Scotty looked better than Tyler. I can only do so much with the raw materials I'm given," Evan says, smiling. He winks at me and I lower my head a bit. Everyone chuckles and then Bear apparently decides that play time is over.

"All right!" he says, slapping the table and standing up. "Let's clean up and get some work done today. Rod, you get that paperwork into district yet?"

"Aw, fuck me, I fuckin' forgot. Cocksucker." Then he looks at me. "Sorry."

"No worries," I say in return. "I love a guy with a filthy fuckin' mouth."

"Goddamn perfect woman here. Jesus!"

Bear pulls Rod away and they head off. Dean gives me a shake as he takes his exit, and it's the kind of loose but elegant grip that one usually receives at a grand ball or the U.N. or some damn thing. I half expect him to kiss the back of my hand.

"Glad you enjoyed it, honey," says Alex the chef. "You're welcome here any time."

"Thanks." I smile at him as he takes my plate and heads into the kitchen.

Then this brooding, quiet guy who was introduced to me as Brandon, and who hasn't spoken a word throughout lunch, steps over and hovers above me, blocking the light with his firefighter-shaped shadow. He doesn't speak, and I decide not to either, so we just kind of stare at each other until finally he says…

"I like your hair." And he walks off.

I glance at Evan again, and he gives me a 'I have no idea' look.

And then the young guy, Jeff, comes over.

"Hey," he says. "I'm sorry about earlier."

"What are you sorry about?" I ask.

"I dunno, I just, I feel like I was kinda forward and maybe a little rude or whatever, and I… Y'know, I'm sorry."

Jesus Christ, he's like a fucking reincarnation. I find myself choking up again, against my will. But I rally and laugh it off.

"Dude," I say, "that is not forward. I've seen forward, believe me, and that ain't it."

He smiles. I continue, "But thanks. Apology accepted." Again, I smile. He smiles back. And it breaks my heart a little bit.

Then he leaves and it's just me and Evan. Which is why I came here. To see him. But I feel instantly anxious as I consider all the things that I want to say. That I *need* to say. And as I debate how to begin…

"So," Evan says, "hi."

I laugh ever so slightly. "Hi," I say back.

There's a moment where we just sit like that, and then I take a breath and say, "Evan, I—"

But he interrupts me before I can say more.

"Don't. It's fine, Maddie. It's fine. It's just good to see you. Really."

"It's good to see you too."

"How're your folks?"

"OK. I guess. They're in Monaco, you know."

"I do."

"So... They're OK. We've been talking a lot more recently because of... y'know, the anniversary. We tend to talk a lot around this time of year."

"When's the last time you saw them?" he asks.

"Oh, um, I don't—I mean it's probably been a couple of years."

"Really?"

"They've tried to visit or have me visit or whatever, but it just feels like... I dunno. Never the right time. It's, y'know, it's fine. You know how it is."

"Sure," he says. "So... Oh! So, what's this drone thing Tyler was talking about? Something with real estate?"

I laugh kind of bitterly. "Yeah, fuck. Was supposed to be. Was gonna be my big business idea that was gonna change the real estate game. Thought developers and agents would be all over me for my revolution in the real estate market, but I think maybe I actually just... wanted to buy a drone." Evan laughs. "I dunno. Nothing's exactly worked out the way I thought it would."

"Yeah," he says, "nothing ever does."

"Yeah," I sigh out. "That's for damn sure. You make plans and plot and strategize and next thing you know you're a morning manager at a strip club in the desert."

Evan just looks at me. Can't tell what he's thinking behind those black eyes of his. Never have been able to.

"Well, not you," I say, to fill the silence. "But some of us are. Me. I am. I'm the strip club manager. That's what I'm saying."

The corners of his eyes wrinkle and he smiles.

"So!" As I try saying something that's not totally stupid. "You're married, huh?" I slap his knee. "That's so awesome. What does he do, your husband?"

Evan takes a beat, smirking at me before he answers. "He's a real-estate developer."

"Really? I ask

"Yup."

"What's his name? I've probably tried to pitch him on my stupid drone idea."

"Robert Vanderbilt," says Evan and my jaw hits the floor.

"Fuck you, dude! You're married to Robert Vanderbilt?"

"You know him."

"Uh, yeah, I know him. His name is on every other property I see listed."

"Yep. That's him. He's a go-getter."

There's a moment of silence because we both know what should happen next, but I'm not gonna ask and he's not gonna offer. So…

After a beat he says, "So, Tyler—"

I hold up a hand to stop him. "I don't know. OK? I don't. I just… The whole thing's such a mind-fuck, I don't know what I'm gonna do."

"Yeah, I get that."

"The guy I had a massive crush on for my whole childhood disappears on me, basically destroying my hope and my heart, and then after a dozen years he shows back up and we sort of fall for each other, but kinda-not-really because neither one of us immediately realize who the other is because he's an unrecognizable version of his former self and I'm now a grown-up, oh, and also dressed like a fucking *stripper* because that's what I am. Jesus. How do you navigate that relationship? There's no roadmap for that. I mean, if you wrote that story, nobody would believe it. It's absurd."

Evan snorts and says, "Life's absurd." He's right. He continues, "But can I tell you something? And you can ignore me or tell me to fuck off or whatever, but I feel like I wanna say it now because who the hell knows if I'll ever see you again."

"Stop!" I say, slapping his shoulder.

"I know, I know, I'm sorry, couldn't resist. But here's what I wanna say." He pauses, looks at the floor like he's gathering his thoughts just so, then takes my hands and looks me in the eye. "Tyler Morgan is one of the best people I've ever met in my life."

I pull back, beginning to protest, but he holds onto my hands.

"He is," Evan continues. "He truly is. He's an idiot and can be fucking impossible—"

"Tell me about it."

"But he has one of the best hearts of anyone I've ever known. And he's loyal. He really is. And he fucked you, yes. He one hundred percent did. But he was scared and he was in the military at the time and he gave over to all that straight-alpha-male bullshit, and he forgot to take care of himself, which means he couldn't even possibly take care of anyone else, but he's finding his way back. And you can choose to be a part of that or not, but—and not to play therapist here, but—I think you're on a similar journey and maybe you two could help each other. That's it. That's all I wanted to say."

I close my eyes, taking it all in.

And then he adds, "Well… And this. If by chance that special place you've been dreaming of leads you to a lonely place… Find your strength in love.'"

He squeezes my hands. I open my eyes and blink at him.

"Is that… Whitney Houston?"

"Yep."

"You're giving me advice based on a Whitney Houston song?"

Evan throws a finger in the air, pulls his head back, and rolls his neck. "Girl, don't you even *think* about talking smack about Whitney."

And I bust out laughing. It feels wonderful. And like a long-forgotten skill.

"I've missed you," I say, the laughter subsiding.

"I've missed you too, Maddie… So, listen, I don't know if this is of any interest to you, since you're killing it in the stripper game and all, but Robert has this huge project he's trying to get off the ground out by the Hoover Dam, and he's having a bitch of a time getting the surveying done and… Honestly, I have no idea. I don't understand this shit at all, but perhaps having someone who can help him with a bird's-eye view might be useful in some way?"

"Are you serious?"

"Yeah. This is my serious face." He gives me the same dark expression he wears much of the time.

"Oh, my God, Evan, I'd… Yes. Please. Thank you."

"No problem. I'll have his assistant give you a call."

"Oh, my God, Evan, thank you so much."

I grab him around the neck and hug him like I never want to let go. Because I kind of don't.

"My pleasure, Mads," he says. And then he whispers in my ear, "I miss him every day," and I start crying. And then he whispers, "And so does Tyler."

And I can't be sure, but normally unflappable and unreadable Evan might be crying a little too. I don't know. Neither one of us lets go of our embrace or pulls back to look.

We just hold each other for several long minutes.

CHAPTER TEN

TYLER

"The Delta, mostly," says Pete.

"Shit, really? The Mekong Delta?" I ask.

"No, the Mississippi Delta. Yes, of course, the fucking Mekong," Pete responds.

I've been sitting in his office asking him about his time in the service for most of the morning. He's not particularly forthcoming, but I like him and I don't wanna leave just yet. It doesn't take Dr. Eldridge, who kinda reminds me of my mom, to tell me that I like Pete because he seems like the kinda guy I wish I had had as a dad, instead of my actual dad. Maybe I can get Doc Eldridge and Pete together! That'd be badass.

The blood on my shirt is mostly dry now and it looks kind of like a Rorschach test. When I stare down at it what I see is the sexiest woman I've ever met wrapping her gorgeous legs around me, and that makes my dick jump. Consequently, I'm not looking down at it, because I don't want Pete to get the wrong idea. Never can be too careful.

"Jesus," I say, "So what kind of missions were you running?"

Pete takes a bite of his corn dog (the lunch buffet at the club features corn dogs, presumably so that the girls can wrap their mouths around them while they're giving lap dances to the lunch crowd. That's just smart marketing) and studies me.

"Classified ones," he says.

"Oh. So you were in Cambodia?"

"How long you serve?" Pete asks.

"Four tours."

"And nobody ever told you what the hell 'classified' means?" he says, as he takes another bite.

I take a bite of mine too and we both chew in silence for a second.

"So how'd you wind up owning a strip joint in Vegas?" I ask him.

"You this inquisitive with everybody?"

"I dunno. I kinda stuffed down my inside voice for a long time, but lately I'm making an effort. Just trying to be a part of society or some fucking thing."

He eyes me, nods. "Yeah… I get that." Then he finishes off his corn dog, throws the stick in the trash, wipes his hands, and says, "Girl."

"Girl got you to Vegas or girl got you to open a strip club?"

"Yep," he says. I really like this fucking guy.

"Where is she now?"

He pauses for a moment. Then he turns in his chair and points to an urn sitting on the shelf behind him.

"Oh. Sorry." I say.

"Nothing to be sorry about. She saved me when I thought I was past saving, we were together for a long time, then she died in her sleep with my arms wrapped around her. That's about as good a life as a man can hope for."

I start feeling kinda misty and I'm not sure why. I didn't know her. Hell, I barely know him, but still something about the way he says it hits me in just the right place.

"There's gotta be more to that story," I suggest.

"There is," he says. Period. Full stop. OK. I can take a hint.

I finish my corn dog too and toss the stick and napkin across the room into the trash can on the far side. (Four years as power forward on my high-school varsity team. You can't fuck with my corn-dog-stick tossing game.)

"So, Pete, can I ask you a question?"

"You have been all morning."

"Fair enough. Can you fire Maddie?"

He looks at me like I'm making him tired. Probably because... "What's that, now?"

"I'm just trying to help her."

"By making her lose her job?"

"C'mon, man," I say, "I don't know exactly what the deal is, but you and I both know that fucking guy is gonna be back. Whatever she's into, she needs to disappear. But she's so goddamn stubborn, she'll just keep showing up until some something gets broken that can't be put back together."

"She's an adult," he says.

"Okay, fine." I decide to change up my argument. "But you and I both know Maddie's not supposed to be here."

"No?"

"No. You *know* her. She's not like the other girls who work here."

Pete leans back, puts his hands on his belly. "Yeah? You know a whole lot about the other girls who work here?"

"Well," I say, somewhat hesitantly, because I can already see where this is headed. "I—"

"Stephanie has a kid and was left high and dry by her old man. She tried about fifteen other things but couldn't cover the bills."

"I know, I—"

"Meredith trained to be a ballerina, got a knee injury, this is a way she can dance and make a living at the same time."

"Okay, I get it, I just—"

"Patricia's just kind of a sexual deviant with low self-esteem, but y'know, they're not all gonna be stories of plucky underdogs." Pete almost cracks a smile. Almost. Then he says, "Stop trying to make up for your fuck-up by forcing yourself on the situation. Looks to me like you and her are finding common ground"—he nods at my bloody t-shirt—"such as it is. So just give her some space and stop trying to play hero. That ship has sailed."

Shit. Pete just knows how to get right to the heart of a motherfucker.

"Maddie's a good girl," Pete says. "She's a smart girl. She's gonna be OK."

"I just wish she'd take some help and not feel like she has to fucking do everything on her own all the time."

"No, you don't."

"What?" I ask, genuinely surprised.

"Because then she wouldn't be her."

Again, right to the fucking heart.

He stands, which I take as my cue to stand too. Pete says to me, "I'm not much of one for telling another man what he should do or how he should be, but…" He puts his hand on my shoulder and walks me to the door. "I know Raven already told you this, but it feels like it bears repeating. Because, you know, you're stupid."

"Thanks."

"If you really give a shit about Maddie, find a way to show her you do. Not get her to forgive you or think anything about you, just show her you're grateful for her. Think of it like giving a gift. You give me a picture to hang in my office, you don't get to tell me where to hang it, or when, or even if I do. You just give the gift and walk away. Give her a gift. You get me?"

I turn to face him. I nod. "Yeah. Like my friend Lobsang once told me. Give of yourself freely. Have no attachment to the outcome."

"Sure. Whatever. Just don't be a fucking asshole."

"That is also a way to say it." I shake his hand. "You're a wise man, Pete—Uh. What's your last name?"

"Don't matter much. And I'm not wise, I just got lucky to know somebody once who helped me learn some shit that set me right." He looks over to the pretty urn behind his desk, then back at me. "Hell, kid, I was probably even stupider than you once upon a time. So… there's still hope."

He nods his head and I walk through the door of his office and down the stairs, thinking about how much I really do have to be grateful for. I mean shit, I'm still alive. And I'm in love with my best friend's kid sister. And she, at the least, keeps letting me fuck her, so I feel like that's an encouraging sign.

I do need to show Maddie how much I'm thankful for her. He's right. I need to give her a gift. One that shows her I understand where she's at. What she needs. Something that's only for her and isn't at all about me.

I just need to figure out what the hell that is.

CHAPTER ELEVEN

I wake up from my after-work nap to the smell of pumpkin pies baking in the oven.

Because it's Thanksgiving. Or will be tomorrow. Annie, Diane, and Caroline are making pies for a dinner they're going to with some old friends from college.

They invited me, but I declined. I don't actually know those friends from college, seeing as how I was a mess almost the entire time I was there and didn't actually get to know *anyone*, Diane, Caroline, and Annie included.

It's been years since I did anything on Thanksgiving. Last year I was just starting the wedding planner stuff, so I pretended it was another work day and kept working. The year before that… I think for a minute. Same thing, only it was the multi-level marketing stuff. I was running online giveaways for an early Black Friday sale. The year before I think I was trying out new recipes for the pet bakery.

Jesus Christ. Thanksgiving is like an endless reminder of how many times I've failed over the past few years.

My phone rings so I turn over, fish it out from under my pillow, and stare at the screen.

My mother.

No, thank you. I force it to go to voicemail and stuff it back under my pillow.

I bet Evan and his husband are having a nice dinner for Thanksgiving. I bet it'll be all fancy and shit too. I bet he wouldn't mind if I invited myself over. But it's all too much effort. The phone call, the asking, the accepting, the everything. It's just too much effort when I can just stay right here in this bed and pretend Thanksgiving is already over.

My phone dings a voicemail notification, and I'm just about to press the icon to see what she had to say—probably something simple, like, *Happy Thanksgiving! We miss you!*—when a soft knock at my door stops the screen tap.

"Come in," I say.

"Hey," Annie says, peeking her head in first. "You awake now?"

"Yeah." I yawn. I've taken to sleeping after work lately. I think it's probably a bad sign because I'm not actually tired when I get home. Just… uninterested in doing anything else but crawling back into bed. Which I realize might be a sign of depression. Which isn't surprising because I think I am actually depressed.

This is not the life I imagined for myself. At all.

"Good," Annie says. "Because I wanna talk to you about something."

"What's up?" I ask.

"I'm not sure," she says, sinking down onto the mattress next to me.

I sit up a little. "What is it?"

She looks out my window, closes her eyes, takes a deep breath. "You know David?"

"Sorry… Which one's David?" She fucks men for a living, so David could be anybody.

"My high school boyfriend? The one I tried to make it work with when I came here?"

"The one getting married?"

"Yup," she says, sadly. "Him."

"Sure," I say. "Yeah, I remember."

"Well…" She hesitates. "He's not getting married anymore."

"What?"

"Yeah. So I called his fiancée last week—"

"Oh, shit, Annie. Why?"

"Just to say congratulations—"

"Oh, Annie…"

She shrugs. "Yeah. But I couldn't let it go. Anyway, I did. And I said all the right things, and behaved like the most reasonable responsible adult, but… it didn't quite work out the way I'd planned."

"Fuck. Did she flip out on you?"

"Noooo," Annie says. "No. That's not what happened."

"Then what the fuck happened?"

"He… called it off."

"Sorry? Called off… the *wedding*?"

She smiles weakly and nods her head. "Yeah. Like… he called me last night and told me that my call to her made him start thinking about us and—"

"Awww, fuck," I say.

"—and even though I didn't mean to, looks like… I broke them up." She throws her hands up. "Shit! I give up, Maddie. I just can't do anything right."

God, I know that feeling. "OK. OK. But it's not your fault he broke it off," I say. "I mean, if he still loves you, he still loves you. And no woman wants to marry a guy in love with someone else."

"I get that," she says, still sounding so defeated. "But he seemed happy enough before I made that call."

I think about that for a second. "No," I say. "No, he's the one who called you to tell you about the wedding. If he was so happy, then why did he bother to do that?"

"I know. I think about that too. That maybe he was feeling me out, or trying to make me jealous, or whatever. And it worked. Because I came apart with that news. So, I think maybe he did do it on purpose. But I could've let it go. Just moved on and let him have his life."

"What's the point in that?" I ask. "I mean, then you'd both be miserable. Like two ships passing in the night. Star-crossed lovers and all that bullshit. No one needs regrets like that."

It occurs to me there's a lesson here. And it's for me, not Annie.

"I don't know why I'm telling you this. Maybe because you always know what to do."

"Me?" I scoff. "Are you kidding? I'm a mess!"

"No," Annie says. "You're like… I dunno, the *Mount Everest* of common sense. You always think things through. You always have a plan. You always have new ideas on how to get what you want. And…" she says, then takes a deep breath. "You have limits. Lines you won't cross just to get something. You're loyal. And honest. And generous." She smiles. It might be the first real smile I've seen on her face in weeks. "I admire that. I admire you. So… I just need to ask you this, OK? And I need your honest opinion, no matter what it is."

I'm still a little dumbfounded that she just called me the Mount Everest of common sense. Not to mention all those other altruistic qualities I absolutely do not possess. But I say, "OK. Shoot."

She draws in an enormous breath, like she needs a lot of courage to say these words, and then she asks on the exhale, "Do you think I'd be a terrible person if I went home and tried to work things out with him? Like, say I'm sorry for not realizing how much he meant to me? And promise to make it up to him if we can just start over again?" She places a hand on my arm, squeezing lightly. "I know I'd be leaving you guys in a terrible spot with the rent. But I'd pay you everything I could. I'd give you my share for two months, so you guys could find another roommate."

I almost laugh. Not because it's funny, but because it's not even a question. "Annie," I say, sitting all the way up to look her in the eyes. "Why wouldn't you? I mean..." And I have to word this carefully, so I don't make her feel worse. "You're selling your body for money. No offense, but there is no way going back to life without *that* makes you a terrible person. And anyway," I say. "You only get one soulmate in this life. And if he's yours, then he's yours. There's nothing you can do about that. So, shit... Go for it."

She smiles, but a tear falls down her cheek. "I'm going to miss you."

I lean in and hug her. "Yeah, I'm going to miss you too."

"And I hope you work things out with Tyler, ya know?"

I put my hands up. "OK. Let's all just slow down." Because I know Annie. Somehow, in spite of all the awful shit she's seen and done, she manages to hang onto the adolescent dream that true love is out there and waiting for us and if you kiss the right frog and all that bullshit, a prince will come to rescue you. I think she has to think that shit to get through her days. Like she's sleepwalking.

But I'm wide awake.

So I change the subject and we talk a little more. Just details about when she's leaving and so forth.

Tonight, she's decided. She's already packed.

Which makes it abundantly clear that she didn't need my permission, she just wanted it. Which I appreciate in some disproportionately affecting way. It means… well, that I mean something to her. And that makes me feel good.

She tries to give me her portion of the rent because Caroline and Diane wouldn't take it. But I refuse to take it too. I have money saved for Carlos. And since that's a losing battle if ever there was one, I decide I'd rather use my money to help people I love. Carlos Castillo can fuck off.

Caroline, Diane, and I see her off a few hours later. We help pack up her car. She doles out things to us she won't be taking with her. And it's not hard to see the sadness on my other roommate's faces when they accept her work clothes and shoes.

They don't want this life anymore, either. They're envious, but not in a mean way. Just… a longing kind of way.

We stand in the driveway and wave until her car disappears into the desert.

And then the three of us sigh and go back inside to the lives we have yet to leave behind. It also occurs to me that I have no car now. So I have to ask Diane for a favor. She agrees, of course. We work totally different hours, and that's what friends are for, right?

But I hate asking. I hate it. I feel like I'm going backwards. Like I'm at the bottom of Mount Everest now, and I haven't even taken one step up yet.

I sleep until my alarm goes off for work, and then I drag myself out of bed on Thanksgiving morning, ready to go out and be thankful for… absolutely nothing.

I don't know if it's surprising or not when I walk into work and find more than a dozen men already there eating breakfast.

I guess it's not. I mean lots of people hate the holidays, right? Lots of people have no one and nothing to look forward to on these days, myself included. But lots of people also have the day off. Which means they can sit at home and feel sorry for themselves or go out to a strip club and pretend for a while.

These folks just seem to be pretending early. I'm betting most of them are broke or drunk by noon and sleep the rest of the day away.

I'll be off by noon too… and then what?

Yup. My life is just as awesome as the customers at Pete's on Thanksgiving morning.

My shift goes quickly because there's a ton of girls in here today. Everyone wants to work a holiday, I remind myself. And the morning shift is popular for some reason. I tell myself it's because I'm such a terrific manager. I've got five extra girls on the schedule and by ten o'clock, the place isn't… full. But it's filling up.

I don't do any dances. I give my stage time to another girl who needs the money. I also need the money, but I don't have kids, and I don't have to take them to their grandparents this afternoon, and I don't have to meet anyone's expectations today at all.

So I just sit in the downstairs back office—Raven's office, but mine when she's not here—and do stupid things like check time cards over and over.

My phone rings just before I'm about to start cleaning up to go… home… and even though it's my mother and I don't feel like talking to her, I answer, because it's a holiday and that's what you do. Smile and be nice. Infamous words from Raquel the Friendly Stripper I have tried to live by ever since she handed them out.

In my most cheerful good-daughter voice I say, "Hey, Mom! Happy Thanksgiving!"

"Did you get my message last night?" she asks.

"Oh…" Whoops. "Yup! Sorry. I'm kinda busy." Lies. Both statements. I didn't listen to her message, but I don't want to admit that. It just seems… heartless. "So can I call you back later, maybe?"

"Call me back? What time are you coming over?"

"Over?" Jesus Christ. What's she talking about? "Sorry. Where are you?" I ask, trying to play this off.

"Honey… The Four Seasons," she says, her high-pitched I'm-frustrated-with-you voice making me wince.

"The Four—? In Las Vegas?" I ask. Dumbly.

"Madison. Did you even listen to my message?"

"Yes, I just—" I insist. Once you lie, you kinda just have to go with it.

"It's fine. Don't worry about it. Dinner. Today. With us, your family. At four o'clock. But we want you to come over early. You know, so we can all catch up and talk before we eat. Your father is so excited to be here. And we can't wait to see you."

What. The actual. Fuck.

"Mom. I—Why didn't you give me a heads up on any of this before *yesterday*?"

"We'll tell you everything when we see you. Can you make it or… Should we come to you? Would that be better?"

"No!" I say, too aggressively, then auto-correct, "No. No. Sorry, just, uh, no. I can make it. I'm… excited to see you." I am, I realize. "So just give me a bit to wrap up a couple of things and change and stuff and I'll be over. OK?"

"Wonderful, we're in room three nine one five. I'll text it to you because I know you'll never remember. Where are you, by the way?"

"Uh, I'm working, why?"

"It sounds like a nightclub."

Fuck. "Uh, sorry, Mom! Have to handle something real quick, but I'll be there soon, K? See ya in a bit!"

I end the call and lean back in my sad, rickety office chair with a confused sigh. Well, that's a strange turn of events. How the hell did my parents get to Vegas?

Who cares, I decide. I might even be smiling. Because… I have family here! On a day meant to be spent with family. Shit. I am not poor Maddie, girl perpetually on her own. What do you know. I have somewhere to go. I have a place I belong. And even if it's just some hotel restaurant, it's still better than sleeping away my day feeling lonely and desperate.

On my way out of Pete's I wish everyone a happy Thanksgiving. I smile as I say it. I might even have a spring in my step.

When I get home, I choose my most conservative outfit—tan trousers, pink silk blouse with a ruffle at the neck and wrists—and put on a pair of shoes that no stripper would be caught dead in. I even put on earrings. And not the kind that droop down to my shoulders. Real earrings. With genuine sapphires and diamonds.

Sitting next to a foil-covered pumpkin pie on the kitchen counter is a note from Diane and Caroline. *For you*, it says.

Sweet. Now I have something to bring. Good daughter.

I gather up my purse, my pie, and get into Diane's car.

It's nearly two o'clock by the time I fight Strip traffic and pull into the valet at the Four Seasons drop-off at Mandalay Bay. I figure what the hell. I'm never gonna get that money together for Carlos, I might as well enjoy life while I still can.

Inside I am a little lost because you can't ever find the elevators in Las Vegas. They hide them, hoping you'll stumble into a casino and spend all your money. A man greets me with a huge smile you only find on the faces of greeters at five-star hotels. "Can I help you with that, ma'am?" he asks, pointing to my pie.

"Um, no. I'm just looking for the elevators for room"—I check the text my mother sent, because she knows me well. I never remember anything—"three nine one five."

His smile grows wider, if that's possible. "Well, let me escort you up." He takes my pie with an assertiveness that implies carrying it myself isn't an option.

"Thanks. I'm here to see my parents," I say, kinda loopy like I'm a little high. I continue to give way more information than the guy needs. "They're in from Monaco. They surprised me," I say, unnaturally excited about the turn in my day.

"Great!" he says, equally unnatural in his enthusiasm.

He flashes his ID badge at an elevator that's tucked into a short, private hallway, and then waves me inside. There's a bench, which is unusual for most elevators in Vegas. I mean, typically they want to cram as many people as they can into these things. But it is the Four Seasons, so that must be what you pay extra for here, right?

The ride up is quick and we make no stops. Just right up to the—I stare at the panel of available floors on the side of the elevator. Just one to choose from. Top.

The doors open to another short hallway leading to a tall wooden door with the room-number placard off to the side. My escort knocks for me, then hands me my pie and says, "Happy Thanksgiving."

I fish a bill out of my purse, pull up a twenty—fuck it, why not—and hand it over with a sweet, "You too," that I actually mean.

The door opens and my mother and father are there. Wrapping me in hugs, talking a mile a minute, saying things like, "You look great!" and, "Do you believe this suite?"

And that's when I see the staircase.

Staircase? Who the hell has a staircase in a hotel room?

And that's when I see who's coming down the staircase.

You have got to be fucking kidding me.

CHAPTER TWELVE

TYLER & MADDIE

TYLER

She looks surprised to see me. No, not surprised—um, what's the word for when someone looks like they're trying to decide whether to turn and walk away, scream at the top of their lungs, or murder something? Whatever that's called, that's the expression she has on.

It's OK. To be expected. *Give the gift. Not about you. Breathe. Stay present. Like your Rinpoche in Nepal taught you. Or just don't be a fucking asshole. Like your Rinpoche in the strip club taught you.*

"Why. Is. Tyler. Here?" Maddie says.

Her mother Georgina—who looks terrific, I must say—answers, "He insisted that we not tell you."

Her dad Simon chimes in, "Well, he also insisted that we come in the first place, so in fairness, the least we could do was to honor the surprise, since Tyler did strongarm us into letting him pay for all this." He gestures around the presidential suite of the Four Seasons to emphasize that this is the "this" he's referring to, and grabs me by the shoulders, giving me a shake in a 'you old so-and-so' kind of a way. Simon's always been a hail-fellow-well-met sort of a guy. I like it. It's festive.

"He. What?" Maddie asks, a little loudly.

There's an awkward beat during which Georgina and Simon look at each other and then at me. I smile and shrug.

"Uh," Simon begins. "Well, Tyler called us a few days ago—"

"Which was such a lovely surprise," Georgina adds.

"Yeah!" says Simon. "It really was. So he calls us up to see how we were doing and we got to chatting and then he asked when we might get to see each other—"

"—and then he suggested that, with Thanksgiving coming up, we should try to see each other now," says Georgina. I don't say anything. They're telling the story exactly right. Also, Maddie just keeps staring at me, so I'm holding back on chatting it up too much.

Evan told me that when Maddie came to see him, she said it had been a couple of years since she saw her folks. So I anticipated the possibility that it might take her a moment to adjust when she found out what an awesome thing I'd done for her. Because it is an awesome thing I've done. It is. I know it is. I've given her a gift. She just has to see it.

Fuckin' Tyler Morgan. Good Samaritan and all-around excellent guy. Pretty much only Evan says so.

But I'm working on changing that.

"Honey…" Georgina begins, as she takes Maddie by the hands, whispering just loudly enough to be sure that everyone can hear. "Tyler told us everything."

Maddie's focused stare on me intensifies a bit.

"Did he?" she says. "What'd he tell you?" she manages to ask through what appears to be a completely clenched jaw.

Again, all totally expected. No need to stress. *All's OK. She'll relax in a minute. Or not. Not your call. No attachment to the outcome. If she kills you, she kills you. Nobody said altruism was an easy ride.*

"He told us that you've been working yourself into the ground with your new business, and that you keep saying how much you wish you could get away, but since you can't, we all agreed that we should come see you," Georgina says sweetly. True. That is what I told them. "And besides—" Georgina now lowers her voice to a more appropriate whisper, but I can still hear her. (I've got amazing hearing, which is wild considering how many times shit has exploded next to me.) "We feel… Your father and I feel like... We've... We've missed you. We feel like we should all make an effort to see each other more often. We love you. We want to be more involved in your life. We just… We love you, sweetheart."

And then Georgina pulls her into a tight hug, and Maddie takes her eyes off me for the first time. She closes her eyelids. I'm no expert on human emotions, but my instinct tells me she's trying to keep from crying. I do know what that looks like.

"Maddie!" Simon bellows as he slaps me on the back, breaking the mood, as is his wont. "You should've told us you've been seeing Tyler! We had no idea he was back!"

Maddie pulls away from her mom now, opens her eyes, which are a bit moist but have no proper tears, and says, "Yeah, well…" I grimace without intending to, unsure what's gonna come next. I made a calculated risk putting this whole thing together, but even though it's calculated, it's still a risk. And then she says, "...Like he said, I've been busy. So… I guess I just forgot to mention it. But yeah. He's back, all right."

And then she kind of smiles at me. Like she means it.

Well, would you look at that.

Namaste, motherfuckers.

MADDIE

My emotions have been getting whipped around by a cyclone for the last few weeks and I'm tired. Beyond tired. Exhausted in a way that doesn't have a word to describe it. So in this moment, even though there are about twenty different feelings coursing through me, I decide to just pick one and let it rule the day. And to my surprise, the one that wins out is… gratitude.

Because right now, instead of sitting alone in the house I share with two hookers, now that the third hooker has driven off into the sunset to be with her high-school soulmate (how is this my life?), I'm here in the presidential suite of the Four Seasons with my parents.

And, of course, Tyler Morgan. Who somehow knew what I needed even though I didn't. And then he made it happen.

Son of a bitch.

"So," I say to him, in an attempt to make this all seem completely normal and not walk my parents into a conversation about anything having to do with me and Tyler, "you convinced Mom and Dad to let you pay for all this? Hell, that's a Thanksgiving miracle in itself."

Mom walks over to Tyler so that she's on one side of him and Dad's on the other. She takes up his hand. "Well," she says, "he's *very* persuasive." She squeezes his palm and nudges him. He grins in his unforgivably charming way and winks.

Is—is Tyler Morgan flirting with my mom? Shit, is my mom flirting with Tyler Morgan?

Dad then makes fists and sort of shadow boxes with him, saying. "Yep! Sure is!"

Forget Mom, is *Dad* flirting with him? Jesus Christ.

"Shall we have a drink before we head down for Thanksgiving dinner?" asks Mom.

"We?" I ask. "Is… Tyler? Are you… having Thanksgiving dinner with us?"

"Well, sure he is!" bellows Dad. "That was part of the deal! We said, 'OK, we'll let you pay for the suite and all, but dinner is on us, and you have to come!'"

I swear to fuck, I feel like I'm in the middle of some bizarre, alternate-universe holiday commercial for… like, long-distance service, or some damn thing.

"Come on," Mom says. "Let's all head into the living room for a cocktail."

"I got it," Tyler exclaims, stepping over to the bar in the corner. "Georgina, still gin and tonic? Simon, you want a Manhattan?"

"You remember!" Mom says, delighted.

"Maddie? Whatcha drinking?" Tyler asks.

All three of them look at me expectantly, broad smiles plastered across their faces.

"Um… Just mix up everything that's there into a glass, and make it a double."

"And then after a few years of seeing what the world had to offer a guy like me, I just kind of wound up back here."

Tyler's wrapping up the story of where he's been for the last seven years. I'm alternately surprised by the little details I didn't know and pissed off that I'm only just discovering it all now. Because it reminds me again of how far gone from us—from me—he's been.

"Wow. That's some kind of a story," says my dad. "And what happened with Nadir's—that was his name, yeah? Nadir?" Tyler nods, affirming the name of the translator he worked with to develop the technology he sold that made him a multi-millionaire. The translator who died before he got to benefit from what he and Tyler made. "What happened with Nadir's family?" Dad finishes asking.

Tyler gets solemn. "Um, yeah. Yeah. I don't really know, actually. I…" Tyler trails off. Huh, it's not solemnity I see. It's shame. "Yeah. I dunno."

There's an awkward pause. Then Dad says, "Well, that's war, huh? Hell, as they say."

"Yeah," Tyler huffs out. "It can be."

"Well"—my mom takes Tyler by the arm—"we're just glad *you're* OK. And that you're back home!" I forgot how much Mom and Dad always loved Tyler. They kind of saw him as a second son. Especially after his mother died. He was at our place all the time. His dad was such a bastard. Probably still is. And for just a moment, I get sad for someone other than myself. But then I stuff it down. Because I can't afford to share my sorrow.

Mom touches Tyler's beard. "And what's all this about? Is this a trendy thing that you're doing, or…?"

"No, Georgina, just too damn lazy to shave." Tyler smirks and everyone laughs. I dunno how he fucking does it, but he does.

"So, Maddie!" says Dad. "Tell us more about this real estate thing you're doing! You've been so hush-hush about it, but Tyler says it's going well."

"Oh…" Shit. I really don't want to have to lie straight to my parents' faces. "Yeah, well, um…"

"Tell 'em about Robert, Maddie," Tyler chimes in, encouraging with a knowing look. Evan must have told him that I came by the station. Fuck.

"Oh, well, yeah, just, um, Robert Vanderbilt and I are maybe talking about—"

"Robert is Evan's husband," Tyler volunteers.

"Evan's married?" Mom asks.

"Oh, yeah," Tyler says. "His husband is the biggest real estate developer in town. And he's working exclusively with Maddie." He smiles a wide smile.

"Honey!" Dad barks out. "That's great! This might be the one then, huh?"

The looks on Mom's and Dad's faces are so hopeful that I want to punch Tyler in the stomach for offering it all up. Because the greater the expectation, the greater the disappointment when they discover the truth. But to hell with it. Right now, here, today, we can all pretend that everything's OK. So I do.

"Fingers crossed!" I say with a tight smile.

"Fantastic!" beams Mom. "And is Evan well? Still fighting fires?"

For the tiniest of moments there is a thick cloud in the air. Because I know every one of us thinks of Scotty. But then the cloud quickly rolls off.

"Yep," Tyler answers. "He's great. Never seen him happier. He's really in love. They're funny to watch in the morning. They have a chef who comes in, but Robert insists on making Evan's smoothies personally, because he knows how he likes them. It's sweet."

"Oh," Dad starts, "is that where you're living?" Which is a good question. Why the hell is Tyler at Evan's in the morning?

"Oh, yeah," Tyler says. "Just for a while. I had an apartment in The Mandarin, but it… Um. I'm... Moving on from there. Time to make a change. So I'm staying with Evan and Robert for a while. That's all. That's why we're here and not there!" He puts on something like a forced smile and I'm not sure what the hell's going on. We fucked in his apartment in the Mandarin like a month ago. I even joked that it looked like he had just moved in because there was virtually no furniture. Something's weird here.

Then he claps his hands and says, "So! Shall we?" He stands quickly, and as he does, he bumps into my mom's hand, the one holding her gin and tonic, and the drink splashes out of her tumbler and all over me. All over my ruffled blouse and my pretty tan trousers. Perfect. Just fucking perfect.

I stand, and Tyler yelps, "Oh, shit, I'm sorry," as he fumbles to try to help wipe me off, knocking over the glass of whiskey I have sitting on the arm of my chair and onto the ass of my pants in the attempt. "Jesus!" he shouts. "Fuck! I'm sorry. Fuck, I'm sorry, Georgina. Didn't mean to say fuck. Fuck."

Tyler Morgan, ladies and gentlemen.

"It's fine," Mom says. "Just… Oh, honey. Your pants."

"Yeah, no, I know," I pretty much growl.

"You need to get some soda water onto those before it sets," offers Dad.

And suddenly everyone has their hands all over me, trying to be helpful.

"Guys!" I shout, and they all back off. "It's fine. Just... Just, why don't you all go downstairs and just like, give me a minute. K? I'll clean off and, Mom, do you have anything I can put on?"

"Of course, dear. Take anything from the closet you want. Oh, I'm so sorry."

The look on Mom's face is way more upset than it needs to be. Except that it's not. Because the fact that some shit got accidentally spilled on me is not what she's apologizing for. She's apologizing for so much more.

"It's OK, Mom. It's OK." I give her a hug, keeping enough distance so that I don't get booze all over her. "I am too," I whisper into her cheek.

She pulls back, tears in her eyes, and smiles. I smile too.

"OK!" Dad merrily intones. "Well, then we'll head down to the restaurant and get a table, and you just come on down whenever you're ready."

"OK, Dad." He gives me a kiss on the cheek and heads off. Mom gives me one last, brief hug, and heads toward the door as well, leaving Tyler standing there.

"Shit," he says, "I'm sorry. I didn't—Fuck. I was just trying to—"

I cut him off before he can say more. "It's OK. I know what you were trying to do. So..."

I pause because I'm still not ready to just fucking forgive Tyler Hudson Morgan for everything he's done. Or hasn't done, more accurately. But I think about what

Pete said to me. "You don't always get a second chance to make things right."

Tyler's trying. Like, he's really fucking trying. And even though I'm still not sure that it's all gonna work out, and we're gonna live happily ever after or whatever weird fantasy it is that Tyler and Annie and whoever else are all thinking is going to happen… Right here, right now, on Thanksgiving, I can at the least offer him this act of generosity. Because he's offered me one.

"So… Thanks," I say and nod to him. "I'll be down in a minute,"

He smiles and nods back, then heads to the door. I watch it close behind the three of them as they make their way out, then I head up the stairs to the bedroom.

Making my way through the master bedroom into the en suite (again, this is a fucking *hotel room*), I strip off my blouse and pants, leaving them on the bathroom floor. I want to make sure the whiskey that got on my ass didn't stain my underwear. It's a new lacy white bra and panty set that I bought because it looked pretty and because I realized I more or less only own really slutty stuff that I can also use at work. Sexy, but not very practical. I thought this set was sexy *and* practical, and I really don't want it stained by Johnny Walker.

I contort myself in front of the mirror to make sure I'm clean—as clean as someone like me can be, anyway—and it looks like it's all OK, thank God. And as I stand in front of the full-length mirror in this gorgeous marble bathroom that looks like it got pulled out of a French castle, looking at myself in my pretty white underwear, red hair styled and coifed and laying over my shoulder, wearing sapphire and diamond earrings that were a present from my parents, and elegant heels that one wears because they make one's calves look good and not because they make men in a dark room want to jerk off to visions of you later, I feel almost like an angel. Again.

In the way that Tyler thought of me as an angel, and for a few seconds when we were together, made me feel like I was one too. Before the truth came out and the clouds got pulled from underneath me, and I came tumbling back down to earth.

But right now, I can pretend. For a little while. I can pretend I *am* working on a successful business that I started myself, and don't owe a bunch of money to Carlos, and don't work in a strip club, and don't live with hookers, and haven't fallen in love with the one guy in the world who really and truly has the ability to destroy my heart, and—

Wait.

What?

Did I say…?

Hold on.

That's not right.

I'm not in love with Tyler. Not anymore. I *was*. Kind of. When I was a kid. But that wasn't real *love*. And I'm not now. No way. That was just… I was just letting my mind wander. Kind of getting lost in the fact that I feel safe right now. But I'm not in love. I'm just… appreciative. At present. I'm sure that once the heady romance of this day wears off, I'll go back to being as justifiably pissed at him as I have been. Once I'm back in the day-to-day of my struggle, I'll—

My thoughts are interrupted by a knock on the door frame of the bathroom.

"Um, sorry… I took off my watch earlier when I was washing my hands and I think I…" Tyler stammers as he half looks at me and half looks away.

"Tyler—" I sigh.

"Maddie, look, I'm not trying to fuckin'—I just… I just want you to understand."

"Understand what?"

"Fuckin'… everything. Jesus. Why I dunno. Like, just why shit went the way it went. Why I am the way I fuckin' am. Just…goddamn… Everything."

"Look, you don't have to—I get it. OK? It's fine. I get it."

"Yeah, well, I don't want you to fuckin' 'get it.' I want you to *understand.*"

"Ty—"

I start to tell him that I do, and to just go back down and I'll be there soon after I've cleaned up and changed into some new clothes.

But before I can get anything other than his name out of my mouth, he's next to me, pulling me close to him, his lips on mine.

"Tyler, Tyler," I work out between kisses.

"What?" he says, panting.

And I jerk my head away, look into his blue eyes, and say…

"Fuck it. I'll clean it up later."

As I kiss him urgently back.

TYLER

"I'll clean it up later" could mean a lot of things, but I make the choice not to analyze.

I did not expect to find her standing here in her underwear. I really didn't. But as long as we're being thankful for shit, this one jumps straight to the top of the list.

Her lips barely touching mine, licking at them as she speaks, she says, "My parents are going to be wondering what we're doing."

My hand finds its way behind the white lace at her hips and my fingers land on the soft, already wet flesh between her legs and I say, "No, they won't. They're adults."

I drop my mouth to her neck and nibble at the skin along her throat and up to behind her ear. She's wearing beautiful earrings and I take them in my mouth along with her earlobe, sucking and tugging at the skin and allowing my hot breath to pulse in her ear, the whole time working my fingers inside the folds of her pussy.

Her head drops back, like it's done every time I reach into her, and with my other hand I force her to undo my pants and take hold of my cock.

She moans as I get two fingers worked high into her and then she pushes me backwards against the wall, kissing and pulling on my shaft. She grabs the hem of my shirt and pulls it over my head, pausing as she sees the fresh splotches of red that have yet to become scars themselves dotting my body along with the long-forgotten scars that have settled into their final resting places.

"Is that what I did?" she asks.

"It's what we did," I tell her. "Did it feel good? To do it? To punish me?"

"No. Yes. I don't know."

"OK."

I finger her deeper and she coos. It makes me harder.

Then she pulls my fingers from inside her and places my arms at my sides. She begins kissing the healing wounds. She rests her palms on my stomach and kisses her way down. Starting at my collarbone, working down my sternum, kissing, licking, nuzzling every rugged edge of me.

She goes down on her knees and pulls off my boots, one at a time, then draws my jeans down to my ankles and pulls them free as I step out. She looks up at me and I run my fingers through her hair.

"You're so beautiful," I say.

She says nothing, puts her hands on my hips, and flicks at the tip of my dick with her tongue.

"Fuck," I gasp.

She slides the very edge of her tongue inside the slit in my tip, wrapping her lips around the head, building pressure as she lets her tongue swirl around. I fist her hair and force her head all the way down my length, and she bobs back and forth, making me dizzy.

I glance ahead and see us in the full-length mirror she was looking at herself in when I interrupted her. Me, battered and bloodied but still here. Her, without visible scars, but no less punctured and bruised. And also still here.

I watch the ocean of red hair push in and out. In and out as she sucks and licks and teases my cock. Her gorgeous ass is propped on her heels and her back arches and bends with every movement she makes to consume me.

I push her head gently back, withdrawing myself from her mouth, and a strand of saliva pulls back with her, like it's a lifeline connecting us and is afraid to let go. We won't be apart for long.

I take her by the shoulders, stand her up, and turn her around so that we're both facing the mirror. I drape one arm around her chest and the other around her waist. I kiss her shoulder, put my cheek next to hers, and say, "I want you to see everything."

"Why?" she asks, a hint of sorrow in the question.

"Because," I say, "I want you to understand."

We stare at our reflection, her looking into my eyes and me into hers. I'm waiting for her to ask, "Understand what?" But she doesn't. She says, "I want that too."

And then she takes my hands and pulls me with her over to the mirror. She places her palms on either side of the frame, sticks her ass out to me, spreads her legs, and, looking up at my reflection in the glass in front of us, says, "Make me understand."

MADDIE

He stands there for a moment, not breaking eye contact with our reflection, then he bows his head down to kiss me on the shoulder again. He presses his cock up against my ass and I take a breath at how hard and perfect his dick is. Each time I feel it it takes me by surprise. Like it's the first time.

He takes my breasts in his hands, pulling the material of my bra down just enough to pinch my nipples as he kisses down my spine. He keeps kissing down, and down, sliding his hands along my stomach as he pulls back. I have a moment of what I can only call separation anxiety when his dick loses contact with my ass, like it's somehow going away for good and I'll never feel it again. I try to shake that notion from my head. Not because it might be true, but because I don't want to care if it is.

And then I'm not thinking anything because I feel something warm. I look into the mirror and all I can see is myself bent over and, down below my spread legs, him on his knees, his massive cock pointed directly north. His face is obscured by my backside and I feel him pulling my panties to the side and then spreading my ass with his thumbs.

His warm breath is on my rear and then suddenly his tongue is inside it. He's reaching around, rubbing my clit, and tonguing my asshole. My eyes squeeze shut tightly and I can feel water gathering at the corners of them.

Now that his mouth is on me, he's burying himself inside me. Lapping and prodding. His one hand is still rubbing my clit in tight, fast circles, and two fingers of his other hand are inside my pussy, spreading me open, massaging my walls.

I let out a sound that's not quite a moan, not quite a cry. A combination of both. A sound I don't recall ever having made before in my life. And I can feel his smile spread across my skin.

He works into me harder. Rubbing, stroking, tonguing. I slap my hand against the wall next to the mirror as I shout, "Fuck! Fuck! Fuck me! Fuck me! Now!"

I no longer feel his smile. I see it. As he leaps to his feet, takes me by the hips, and pushes himself into my dripping wet pussy.

"Oh, Jesus," he says, sliding all the way inside.

And now our eyes are locked onto each other's in reflection as he works his way in and out. Back and forth.

"Make me," I cough out as he thrusts. "Make. Me. Un. Der. Stand," I grunt with each push, never breaking eye contact with him. I'm tempted to glance away, to look at the rest of him, or to look down at the floor, or just to close my eyes, but I don't let myself look away from him. And he doesn't look away either. And with each slap of his hips against my ass, he drives in harder, pushes deeper.

I can feel myself on the verge of coming, but I'm forcing myself to wait, to hold out. I want to come with him. I want to see what it feels like for us to come at the same time.

I want to understand.

TYLER

Fuck me, I'm going to come. But she hasn't come yet, and I won't do it until she has. I'm trying hard to maintain eye contact with her, but it's so goddamn intense that I'm afraid I'm not going to be able to hold out. I can't look anywhere else though, because when I catch even a glimpse of her body, grinding back and forth along my dick, or her hair bouncing as she pumps, it's even more unlikely that I can keep it inside me.

So I take things down a notch. I draw out slowly, pulling myself completely out of her. As I do, I see a hint of confusion and disappointment in her gaze. I smile, then slide back inside her again, just as slowly, and she lets out a long moan. So I do it again.

I draw back. Back, back, back, pulling out until just the tip is resting on her entrance. I reach down, take hold of the shaft, and rub the thick end of my cock up and down against her soaking wetness. Teasing. And then once again, I slide deep into her, giving an extra push at the end that drives her forward a step and makes her squeal and giggle.

It's the giggle that does it.

Fuck it. I'm done.

I continue pulling out of her all the way and driving in, but not slow and methodical. Hard. And animal. My grip tightening around her hips, making her creamy, white skin redden under my touch.

And now I stop pulling out and stay in her. Back and forth. Stiff. And fast. Almost lifting her off the ground with the tension in my grasp and the strength in my pull as we crash into each other.

"Oh, fuck, fuck, baby… I'm gonna come," I call out.

"Yes," she says, "Yes, do it. Come. Come now."

And I remember what she said when she was driving away last week. "Next time, just come inside me."

And so I do. I come.

Inside her.

And I never want it to stop.

MADDIE

I can feel the contraction of his dick as his come throbs into me. And it drives me insane. I let go and a flush of wetness pours from me.

"Oh, God. Oh, God. Oh, shit," I cry.

"Yeah, yes, baby, come, come on me," he says. And do I fucking ever.

I tense and release around him, never breaking eye contact, moaning and wheezing, knees buckling, legs shaking, but refusing to fall. I refuse to fall.

I push my ass back into him so that I can take even more, if that's possible. He apparently assumes that's a sign that I want him to shove his thumb into my ass, which is fine by me, and then what I thought was an orgasm pales in comparison to whatever the hell is happening to me now, the way a dwarf star looks weak when compared to a supernova.

"FUCK. YOU!" I scream, no longer able to keep eye contact. My eyes close and my head falls forward as he just keeps shooting his come inside me and I keep spilling myself around his dick.

My forearms tense against the wall to keep me upright, and behind me, I can feel his knees buckling against mine, like he's about to collapse too.

"Jesus!" he calls out as, with one last push, he *finally* empties what he's got left inside him into me.

I swallow, and then gulp in air. I lift my head to look in the mirror and see him, his head down now, his eyes shut tight and his body twitching with small spasms.

When he finally lifts his head again and opens his eyes, they immediately find mine. We stare at each other. Neither one of us says anything. Neither one of us wants to. Both of us are aware that we have crossed over somewhere. Both of us seem to know that even though there is still much to figure out, we are perhaps one step closer. On this day of giving thanks, we are unexpectedly and incomprehensibly edging toward something with each other that we have both lacked for a long time and that we both very much need.

Understanding.

CHAPTER THIRTEEN

TYLER

"Why are you staying at Evan's? What happened with your place? I thought you liked it." she calls to me. She's in the walk-in closet, looking through her mom's things for something to wear. I'm sitting in one of the chairs in the… I dunno. Parlor? I guess? This place is pretty sick. I should see if they'll just let me live here.

"Um, my place got…" I stop short because for whatever reason—maybe it's because her parents are here, maybe it's just because my dick has magical powers—things seem to be real cool between us right now. And I don't wanna ruin it. And call me crazy, but telling her that I burned my apartment down during a psychotic fever dream after I found out that she, Maddie, was the person I was fucking seems like it *might* just set us back a step.

"Got what?" she asks from the other room.

"I just… felt like it was time to move on from that joint, honestly. It was so, y'know, hectic in the middle of the Strip and all. So, I dunno, I'm thinking of moving out to the desert. Quiet feels like the right play for me right now."

"Yeah? Well, if you need somebody with a twelve-thousand-dollar drone to scout territory for you, I may know someone." She steps out into the main bedroom area wearing…well, mom pants. And, like, a flower shirt thing. "How's this? OK?" she asks.

Fuck. Do I lie? Do I tell her that it makes her look a fifty-five-year-old? Albeit a sexy-as-fuck fifty-five-year-old, but still. Or do I—?

"OK," she says, and marches back into the closet.

"What? I didn't say anything!" I call after her.

"Yeah, you did," she shouts back.

"Do you want help?"

There's no response. I take that to mean that she doesn't want any help. That's cool. Two can play this silence-implies-information game.

I sit there quietly for a moment, thinking about how…normal…this feels. Almost like she's my girlfriend or whatever and I'm waiting on her to get ready so that we can go have Thanksgiving dinner with her family. All of which is, of course, what is happening.

Except that she's not my girlfriend.

She's… I'm not sure what. I mean I know who and what she is to the world, but I don't know who and what she is to *me*. But I've been given the advice to back off and let her be by enough different people now that I'm gonna try to just shut up and not fuck it all up. (Good luck, bro.)

After a few moments of quiet (Which is nice, I'm realizing. As long as my brain plays along and doesn't disrupt the peace) she steps back into view and leans against the doorway. She's down to just her underwear again. Is she trying to do me in? Maybe so. Maybe her plan for getting back at me for everything is to sexy me to death. Fine. I'll take it. About a trillion times better than the other ways people have tried to kill me.

"Can I ask you something?" she asks.

"Yes, we can do it again," I say as I stand, start unbuckling my pants, and move toward her.

She puts her hand out to stop me. Shit. Well, worth a shot. I put my hand up in return and take my seat again.

"Yes. Please. Ask away," I acquiesce.

"Why did you do this? All this, with my parents? Why?"

"Um…"

"Don't get me wrong, I appreciate it. I really do. I think I just showed you that."

"Yes, and I appreciate *that.*" I bounce my eyebrows at her. I'm so fuckin' charming.

"But why did you do it? What made you? Was it just so I'd fuck you again?"

Jesus. Is she serious? I can feel myself starting to get hot. I tried to do a nice fucking thing and she thinks… She thinks…

Shit. It's hard to focus with her standing there looking sexy as...a...um...shit, I got distracted again. Fuck. But, oh! What made me do the thing with her folks? Got it."Was it so I'd fuck you?" I laugh a little. "Um, well, I guess… OK, So, lemme say a couple things. First I talked with Pete—"

"Yeah, he told me."

"Did he? Well, yeah, I did. And he's kinda awesome and he basically just said that if I really gave a shit about you that I'd think about what you need and, like, give you a gift and stuff. And I do really give a shit. I give several shits. I know you don't believe me, but…" I pause to give her a chance to tell me that she does, in fact, believe me. But she doesn't say anything, So I continue…

"So, yeah. So, I tried to think what I could give you. Give YOU. That would be something you would like and could…use, or… Fuck. I dunno. Whatever. Evan told me you came by the station and you said it'd been a couple years since you'd seen your folks, and Thanksgiving was coming up, and shit, I figured it was the right thing to do. If you won't let me into your world, you should have somebody here. You don't have to do fucking everything alone. That's all."

She doesn't say anything. Fine. I'm not done anyway.

"So, second… You can think I'm a selfish prick or whatever you want to think, but I gave you a gift because I wanted to and because it seemed like the right thing to do. That's it. So, no. I didn't expect anything from it. I certainly didn't do it so that you'd fuck me. Hey, fucking you is a nice treat, but it's not what I was looking for, and besides, I haven't needed to do anything to get you to fuck me before now, so why would I start?"

She gets a steely look in her eye and kind of chews at the inside of her cheek and simmers a little while she assesses whether or not I'm full of shit.

"Believe me or don't. Up to you. I did what I did from a sincere place. You made the *choice* to let me fuck you. So that's on you. If you didn't want to you didn't have to. 'Thank you' would've been just fine. So as far as me getting your parents here goes, y'know… you're welcome."

Funny how easy it is not to give a fuck whether or not somebody believes you when you're telling the truth.

She breathes in and out of her nose while still chewing the inside of her mouth, her tits rising and falling with the breath, causing me to imagine my cock sliding back and forth between them. Which is, in my opinion, an unfair advantage in an argument.

After a moment she says, "Do you think it makes me hot when you get pissed?"

That is so totally not anything I was expecting her to say.

"I—Uh. I don't… Um. Why? Does it?" There's probably a little hope in the question.

She smirks. "A little."

Holy shit! This day is getting dysfunctionally better by the second!

"Fuck," she says, hanging her head. "What the fuck are we doing?"

I stand and approach her. Carefully. "We are figuring it out. I guess."

"Figuring what out?"

I reach her and lift her chin with my finger. Her eyes are wide and seeking. "It. All of it. This shit. Why it's happening. What it all means."

She laughs a tiny, mirthless sniffle.

"What?" I ask.

"I have this shrink, who's fucking *terrible,* by the way."

"Oh, you should see mine," I tell her. "She's the balls."

She ignores me, and keeps talking. "—and this shitty shrink told me something that has kind of stuck with me."

"Which is?"

"Basically, that things have no meaning. Good things. Bad things. They just… happen. And if that's true, I don't know what the point is in trying."

"Wow, somebody said something like that to me too," I say.

"Yeah? Who?"

"Um… James Franco." (Oh, boy. Here we go.)

"You know James Franco?"

"Uh, a little," I say. "Not the point. Point is that maybe… Maybe, yeah, things just happen. Maybe that's true. And maybe they don't objectively mean anything.

But we can give them meaning. If we want. It's up to us to decide what something means."

Her eyes squint slightly, like she's deciding how full of shit I am.

"Look, I don't know why all of this is happening either. Why this is you and me, and why it's happening now, and what's gonna happen in the future. I've definitely learned I suck at predicting the future. But I do know that I'm fucking tired, Maddie. I'm tired of fighting. I'm tired of fighting everyone and everything all the goddamn time. So… So, I'm choosing to see that you and me… Here… Now. That… That it means I can stop. For a little while, at least. Because I'm not all alone. There's somebody out there who… understands. And that, if we choose to, we can help hold each other up. That's the meaning I'm deciding to assign to all this."

Her breathing speeds up again a little.

"That's it. That's all I've got. And not only was that a good fucking speech, it has the added benefit of also being true. So fuck it. I'm gonna stop while I'm ahead."

She laughs a bit, which makes me realize I've been holding my breath, and now I let it out on a long sigh.

She smiles with her lips but not her eyes. "I'm tired too," she says.

"I know."

"You hurt me real bad."

"I know." I want to tell her I'm sorry. But it feels small. And besides… She knows.

Then she says, "Pete said something to me too."

"Yeah? What?"

"He said when you're young and haven't fucked your life up so bad it can't be fixed yet, you think there's always a next time. And that there isn't always a next time."

"Jesus, Pete's like Santa Claus meets the Buddha meets Rambo," I say with astonishment, and she laughs. So do I. And fuck, it feels good. But not as good as her taking my hand in hers, which she does now.

"Tyler?"

"That IS my name."

"I don't know if I can do this right now."

Fuck.

But, yeah, I get it.

"I know. I do. I know. We don't have to...y'know. But maybe we can just... There's a lot we need to catch up on. Maybe we can just hang out and at least... Do that?"

She closes her eyes and says, "...Yeah. Yeah. We can...do that. I mean, fuck, dude, that story you told about living in Rio HAS to have more to it."

"Oh, hell yeah, it does. But I'm not gonna say that shit in front of your *parents*."

She gets an impish grin and says, "Yeah, well, I wouldn't worry about that. C'mere." She grabs my hand and pulls me into the closet with her, opens a dresser drawer and pulls out something that looks like a woman's fur stole with a piece of metal attached to one end.

"What is that?" I ask. "A...? Like, a boa, or...?"

She laughs loudly. I love her fucking laugh. "You don't know what this is?" she asks. I shake my head. "It's a fox tail!" she says in a whisper for some reason, even though nobody else is here.

"Well, yeah, I get *that*. I mean it kinda looks like a—"

"No. A fox. Tail." Now she says it like putting extra emphasis on the words will help me understand better.

"I don't—" I start.

"It's a sex toy! This"—she holds up the metal part—"is a butt plug. And then this part"—the furry part, she means—"just hangs out the back and kinda makes a woman look like a…y'know…fox. Or kitten. Or whatever."

"Uh, OK, well, first, that's the hottest thing I've ever heard of. How do you know about it?"

"I work in a strip club."

"Right. Copy that. But then second, that means that…your—"

"—MY prim and proper MOM is rocking some freaky fox tail action in the sack!"

"Holy. Shit." I can't stop the grin from spreading. "I don't know how I'm gonna look at her the same way now."

"Oh, please. You were already flirting with her downstairs, this just reinforces that she probably wants you to."

"Hey! I'm pretty sure she was flirting with me. Which isn't my fault. I'm mad flirt-worthy. Everybody says so."

She grins, grabs my shirt, and pulls me in for a kiss. A long, sweet, hot, perfect, almost too perfect kiss. Then she pulls back and says, "We better get downstairs. They did fly all the way here for dinner."

She smiles. And I'm fucking happy.

"Cool." I smile back. And then, as I push her hair out of her face, I take the fox tail from her, hold it up, grin, and offer…

"And your mom *did* say you could wear anything of hers you wanted…"

CHAPTER FOURTEEN

MADDIE

As we exit the elevator, I'm terrified. Because this feels…not at all terrifying.

Tyler next to me, heading to have Thanksgiving dinner with my family, feels as familiar and normal as anything in the world. Because, in a way, it is. It's not the first time Tyler and I have had dinner with my folks. But it is the first time we've done it since Scotty died. And it's obviously the first time we've done it since we've become… whatever the hell we are.

And that's what's scary. Because with all the unknowns, there's no way to predict what's going to happen. And I know there's never any way to predict what's going to happen in life. I know that. But the good thing about everything being shitty and broken is that then you can believe that whatever's waiting to happen will be a good thing. Will lift you up. When everything's going OK, the uncertainty of the future tends to come in the form of the good things being burned to the ground.

It takes a really long, hard time to build something up. And almost no time at all to tear it down. Just ask the guys who built the World Trade Center.

This is a pretty morose thought to be having right now, but I've got to protect myself. This day will end, my parents will leave again, and who the hell knows what will happen with Tyler. He's still totally Tyler. Which means unstable. And unpredictable. And as uncertain as an uncertain future can be. And I have to guard my heart. I don't want to. But I have to. Because I won't be broken again. I won't let it happen. I've had enough tragedy and heartbreak for this lifetime.

And then, of course, there's Carlos. Which is its own special brand of anxiety. Yeah, the climb continues. No resting yet. I'm nowhere near the top.

Mom and Dad are sitting in the lobby, near the restaurant, waiting. As we approach, Dad says, "We were getting worried maybe you got lost in that suite!" He and Mom and Tyler all give a hearty laugh. I give a half-hearted one. I still just don't wanna risk having to talk about me and Tyler.

Mom sees what I'm wearing—one of her wrap dresses; a black one with pretty flowers on it—and gushes, "Oh, honey. That looks fabulous on you. You should keep that. It looks better on you than it does on me! Why don't you go through and see if there's anything else that would look good on you?"

"Yeah. I mean, I saw a couple of things…" Tyler says, with a shit-eating grin on his face. I swear to God, I will punch him in the dick.

"Nonsense!" Dad says. "George, you look amazing in that dress. Why don't we just take Maddie shopping tomorrow and get her some stuff? Black Friday!"

I feel like I'm gonna cry, and it's totally unexpected. But my folks wanna take me shopping. For clothes and shit. Which I don't really care about in and of itself, but they want to take care of me. And suddenly I start thinking…what's wrong with that? Why not let them? Why not just tell them what's going on (or at least as much of it as I think they can stomach) and get their help? They're my family after all. They love me. They want to help me. What's all this pride about anyway? It hasn't done shit but jam me up.

That's right, Maddie.

Fuck. What is that?

It's me. The angel.

Oh, Jesus. Are you still here?

Yep, bitch, and I am too. You can't get rid of us that easy.

Fucking hell. Why now?

Maddie, the angel says, *Yes. Let them help you. There's no shame in it.*

Sure, you fucking quitter. Let somebody else bail you out, says the devil.

This is confusing. I figured the devil would be all like, 'Yeah, fuck them, get what you can, take what's yours, etc.'

That's not my job. My job is to argue with the angel. Point-counterpoint. Basically, I'm just here to make sure you don't turn into a total fucking dishrag. And if you take shit from people, you owe them. You wanna be indebted to your mommy and daddy? You're twenty-five, bitch! Fuck is wrong with you?

They are family. Family is there for each other, says the angel.

Yeah? Satan and God were family once too, and look how that turned out.

That doesn't even—

Fuck you! It makes sense!

I don't need this shit right now.

"Everybody ready to eat?" Mom says, jolting me back into the present.

We all nod a 'yes' and are just about to head into the restaurant when from behind us, I hear…

"Georgina? Simon?" We all turn to see a man approaching from across the lobby. He's wearing a kind of ill-fitting suit with a Mandalay Bay nametag on it that says "Jack." The Four Seasons doesn't have a casino in it, but it connects to Mandalay, which most certainly does. Jack is one of the pit bosses there. I know because I know him. Or used to anyway.

Jack Morgan.

Tyler's dad.

He reaches the four of us, walks right past me and Tyler and straight up to Mom and Dad. I look at Tyler to see if I can get any read off him at all.

Nothing. His eyes are dead. All the light is gone.

"What's up you guys?" Jack wheezes, wrapping them in a hug. Mom, in particular, cringes. "Whatcha doing in town? You're not still in Monaco?"

"Oh, yeah, we are," Dad says. He kind of steps in between Jack and Mom. Jack Morgan was well known to have tried lots of inappropriate things in inappropriate ways with many women. Oftentimes the mothers of his sons' friends. To the best of my knowledge, nothing ever happened with Jack and my mom, but there were some whispered stories that maybe something almost did. A couple of times. "But," Dad continues, "we're just in for a few days for Thanksgiving to see, uh—" He nods in my direction.

Again, I look at Tyler. Again, nothing.

"To see…?" Jack echoes as he turns and sees me and Tyler standing there. And suddenly, there is recognition in his eyes. "Oh. My. God. Is that Maddie?"

He grabs me in a hug and I can smell the cigarette smoke on his clothes. Not new cigarette smoke. Years of cigarette smoke. I gag a little. Which is entirely to do with the hug and not at all to do with the smoke.

"Jesus, look at you," he says, backing up to take me in. "Wow. I ain't seen you in, hell, must be, what? Ten? Years?"

"Um, probably more like twelve," I say. "At least."

"Ho-ly cow. Ain't that something. Look. At. You. Look just like your mother, which is a compliment! Believe me!"

The light in the usually sunny lobby seems to have almost all but disappeared.

"So you're all staying at the Four Seasons? Well, ain't you in high cotton?"

I don't even really know what that means.

It is notable to everyone present that he hasn't yet acknowledged Tyler.

And then… He does.

Kind of.

"Hey, I'm sorry, man," he says to Tyler. "Jack Morgan. How ya doing?"

He sticks his hand out to Tyler for a shake.

Time stops.

Jack's hand just hangs there in the space between him and Tyler. Tyler stares down at it, still not moving, his eyes still dead. I can see Mom fading further and further back from the scene. She's almost at the wall. And Dad is fidgeting, clearly debating whether he should turn on his politician smile and make a joke, or just let this play out on its own.

For my part, I don't know what to do. Part of me wants to take Tyler's hand, tell Jack that this is Ford Aston, a guy I'm dating, and make it go away like that, so we can (maybe) joke about it later. But not only is that stupid, if I do that Mom may remember the phone call we had a few weeks back when I told her a story about a soldier that I was seeing whose name I refused to give her, and start putting two and two together.

Another part of me wants to grab Tyler and run. Again, stupid.

And another part wants, for reasons I cannot even begin to understand much less explain, to help Tyler beat the shit out of his dad here in the lobby of the Four Seasons.

None of these seem like any good will come of them, so I do. Fucking. Nothing.

Finally, Tyler takes Jack's hand, shakes it slowly, and says, "Hey. How's it going?"

"Good, good," says Jack. Then, "Sorry. Didn't catch your name, chief…?"

I know that I don't, but for a second I swear I can hear a clap of thunder somewhere in the great, wide distance.

I see the place on Tyler's cheek where his upper and lower jaw connects tensing and releasing. It looks the way a fish's gills do when you pull it out of the water and it's gasping to stay alive.

"My name?" Tyler asks.

I swallow.

"Yeah! I didn't catch it."

Tyler blinks. Once. Slowly. "I'll give you a hint," he says.

Jack's brow furrows and he snorts out a laugh. "OK," he says.

"OK," Tyler says. And then, still holding Jack's hand, he draws him in close. Tyler's a good five inches taller than his dad, so he has to lean down to put his mouth next to Jack's ear. Which he does. And I hear him whisper… "I'm your son."

Unconsciously, I hug myself around the waist, like I've been kicked.

Jack's eyes narrow and then widen, and he says, "Tyler?"

"You got another kid you need to tell me about?" Tyler says.

"I—Jesus. Tyler. What the fuck are you doing here? I thought you was…"

"Yeah? Thought I was what? Please. I'm curious to know."

This is awful.

"I didn't—uh…" Jack stammers.

I notice that Tyler still grips his father's hand. His father's hand that looks like it's being crushed. Tyler hasn't moved otherwise. Or blinked. Or breathed, I'm pretty sure.

Suddenly Jack lifts his free hand to the ear piece he's wearing.

"Uh, yeah, yeah, this is Jack. What's that? Oh, yeah? OK, I'll be right there."

It's a pretty lousy performance.

"Guys, I'm sorry, I, uh—" Jack mutters out. "I, uh, shit, it's so good to see ya, but I gotta, dammit…"

He wrenches his hand free from Tyler's grip, which is not easy and looks painful, and continues his bullshit.

"I wish I had known you was…I'm sorry I gotta…but somebody's…" He goes on like that as he scurries across the lobby and out of sight. It doesn't really matter what he's saying, so none of us try to say anything back.

Mom is so close to the wall she could be wallpaper. Dad is a lost satellite, trying to figure out if he should go to Mom or come over to Tyler or what.

I stand as close to Tyler as I can, letting my fingers touch his. He makes no attempt to take my hand. Just continues to stare ahead, unmoving.

"Tyler…" I say.

He doesn't look at me or shift his eyes in any direction, in fact. He just takes a step forward, says, "Sorry, guys. Please have a good Thanksgiving," and with four long, purposeful strides, he's out of the lobby, onto the street, and out of sight.

Halloween night, when I found out the guy I'd been having sex with was Tyler, I was… knocked into another dimension. Pulled completely out of my body and thrown to the wind. This isn't like that. Now I'm hyper-aware. Because this has nothing to do with me. And yet, in my gut, it feels as though it does. I'm in suspended animation.

It's a perverse scene with Dad trying to figure out what he should do to help, Mom hiding in the corner, trying to disappear, and me stuck in a space between going after Tyler, staying here, or closing my eyes and hoping to make time spin backwards a decade or so.

People buzz by, coming in and out of the lobby, smiling and patting each other on the back, puttering along, happily lost in their own worries and concerns. And we. Are. Statues.

And suddenly the devil appears on my shoulder and says, *Gee whiz. Know what? I was wrong. Family's fucking hilarious.*

CHAPTER FIFTEEN

TYLER

"Tyler? What're you—?"

I put my hand up to silence Evan as I march past the fancy holiday dinner he and Robert are having with all the well-to-do gays of Las Vegas. I glance to see if Siegfried and Roy might actually be there in person, just because I'm curious, but they're not. I don't think.

"Sorry to interrupt," I say. "Don't mind me." I keep marching down the hallway to the guest room (there are like five guest rooms, but I just mean the one I'm staying in), and stomp inside, slamming the door behind me.

I start looking for things I can punch. But it's not my house. I just know I can smash through the drywall. No question. But it ain't mine to smash. So instead, I wind up stalking the space like a caged tiger. (Shit, if Siegfried and Roy are here, I hope they stay away. I don't want whichever one it was who got attacked by the tiger back in the day to have a flashback and freak out. With everything else I'm dealing with, I don't need that guilt too.)

My fingers dig into my palms as I clench them into fists, and since I've stopped cutting my nails too, they draw blood that trickles down my wrists.

There's a knock on the door as it opens.

"Dude? What's—Holy shit, did you cut your wrists!?" Evan shouts, darting into the room, and grabbing at my hands to look.

I pull away and try to swat him off me. "No! No! I didn't! Will you stop fuckin' grabbing at me?"

He puts his hands in the air and backs away. "What's going on?" he asks. Then his eyes widen and he leans his head back. "What happened? Did Maddie—?"

"No. No. God, no. That was great. We fucked."

"You… fucked?"

"Yeah."

There's a moment. Evan nods as if processing.

"Were… her parents there?"

"When we fucked? No! Jesus. They were in the lobby."

"OK. So?"

"We saw my dad."

"Your—? You saw your *dad*?"

I nod.

"While you were fucking?"

"No, dude! In the lobby!"

This is the most ridiculous conversation I've ever had.

"OK, OK, got it," he says. "So… Shit. How'd that go?"

"Fuckin' great, man. We hugged and kissed like it was old times. Then we tossed a baseball around like in *Field of Dreams*. It was a goddamn Thanksgiving miracle."

Evan sighs and nods. "Yeah. OK."

"He didn't recognize me."

There's a pause and Evan cocks his head.

"Come again?"

"You heard me."

I sit down on the edge of the bed. After a second, Evan sits beside me.

"It's weird," he says. "I haven't even really thought about your dad. It never occurred to me that you were bound to run into each other sooner or later."

"Yeah, I hadn't really thought about it either."

"Do you wanna—?"

"Whatever you're gonna ask… no, is the answer. I just wanna fucking sit here for a second and get my shit together. Fuck! Maddie and I had like a breakthrough, or whatever, and… shit."

Evan sighs. (It strikes me suddenly that people sigh around me a lot. Like I make the whole fucking world exhausted.) "She was glad to see her folks?" he asks.

I nod. "Yeah. And then she and I talked and… But fuck it. There's no chance she's gonna wanna deal with this shit too, on top of everything else she's already carrying."

"Well, that's stupid."

"Yeah? Is it? If you were her and struggling with all your own crap, how would you like to take on somebody else's bullshit problems too? I was trying to fucking *be there* for her. Not make her take care of a six-foot-three-inch man-baby."

Evan kind of laughs, which sort of annoys me.

"What?" I spit out.

"I'm just picturing you in a diaper. Shit's funny."

I don't know how he does it. I really don't. But I kind of smile.

And then there's another knock on the door and it swings open.

"Hey," says Robert, standing there looking like the most well-put-together guy at the polo club. (I'm not just saying that. I know. I went to a polo match in Dubai.) "Sorry to interrupt," he continues, "but—"

"I know," Evan says. "We have guests. I'll be right out."

"No. That's not… Maddie's here."

Evan and I both give looks that would best be accompanied by that sound Scooby-Doo makes.

"Seriously?" I ask.

"Yep." Robert nods. And that's all he says. (Something I've learned about genuinely successful people—as opposed to accidentally successful ones like me—they don't use five words when one will do.)

I stand. Evan stands. Robert smiles, turns on his heel and heads down the hall.

I look at Evan. He shrugs at me. I start off to follow Robert. Evan stops me. He grabs one of my dirty t-shirts from off the floor, wipes the blood off my hands and wrists, throws the t-shirt down, pats me on the back, and sends me out into the hall.

As I reach the foyer (which I pronounce foy-YAY, because Robert does and I assume he knows), I find Robert standing with Maddie, who looks so beautiful to me that I want to fall on my knees. Because that's what you do in the presence of beauty.

"Hi," I say.

"Hey," she says back.

OK. Salutations are out of the way. What now?

"How did you know…?" I begin.

"Just took a shot," she says. "I, uh, Evan gave me the address when we saw each other and so…"

Evan steps over and gives her a hug. "Great to see you," he says. "Oh, um, you met Robert, obviously."

"Yes," she says, nodding to him. "Hi. Beautiful home."

"We like it." Robert smiles back. "Evan, we should…"

"Yeah," Evan says, "Sorry. We have… Um, if you guys wanna… you know, we'll be in the dining room. Just, y'know, if you wanna."

Then he and Robert head off, leaving us standing there. A beautiful red-headed angel, and Brad Pitt at the end of *Kalifornia.* (He looks pretty fucked up by the end of that movie, is the point I'm making to myself.)

"He really loves you," Maddie says, meaning Evan.

"I love him too." I do. I follow up with, "Where are your parents?"

"At the hotel. I told them to go on and eat without me."

"Maddie, no. I—"

"It's OK," she says, stepping in toward me. "I'll see them tomorrow. It's fine."

She looks down like she wants to maybe take my hand. Or maybe it's just wishful thinking on my part, because she doesn't.

"You didn't have to come here."

"Yeah," she says. "No shit."

"Yeah. So why are you here?"

"I dunno." She shrugs. "To show you what a person is supposed to do when someone is in need, and make you feel guilty?"

A hint of a smile skitters across her lips.

"Oh, yeah?" I ask, also smirking.

"Maybe," she says. "Does it?"

"What? Make me feel guilty?

She nods.

"A little," I say.

"Good."

We are now both smiling genuinely.

"So, what do you want to…?" I start to ask.

"Can we eat something?" she says. "I'm fucking starving."

"You are so full of shit!" the big guy with the polka-dot bow tie and tan blazer says to his equally big and mustachioed boyfriend in the paisley smoking jacket.

"I swear to God," says Mustache, "Gerry knows Cher's stylist and he told Gerry that it looks just as good as a nineteen-year old's!" (If someone heard just *that* part of the story, without context, Lord knows what they would think it's about.)

Everyone laughs uproariously. Me and Maddie included. Evan and Robert's friends are the most fun group I've been around in a long time. They keep giving me shit about my beard. Mustache is a salon owner and tells me that he's "dying to get his hands on me." Which in turn led his bow-tied boyfriend to shout, "Me first!" and again, laughter ensued. They just seem like a fun bunch.

They're also all pretty drunk on wine and turkey.

"So, Maddie," a bald guy with more rings than fingers says as he leans across the table, "what do you do? Model? You must be a model. You're gorgeous! I would kill for that hair!"

"Bitch, you'd kill for any hair," says a short African-American guy.

More laughter. But not from Maddie. Shit. What's she supposed to say? She's a stripper? She can't tell them that she works in real estate drone…ing, or whatever it's called. She doesn't really. And if she presents that in front of Robert, like this… Fuck. She's in an impossible position.

I'm just about to knock over a glass of wine on purpose to distract everyone when Robert chimes in and says, "We're working together."

If I could capture the look on Maddie's face and hold it forever, I absolutely would.

"Really?" asks Mustache. "On what, do tell?"

"The Hoover Dam project."

If Maddie had wine in her mouth at this moment, I swear she'd do a spit take.

The look on Evan's face as he looks at Robert is one of absolute, unequivocal, pure love. Hell, the look on my face as I look at Robert is probably the same.

"In fact, Maddie," Robert says, cool as the cucumbers in the cucumber salad (Which was really very delicious. There must have been some mint in the dressing. Anyway. Not important), "What I really need is some topographical coverage of it at night. Which is impossible to get any way other than the drone. When do you think you can make that happen?"

It's like one of those old commercials where everyone stops what they're doing to hear what the broker's advice is. All heads turn to Maddie.

"Uh," Maddie says. "This…week…end?"

"Great," says Robert. And then just like in the commercials, everyone goes back to laughing and joking and eating.

Maddie turns to me and kind of whispers, "What. Just. Happened?"

"I think you just got into business with Robert Vanderbilt," I whisper back.

"Jesus," she says.

"Can I take you?" I ask her.

"What? Whatayou mean? Take me where?"

"The dam. If you're really gonna go there this weekend, can I take you? I know one of the guys who watches it at night. I can get him to let us have full access."

"I have a drone. I don't need full access."

"OK. Then can I take you because it'll be pretty and nice and I've always been kind of obsessed with it and I just kinda wanna take you someplace and like do something with you and have it be cool and not weird and please don't make me beg and come on don't be an asshole lemme please just take you on a date to the Hoover Dam?"

She stares at me like I'm crazy. Which is the right stare to have.

"Did I say all that aloud?" I ask.

She shakes her head a tiny bit and laughs.

"My parents are here until Saturday afternoon," she says. "And I have to…um…work…Saturday night, so…"

"Awesome. I'll pick you up from work on Saturday."

"I get off at five AM."

"I'll bet I can talk Pete into letting you off at midnight."

Somebody asks me to pass the rolls. I do. I'm a gentleman.

"Tyler…"

"Come on. This is incredible and totally weird but still incredible. You just got conscripted into service by the most powerful real estate dude in Vegas. I thought this is what you wanted."

She looks down at her plate. Pushes some peas around. "It is."

She doesn't sound sure. But before I can say anything to her, Bow-Tie tings his butter knife against his water glass. "Everybody. If I may…" He lifts his wine glass. "To Evan and Robert, for having us over to their warm, wonderful home. And to this glorious table of gorgeous people." There's some assorted joking about how gorgeous we all are. Then, "All of us here truly have much to be thankful for."

I look at the table of happy people. I look at Robert. I look at Evan.

I look at Maddie.

Bow-Tie raises his glass high in the air and we all toast that which we have to be thankful for.

And for the first time in a long, long fucking time, I'm not faking it.

CHAPTER SIXTEEN

MADDIE

Saturday nights at Pete's are starting to feel strange. I mean, the money is still here. Better than ever actually. I think the devil outfit is a hit because tonight I've made a little over a thousand dollars for two stage slots and a handful of lap dances, and it's only eleven thirty. But money… I just don't seem to care about it much anymore.

That's because you're in love with Tyler, my angel says.

If she's pissed off that I'm channeling her nemesis and not her for slut-time, she doesn't show it. In fact, she's really on this whole *Tyler's your one-true-love* thing the past couple days.

Ever since Thanksgiving.

Which didn't go anything like how I expected it would. I mean, who could've predicted I'd see my mom and dad again? They've invited me to France a million times but I never had any intention of going. I had this whole waking nightmare about going to France, seeing them living their new lives, and I'd just feel… left behind.

With Scotty.

I think that was the problem.

People move on after they lose loved ones. And that's exactly what seeing my parents in France would mean.

And since I had not moved on, well, that was a problem for me.

And then the fact that Tyler flew them over to surprise me. And he put them up in that penthouse at the Four Seasons. And… I smile thinking about the sex.

You should let him help you, my angel continues. I didn't tell her to shut the fuck up, so she must be getting brave.

Devil? I ask. *You got anything for me tonight?*

He pops up on my empty shoulder holding a half-eaten ham sandwich, chews slowly for a few seconds, then shrugs. *He's gonna fuck things up sooner or later. You watch.*

I am watching. Very closely. But Tyler is making all the right moves lately. He gave me space, but stuck around. Like… that's not normal. That's almost… considerate, right?

Right! Angel says.

He just wanted more putang pie, Devil chimes in.

Did you just say putang pie? I shake my head and he disappears. He's losing and he knows it. Tyler is being pretty understanding about my stripper job, after all. Like, I'm sure he hates it. I'm sure he wants to tell me to quit. Hell, he probably wants to throw me over his shoulder and carry me out of here, then lock me up in his bedroom and never let me leave.

Which lately doesn't sound all that terrible.

But he's holding back on all that stuff. Giving me space or whatever. Letting me figure shit out on my own. Which I appreciate because I'm not *actually* stupid. I've just made a lot of stupid mistakes these past few years. My life since Scotty died has been one long string of pure panic. Like I was underwater and couldn't breathe. Stuck under ice.

And I think I showed Tyler something about me too. That I can forgive. That I can understand. And that I can be there for him the same way he's just kinda being here for me.

His dad, God. What an asshole. But Tyler's so strong. Not like me. If that'd been my dad—unable to see me standing right in front of him because we hadn't talked in so long and life had changed me beyond recognition—well, let's just say I wouldn't have been able to put it behind me that same night. Let's just say I wouldn't have been able to accept the kindness of friends to help me do that. Let's just say… I'd have let that little encounter derail me for months, if not years.

He's not like me at all. And maybe I need that in my life? Someone who fills in all my vacant spaces. Someone who makes up for what I lack. Someone who gets me, doesn't judge, and makes me better.

Someone who completes you, Angel says.

Yeah. Someone like that.

Raven comes into the little office, which is where I've been hiding since I changed into my jeans and t-shirt because Tyler should be here any minute now to take me out to the Hoover Dam project and do the drone work.

Maddie—this is me talking—*he's taking you to the Hoover Dam for sex, not the drone work.*

Yeah… I think I know that. And once again, things that had me uptight and angry last week just don't seem to rattle my chain like they used to. Sex with Tyler tonight sounds perfect, actually.

But date night aside, I really hope Tyler can fly my drone. Because I'm not all that good at it. And even though this whole drone thing is a long shot, I feel attached to it. The idea of it. Like somehow the drone is part of this whole healing process I think I'm going through. Symbolic or whatever. Wings. Flight. Freedom.

Which is a very naïve association, Devil says, back now, sans sandwich. *Because Carlos is still after you. And Logan—*

Yeah… that fucking Logan asshole. There's a part of me that thinks he's the real problem here, not Carlos. Like Carlos is a bad dude and all. And he's definitely gonna kill me, or kidnap me, or something equally horrible if I don't come up with a plan real quick. But Logan… he's worse somehow. Evil. I can almost *feel* his wickedness—

"Maddie!"

I snap out of my thoughts and find Raven and another girl staring at me. "What? Sorry, I wasn't paying attention."

"Jesus." She sighs. "Your man is upstairs talking to Pete. So get outta here. I got business to do with—" She looks the new girl up and down, then says, "Rose?" Shakes her head. "Lola? No, I hated the last Lola. How about… Aspen?"

The new girl is wide-eyed and still. Like she's got no idea what's happening.

God, I kinda felt that way too when I first started. I wonder what her story is? Why she needs money? She looks too young to have a daycare bill. Maybe school? Maybe she's paying her way through school?

"Aspen?" Raven snaps. All business—which translates to bitchy—just like she was with me that night I got hired. "You're a grown-up. Use your words."

"Sure," she stammers. "Aspen. Whatever."

Raven turns her back to newly-christened Aspen, and she's smiling. Deviously. I squint at her, but she gives me a small shake of her head that says, *Later*, and forces her smile back down to a frown. "Well, have a good time tonight with Tyler."

She's been weirdly... nice to me lately. In fact, I've noticed she's like this a lot. Meaning she's mean and bitchy to everyone at first. Like your older sister who feels it's her job to set you right when you wander off the straight and narrow. But once you get into the groove—like become part of Pete's little stripper family or whatever—she's kinda friendly. Comes off as just... protective.

"Thanks," I say, meaning it. "It's actually business and pleasure. But I think the business is actually pleasure too."

Raven lets her smile loose again. She softens, just a little. And she looks younger all of a sudden. Not washed up at all, but just wise. "Go on, get out of here."

I nod, pick up my backpack, sling it over my shoulder, and leave them to their own business.

Walking down the hallway towards the stairs to Pete's office, I spy Candy working a group of guys. She just got promoted to Saturday nights. Couple girls just kinda disappeared over the last week, which is pretty common around here. And I'm the one who told Pete and Raven that Candy deserves a chance for weekend shifts.

It makes me feel good. I mean, I got her a better stripper job, not a career in banking. But it's a chance she needed. She does have kids. And a huge daycare bill because she's a single mom.

But it makes me feel sad too. I look around at this place—a place that's kinda become like a second home to me over the past few months—and it suddenly feels... over. Candy moving up, the new girl... it's like I had my shot and now I'm done. It's their turn now.

That's not rational, I know this. Carlos still thinks I owe him a shitload of money, but I know the truth. I know

I don't owe him that money. I know I'm right. I know I've been doing the best I can. I know that strippers are just people—struggling with past mistakes, or bad relationships—who have few options left.

So I sucked it up, came here, and made the most of my mediocre opportunity. Just like Candy's doing.

I also know… I'm not the same person I was a few months ago when I started this job. My past came back to haunt me, for sure. But sometimes the scariest things are the ones you're running from, not the reality they bring when they catch up to you.

I'm stronger today than I was yesterday because I think I might be able to let Scotty just…die his death and deal with it.

I think I might be ready to move on.

Tyler did that, Angel says.

And for once, as I climb the stairs up to Pete's office and hear the murmur of him and Tyler talking at the top, I don't call the devil to get his opinion on the matter.

Because she's right.

I'm right, because I'm her.

Tyler did do that.

Sometimes angels fall.

And that's OK.

Because there are lots of people who still give a shit. There are lots of people willing to extend a hand and lift you back up.

I'm not Tyler's angel.

He's mine.

CHAPTER SEVENTEEN

TYLER

There's a soft knock on Pete's office door. From where I'm sitting in my Pete-facing chair, I turn to see Maddie swing the door open and poke her head in right as Pete answers the question I just asked him. "Shit, kid, I dunno. Maybe a couple hundred? Not all confirmed. It was the fuckin' jungle."

Maddie gives me a 'what the fuck are you talking about?' look. I shake my head the tiniest bit in a 'you don't wanna know' response, and smile. She smiles back. Which makes me hard.

Jesus. If I don't stop getting hard in front of Pete, I'm worried he's gonna get the wrong idea. I mean he's a cool old guy and all, but—

"Scarlett." Pete waves to her and says, "Can you do me a favor?"

"Uh, sure. What's up?"

"Can you take this guy off my hands? I got accounting to do."

Pete…

There's almost the hint of a smile in his question. *Almost.* That's OK. I know Pete likes me. I'm not sure why it's so important to me what Pete thinks of me, but it seems to be, so I'm glad I'm confident he thinks I'm so excellent.

"Sure," Maddie says. "Thanks for letting me off early."

Pete shrugs. "It ain't Starbucks. If you don't steam the milk, there's a buncha other girls who'll heat it up instead."

"Ha!" I laugh. "Fucking killer metaphor, man."

Pete sighs. "See? Seems like the only way to keep this asshole here from bugging me all night is to send him off with you."

I smile. I knew he liked me. I slap his desk, stand, extend my hand.

"You're a good man, Pete."

Pete forces himself up from his chair, seizes my grip.

"I'm a no-good son-of-a-bitch. I'm just your kinda no-good son-of-a-bitch."

We shake. And for a second, I feel like I can glimpse what Pete might have been like as a younger man. There's a ghost behind his eyes that peeks out at me.

Like, you wouldn't know it meeting him on the street, but the guy has one of the kindest hearts you'll ever encounter. You can tell he just wants to do the right thing by people. Even if he doesn't always know what that is.

Something about that gives me hope.

I smile and say, "See ya, Pete."

He nods at me. "Tyler."

I turn to Maddie. She's so sweet, and pretty, and fucking sexy, and her jeans look good, and her tits look amazing, and she's watching me with a look that says she's nervous but excited, and I'm still trying to hide my fucking erection from Pete, and I start to take her hand, but then I stop because I'm not sure if I should in front of Pete, but then I go to take it again, stop again, step past her to the door, open it for her, and wave her forward to take her leave.

She smirks at me and shakes her head. I assume because she can't wrap her brain around how I can be so sexy, dangerous, indestructible, hot as shit, and adorable all at the same time.

As opposed to not being able to wrap her brain around what a fucking dipshit I am. Y'know, could go either way.

Maddie grins back at Pete and also says, "See ya, Pete."

There is an honest-to-goodness smile in his eyes (if not on his lips) as he looks at her, then at me, then back to her.

"What?" she asks him on a tiny chuckle.

He shakes his head, says, "Nothin'," then nods at her, offering a, "See ya, Maddie."

She walks past me through the open door, and just as I'm about to pull it shut and go, seemingly out of nowhere, Pete says, "Flanagan."

"What?" I ask, looking over my shoulder in time to see him spin in his chair and take the urn off the shelf behind him and begin polishing it with a cloth.

"My name," he says, not turning around to face us. "It's Flanagan."

A big grin spreads across my face, and Maddie looks at me, quizzically. But I just shake my head slightly and let the smile live there, unexplained.

Pete…

With his back still to us, he raises his meaty hand in another goodbye, and as I close the door shut, and he disappears out of sight, I find myself… unexpectedly nervous too.

We pull into the empty parking lot and, looking out the window, Maddie says, "Wow."

"I know, right?"

"People made this. People, like, *made* this," she says.

"I know."

The Hoover Dam *is* incredible. It's the perfect blending of the enormous power of the natural world and the ingenuity and effort of the human animal.

Or else it's the perfect symbol of our struggle to control the seemingly uncontrollable.

Or else it's just a big fucking hunk of concrete and steel that looks really cool and is, like, super pretty at night when it's all lit up.

Maybe it's all three.

"Yeah," I say, throwing the car into park. "When Evan got his driver's license, we'd come out here at night sometimes and like, sneak around, drink, bring girls. Well, Evan wouldn't. Bring girls, I mean. Obviously. But, yeah, we'd do that shit."

"Really?" she asks.

"Yeah… Scotty probably never said anything about it, huh?"

"No. He didn't." She's wearing a frown, now.

"Well, I mean, you were, like, eleven. That'd be a weird thing to talk to your eleven-year-old sister about."

"What? Trespassing, underage drinking, and hooking up with skanks?"

"Hey!" I point my finger at her. "They were not skanks! They were delicate flowers just starting to blossom into womanhood!"

She drops her chin and gives me a bored expression.

"And Maybe... Like... Five. Skanks. Tops," I say.

She pats me on the knee and opens the door, letting in the chilly night air.

I hop out of the cab and open the rear door to grab the drone from the back seat. She opens the rear door on her side and snatches up her backpack.

"Careful with it," she says.

"What am I gonna do? Drop it? Oh, shit!" I shout, as I pretend to drop it. I'm a practical joker. Everybody loves it. Except Maddie, I guess.

"Dude, don't be…you. With my drone, please."

I nod and proceed to be overly precious about handling the fancy flying machine. She rolls her eyes and pushes the door shut. I'm killing this date so far. Fucking killing it!

A guy in a security guard outfit comes strolling up to us. As he approaches, Maddie asks, "This your friend?"

"Uh… Yeah," I offer back, probably too tentatively.

"What?" she asks, sharply.

"Nothing. Just he's not exxxxaaaactly my friend… Exactly," I draw out.

"Fuck does that mean?"

"Nothing, just—Hey, man!" I say convivially, putting up one hand. "You Terry?"

"Yup," he says back.

"Hey, man, I'm Tyler," I say, offering him a shake.

He's a young guy. Early twenties. Kinda skinny. Dressed in the poorly-fitted, not-quite-brown, not-quite-grey garb of privately contracted security personnel. He doesn't take my hand. That's fine. I don't need him to be my BFF.

I set the drone down on the hood of my car, open the driver's side door, reach over into the glove box, and pull out a manila envelope. One of the ones with the clasp closure. Not the self-adhesive kind. Those suck. I mean this one has adhesive too, but it also has the clasp. Because that's how you can be sure it stays closed. This isn't my mind rambling. This is the process I went through briefly when deciding which envelope I should stuff ten thousand dollars in cash into.

"Here you go." I hand it to him. He sticks his finger in the flap and just rips it open. (Jesus. Don't even know why I try sometimes.) He looks inside. Then casts a glance at me while still looking inside. Then twists his neck like somehow he'll be able to see it better from a different angle. Weirdo.

"We good?" I ask.

He makes a sucking sound with his teeth and nods, then wanders back to the security station and closes the door. Sweet. That was easy. Now we'll just—

"What the hell was that?" Maddie asks, rounding the Defender.

"What? That's Terry. Me and him go way back."

"Uh-huh. And what was in the envelope that you handed your old buddy Terry?"

"We gonna fly this drone or what?" I ask with excitement. Because, y'know, fun-loving Tyler. That's what they call me.

"Did you just pay that guy so that we can be here?"

"Um, NO." She looks at me with… not skepticism. What do you call it when…? Oh! Yeah. Like I'm full of shit. That's it.

"No," I almost plead. "Honestly, NO. I did not pay him so that we can be here."

"…O…K," she says reluctantly.

"I paid him so that we can go down into the tunnels."

"Jesus, Tyler—"

"What? It's cool. It'll be cool. I mean, yeah, we'll do the drone thing and whatever, blah, blah, blah, but the TUNNELS! The tunnels are so COOL!"

I kinda do a little dance for her, like John Belushi does as Bluto in *Animal House* when he's trying to cheer up Flounder.

And she is as unmoved by my attempt at frivolity as Flounder was.

"Fuck," I say as I stop my jig. "Look, I—I haven't been on a, y'know, a *date* in like…well…maybe ever, when I come to think of it. So—"

"You've NEVER been on a date?" she interrupts.

"I—Like, no. I don't think so."

"How is that possible?"

"What? How many dates have you been on?"

"Dates? I, uh…" She pauses. "Well… Shit. Have I never been on a real date?" she asks herself, presumably rhetorically.

"See?" I almost accuse. "Like, y'know, I'd just hook up, or like meet someone at a party, or, y'know… accidentally get it on with my friend's sister in the VIP room of a strip club…"

Oh, shit. I was making a joke but that may have been a bridge to far. That's what the look on her face is telling me. Gotta walk this back. Quick.

"Hell, I'm sorry. I'm…stupid."

"Noooooo. Really?"

"Fuck. I was… I just… I just wanna show you some cool shit that meant something to me when I was a kid. That's all. It was important to me, this place was. For a lot of reasons. And not to be too… whatever… but I had some really good times with Scotty and Evan here too. Like fun, innocent kid shit. And I know you can't go home again, like Tom Wolfe said, but—"

"Thomas," she interrupts.

"What?"

"Thomas. *You Can't Go Home Again* is a book by Thomas Wolfe. Tom Wolfe wrote *The Electric Kool-Aid Acid Test.* Not the same guy."

"Oh… Well, which one were people supposed to be afraid of?"

"That's Virginia Woolf."

"Whatever! The point is…" I take her by the hands. "I wanna share something with you that was special to me. And that was special *for* me… with Scotty. And, like, we don't even have to do anything sexy or whatever. I mean this is our first date, after all. Literally. Our first date." (I don't even care that she doesn't laugh. I know that's a solid joke.) "And so I just wanna be with you. Here. With you. That's it. I mean it."

She gives me a side-eye. But it's accompanied by a little smirk, so I take that as a cue to start doing my little Bluto dance again.

"Don't," she says. "Just don't."

"K." I stop.

She shakes her head. "You are just…"

I snake my head around to meet her eyes.

"Yeah? Something good?" I raise my eyebrows.

She laughs. "Show me the fucking tunnels."

"Tunnels? But I thought we had to do the drone—" That's all I get out because she smacks me on the arm.

And then I grab her, pull her in, and give her a long, hungry kiss. Under the late November moon. On top of the Hoover Dam. The dark, murky blackness of The Colorado River below our feet. The same murky blackness that I used to fantasize about hurling myself into when I was a kid and things would start to look bleak.

The reason I never actually did that is because I hate quitting and I hate giving up. If the world wants to take me out, it can do it on its own, it's not getting any help from me.

And in Maddie, I recognize that same thing. She's one of the strongest people I've ever seen. I felt it when we reconnected, and it was confirmed when I found out it was her. She doesn't have to forgive me for not being there for her. Shit, I don't know if I'd forgive me. But if she's really gonna give me a chance, I'm gonna make goddamn sure she doesn't have to shoulder anything alone ever again. Fucking bank on that shit.

And the only thing I wanna throw myself into now… is her.

My hands draw down to her ass and pull her hips into me, into my already hard cock, and she stops kissing me and pulls back.

"Oh, hello." She smirks.

"Hi," I say, stroking back strands of hair that are being pushed into her face by the wind.

"We don't have to do anything sexy, huh?" she asks.

I fight the urge to grimace. "Nope!" I work out of my lying mouth.

"But can we?" she says, putting her hand on the growing bulge in my jeans. "If we want to?" Her mouth is millimeters from mine.

"Uh…yeah. That would be… that would be fine," I somehow manage. Like a fucking BOSS.

She closes her eyes and smiles.

"And then we… droooooone?" she hums out, turning the word into an onomatopoeia.

"Oh, yeah," I say. "Hell, yeah. We'll drone the fuck outta some shit," I pant back, just about ready to burst through the zipper of my pants. "We'll drone this motherfucker like *Three the Hard Way*… I just wanna explore a *tunnel* first," I say, the corners of my lips turning up.

Her smile widens, she grabs my beard, pulls me against her mouth, flicks her tongue out, licking at my lips, and says, "I'll bet."

OK. That's it.

I grab the drone in one hand, her hand in the other, and we gallop over to the elevator that will take us five hundred feet below the earth so that we can… explore.

MADDIE

The elevators are huge. Built to take whole crowds of people down in the dam's interior. And the thrum of power churning through the whole structure vibrates under my feet. We stand alone in the center of the elevator as it descends. Tyler's hand still has mine and it feels a little… sweet. Our first date. A real date.

I glance up and find him smiling.

"You're like… Mr. Happy tonight," I say. But in my head I think, *Just wait. Pretty soon you're gonna be a whole lot happier.*

He shrugs, still smiling as the elevator stops and the doors open. He leads me out into the dimly lit tunnel, which really is an actual tunnel. With jagged rock walls and a coolness that feels a little humid. The entire place feels like pent-up energy—appropriate, since that's what it is.

"So the tunnel—" Tyler starts, then stops when I take the drone out of his hand and set it down gently on the concrete floor.

"Yes, it's a very nice tunnel," I say, pushing him backwards. "Super nice tunnel," I continue, setting my backpack down next to the drone. "But these tunnels have been here for decades." I place both hands on his chest, palms flat, and look up into his eyes. "We've got lots of time to see the tunnels. They're not going anywhere."

"Hey, Mads," he says, his hands slipping down to rest on my hips, pulling me closer. His stare intent on mine. "I'm not going anywhere either."

I swallow hard, then force a smile back that, it turns out, isn't really forced. There's time for all that serious talk later. Tonight is just gonna be fun, I decide. So I say, "OK." Because maybe I really believe him.

He leans down, his mouth on mine, his hands slipping under the hem of my t-shirt and jacket and sliding up my ribcage, and we seal his promise with a kiss that means more than OK.

"What should we do now?" he whispers into my mouth, his fingertips pulling my bra down so he can play with my nipples. That sends a shudder of desire through my whole body, making me smile back into our kiss.

"I have a surprise for you," I say.

He laughs a little, pulling out of the kiss. "I love surprises."

My tongue slips out between my teeth like a secret. Sweeps against my upper lip. Which I think he loves, because both hands grip my breasts harder.

"But first," I say, looking up at the security cameras as I slip my jacket off, "I need to know if those are on."

Tyler glances up at one nearby and shakes his head. "Apparently there's been a minor malfunction in the security control room."

"Has there?" I tease back.

He nods. "Some kind of electromagnetic interference, I've been told. So, unfortunately, no. They're not on."

"Well, that's too bad. I was hoping you had plans to bribe that guy outside to get a copy of what's coming next."

"What's coming next?" he breathes.

Sex, obviously. But I like this new easy relationship we're developing. The teasing. The jokes. The flirting. So I say, "Let's call it Tyler Morgan's Tunnel Fantasy."

He laughs. Just a little chuckle that says he's ready to play along. "OK, sounds good, let's definitely call it that."

I slip my hands up my shirt, grab both of his, and slide them back down as I step backwards, my gaze never leaving his face. And then I laugh. Because I can't *not* laugh.

He cocks his head, still grinning. "Maddie?"

I let go of his hands and hold up a finger. Then I slip my t-shirt over my head. My breasts are exposed, my nipples peaking in the chilly tunnel air, my bra pulled down, which pushes them up and makes them even more spectacular than they normally are.

Tyler's hard-on—which never completely faded on the trip down—presses against his jeans. His thick shaft outlined underneath the denim. His eyes not on mine now, but right where they need to be.

I bend down, never taking my eyes off Tyler, pick up my backpack, and open the zip.

"Jesus, Maddie. You're grinning like a fuckin' kid on Christmas. What could possibly be in that—" But then I pull it out and he says, "Ohhhh," blinks at me, grins wider, if that's even possible, and tilts his head again, as if to say, *You sure about this?*

I nod my head, stroking the soft, rust-colored fur of the fox tail butt plug. "So sure, Mr. Morgan. And look, I have these too!" I pull out the little furry ears and slip the headband over my hair. "I'm a little fox," I purr. "All I need is my tail."

Tyler slips one hand under his arm, while the other hand covers his mouth to hide the chuckle. But he's the one who looks like a kid on Christmas now.

"Here," I say, handing him the tail. He takes it, his hands automatically stroking the fur, just like I did, and I begin to unbutton my pants.

"Where did you—?"

I'm the one who tilts my head now. "I'm a stripper, Ty. I have people. You seemed to like the one I found in my mom's closet. Maybe a little too much." I waggle my eyebrows at him. "Your first and only experience with a fox tail can*not* be imagining my mother. So I thought to myself, *Madison, what could you possibly do to wipe that thought from Tyler's mind?*" I grin. Wide. "So here we are. Surprise!"

"Here we are," he says, staring at the furry tail while his free hand unconsciously reaches down to grab his cock. "Surprise."

I'm already kicking off my shoes and unbuttoning my jeans. Zipper down, wiggling them over my hips, stepping out, before he even has a chance to catch up. I fuckin' love that for once, Tyler Morgan is speechless.

And just as that thought leaves my mind, he snaps out of it and crosses the short distance between us in one step, both hands reaching for the elastic of my panties. The tail brushes against my bare thigh as he drags them down my legs and I have to close my eyes for a moment to enjoy the feeling.

I step out of the panties, the heat between my legs building as I reach for the thick outline of Tyler's cock under his jeans.

"Fuck," he mutters as I squeeze him. "Have you ever done this before?"

"Not a fox tail," I say, turning my back to him and pressing my ass against his cock. "But I can't wait to try it with you." I wiggle a little, which makes him brush the hair off the side of my neck and kiss me just below the ear. His arms wrap around my body, the soft fur caressing my ribs as he lifts my breasts up and grips them until I moan.

"Maddie," he whispers through the kisses on my neck. One hand slips down between my legs, his fingertips pressing against my clit.

I bend over slightly to keep his attention on my ass. He grips both my hips and bumps me back into him, muttering out a soft, "Fuck," as he grinds against me.

My hand takes the place of his, and even though I *know* I'm fuckin' horny—practically vibrating with anticipation—the wetness I find between my legs is surprising. I play with myself until I'm practically gushing, then reach for the lube in the discarded backpack near my feet.

Fox tail. Jesus, it's not even in yet and it's turning me on. "Come on," I whine, urging him to continue as I hand the lube back to him. "I'm ready."

He's muttering behind me. Something along the lines of, "Fuck, yeah," and "Foxy little slut," which makes me giggle, because I assume it's an affectionate endearment at this point.

The lube cap drops to the floor and rolls out of sight. "Ahhhh," I say, as the viscous, cold gel drips between my cheeks. But it quickly warms as he begins massaging it into my ass.

I have to close my eyes, because the feeling of his pressing fingers back there in combination with my own strumming from the front is *so* good.

One finger slips inside me. I grit my teeth and stiffen, but Tyler's other hand is sweeping up and down my spine, distracting me from the sharp initial pain until I relax and allow him access.

He pumps in and out and then two fingers find their way inside. I grit my teeth this time, thinking of the plug's girth. It's medium-sized, not too large. But not too small, either. Because, hell, if I'm gonna stick a fox tail in my butt, I wanna get the full experience when he fucks me.

I suck air in between my teeth as he continues to pump his fingers. They're sliding in and out easily now, and I'm just about to urge him on when he pulls out and the cold, hard, stainless steel takes the place of his warm, pliable fingers.

"*Ho-lee*," I hiss.

"Shhhhh," he says back.

I smile. Close my eyes. And then take a deep, deep breath as he works the plug in and out just a tiny bit, allowing me to get over the shock of cold and relax.

He presses a little harder as he plays now, easing the plug in deeper each time. And then, when I realize he's going to keep going this time, I hold my breath.

Tyler says, "Breathe, Maddie, Relax," as he strokes my spine with his fingertips again.

So I do. I let it out, and in that instant he presses hard, not giving up, and slips the plug in until my muscles widen, then clamp down on the thin ring of metal near the end.

Relief floods through my whole body, the pleasure replacing the pain as the fur tickles my ass. I wiggle, fully exploring the feeling as Tyler's hand reaches in front of me, pulling my hands away from my pussy, and then holds my wrists together behind my back as he urges me to stand up straight.

He leans into my ear, kisses it, dropping my wrists. But I leave them in place as he reaches around to firmly grip both breasts.

"Yeah," he says. "This is about to get fun."

TYLER

I pinch her nipples tightly and she squeals and jumps. I slide my hands around her ribs to her back, never letting my touch separate from her skin. I unfasten the clasp on her bra and the fabric drops to the cold, hard concrete walkway. Her shoulders pinch together as she shivers a bit.

I turn her around to face me, and step back. Here's what I see:

Her long, red hair is crowned with the tawny fox ears; her nipples are puckered and taut; she pulls the fox tail around the side of her hip to where it just obscures my view of her bare pussy, and slowly strokes the fur; oh, and she's still wearing white, knee-high socks with red stripes around the top.

She shivers once again, rubbing her knees and thighs together partially in an attempt to keep warm and, based on the knowing expression she wears as she nibbles at her bottom lip, partially to make me lose My. Fucking. Mind.

"Meow," she mewls out.

I close my eyes and swallow, my hands clenching into fists. "Mmmm," I growl at her. "What the fuck are you doing to me?"

She shrugs one shoulder and says, "Dunno. I don't actually know the sound a fox makes, so I'm just going with kitten. Meow."

My boots are off, my jeans are off, my jacket and t-shirt are off, and I spin her around, slamming her into the tunnel's jagged rock wall. She gasps, then laughs and turns her cheek so that I can see her smile. I press into her, spreading her legs so my erection can slide in between them. I stroke myself back and forth, back and forth, not yet entering her, just letting the shaft skim along the lips of her pussy and get coated with her wetness.

I'm working the fox tail, too. Twisting the base, rotating it around inside her ass, pulling and pushing lightly as I do, and she whimpers, still fucking meowing as she does.

"You are a dirty fucking trick, you know that?" I whisper into her ear.

"Meow?" She says it like a question. Fuck her. It's on.

I rip her hips back, lift the tail out of my goddamn way, twist a fistful of hair around my fingers, and slam myself into her.

Her scream echoes long and loud in the otherwise empty tunnel.

I pull her hair harder, drawing her neck further back as I hammer into her over and over again. She continues making her "meowing" sounds with each thrust, and I feel like I'm going to pass out from a lack of oxygen, because I keep forgetting to breathe.

I press into her, forcing her to straighten her body and go flush against the rock. My chest is flat upon her back and I can feel the soft fur of the fox tail on my thigh as I drive up and into her. One hand still fisting her hair, I place the other around her neck, just below her chin, and I can feel her pulse pounding in frantic time with my throbbing cock moving inside her. I squeeze her throat and she chokes out, "Yes." I grip just enough for her to want it, but not enough to harm her.

Because I will never harm her. Not again. And I will never let her be harmed by anyone else. I will lay unforgiving waste to anyone who so much as sneezes too close to her and risks her catching a cold. I will rip off my own flesh and offer it in exchange for hers. I will walk through fire.

Whatever I have to do to see to it that she is safe, and happy, and free from pain, I will do. Whatever it takes. Whatever the cost. I will suffer for her, if there must be suffering. It will be a privilege.

She's bending and lifting her knees, helping drive me into her as deeply as she can, the bouncing of her ass on my cock making the tail jounce and bounce along with it. As deep as we are underneath the world above, that's how deeply I want to put myself inside her. The neon work-lights illuminating the uneven rocks around us cast broken shadows up and down the seemingly endless expanse of earth that disappears into blackness on either side.

"Does it feel good?" I moan out.

"Meow," she groans back.

I smile and let go of her hair and throat, taking her by the hips once again, sliding myself out of her and turning her to face me.

"Where'd you go?" She pouts, her brow furrowing.

"Don't worry," I say. "This fox hunt isn't over yet."

She rolls her eyes. "You proud of that one?"

"Little bit," I admit and grin. "I wanna see you. I wanna see your face," I say.

She gets a darkly sexy grin and says, "Good."

Now she pushes me back against the opposing wall and kisses my collar bone. She kisses my chest, as ever, taking her time with the traumatized skin that lives there. She reaches for my cock and massages it with her hand, still licking and kissing my stomach and chest, and—

"Fuck!" I shout. "That tickles!"

She steps back and blinks. "Seriously?" she asks.

"Yeah. Why?"

"Because I just bit the shit out of your nipple. Like really hard. It… tickles?"

I shrug and raise my eyebrows.

"You're unreal," she says.

"Thank you," I say back, proudly.

"It wasn't a compliment."

"I know."

I slap my hands on her ass and pull her to me, kissing her like a wild animal. I keep kissing as I play with her tail, moving it in and out of her asshole as she gasps and moans. I touch her face with my free hand and let my fingers find their way into her mouth. She sucks on them, still jerking wantonly on the hilt of my cock as I work the metal stem that's in her ass back and forth, around and around.

Her breathing accelerates and she starts shaking. I know what this foretells. I've been with her enough now to know the exact moment she's going to come. I yank my fingers free from her mouth, and let them work themselves up into her pussy, stroking the inside of her walls as I continue forcing the tail deeper into her ass.

"Oh, shit. Oh, shit," she squeaks out. I punish the walls of her pussy more urgently, work the metal at the end of the fur hanging between her legs a little harder, and suddenly…

She is squirting all over me.

All over my fingers, all over my legs, all over my stomach, and as I finger her harder, trying to snap off my own wrist in the process, she keeps drenching us both.

The wailing moan that comes from within her seems to last for minutes, and the amount of wetness that's pouring from her onto me rivals what's happening with the rushing river outside. And it's even more beautiful.

"OK! OK! Whoa, whoa. I gotcha," I say, as she begins collapsing to the floor and I hold her around the waist, lowering her carefully to the ground. Once she's all the way down, she slaps at my hands, unconsciously, and I pull them away, palms up. She's still twitching and shivering, still leaking out onto the concrete, and I'm still as hard as the rocks in the wall and still smiling like a maniac.

"Looks like we broke the dam." I chortle.

She slaps the ground with her palm and says, "Fuck! Fuck me! What. The fuck. Was that?"

A thought runs through my mind. A joke actually. And I debate with myself for a second before saying it, I really do. Because the thing about being a smartass like I am is that I'm aware of the shit I'm saying, I just can't help saying it. It's not that I don't know I'm probably gonna get myself in trouble when I open my mouth. I do. But I always weigh the consequences of what's about to take flight from my lips, and then almost always decide that the risk is worth the cost.

So I take a breath, bend down close to her, stroke the hair half-covering her flushed and spent face, and say…

"I dunno. Maybe you could ask your mom."

CHAPTER EIGHTEEN

MADDIE

I just blink at him. I feel like I do that a lot with Tyler. Like he's an ever-moving maze, a puzzle I'm trying to find my way through. "What?"

"Too far?" He winces.

And then I laugh. Because, well, the joke was funny if you were there. And I was.

"See," he says, kissing my lips, then giving one a little nip with his teeth. "I am funny. At least, I'm your kind of funny."

I reach up, place both my hands on each side of his face, and smile. "Thank you,"

"For…? Because I think I should be thanking you right about now."

"Later," I say, letting my hands fall to his shoulders. Because I have a very long answer for his question and now isn't the time. I dig my nails in the hard muscles of his back, just enough to make him draw in a breath and close his eyes for one prolonged moment.

He opens them back up. The joking is gone and the wild side is back.

I like his jokes, don't get me wrong. Tyler Morgan is as witty as they come. Always has been and I absolutely love that about him. But sometimes I just want the raw and the real.

Like now.

I climb into his lap and he adjusts the both of us so he can lean back against the hard, jagged rock wall. It's gotta hurt—all those ragged edges digging into his skin—but maybe he doesn't feel pain? Or maybe he likes it?

I lift my hips up, letting that thought trail away for another time too, and reach for his cock. "We're not done yet," I say.

"Not even close," he whispers back. Our eyes are locked as I position him underneath me, our breathing matched. We smile simultaneously. And then I lower myself down on top of him.

I want to close my eyes as he enters me again. And the fact that he's playing with the tail as this happens makes it almost impossible to keep them open. But I do keep them open. I don't want to miss a single second of this.

"Relax," I say. "I got this now."

He chuckles a little. "I'm about as relaxed as it gets, Maddie."

"Not quite," I say, placing the tip of my finger above his eye and softly tracing downward so he has to close it. Being Tyler, he complies. Sorta. Because the other eye stays open in a wink. Which is cute, and adorable, and so genuinely him, I want to laugh. But I don't. I just close the other eye too, then lean into his neck and whisper, "Let me take care of *you* now."

He huffs out a little bit of air, but he doesn't open his eyes. So I start moving on top of him. My hips slowly rocking forward and back, my clit skimming against his lower abs just enough to drive myself wild without meaning to.

I grab his shoulders again just as his hands squeeze both my ass cheeks, trying to pull me forward. Trying to get deeper inside me.

The fur of the fox tail brushes against my skin, and the feeling of being filled up from both ends is starting to make me crazy for him again, but I suck in a breath, hold it, and stay calm as I hover above him, just slightly, just enough to deny his silent request.

"You're fucking torturing me," he says, hands on my hips now, urging me to just sit down. Let him fully inside me.

"No," I say. "I'm making you slow down, that's all. Take a look around. Enjoy it, moment by moment."

The hiss of air he exhales has a touch of frustration in it. But only a touch. Because sometimes slow is good. Sometimes you just gotta let go. And he knows this is one of those times.

It's perfect. I mean, nothing's perfect, but this feels perfect. Like all the bad stuff is gone now. Like we've got a handle on all this shit. Like maybe… maybe we're even in it together.

Which would be nice, for once. To have a partner. To rely on someone. To know I'm not alone.

I bet he feels that way too.

I continue to move my hips, letting him stay inside me, but not giving in completely. Not yet. My fingertips thread up through his hair as I lean down into his neck and begin to kiss. His earlobe, which makes him sigh. Then down his neck until I'm kissing the base of his throat.

He holds absolutely still, his large hands gripping my ass in a hard squeeze. Maybe it's because my position has him deeper inside me? Maybe it's because it feels so good, he just goes with it? Kinda surrenders. Or maybe it's because he wants to remember this moment for later? Burn it into his brain and keep it there like a good-luck charm.

That's why I go still.

I want to hold this moment in my head forever.

"Maddie," he says.

But I keep kissing him, letting my name fade into the darkness.

His eyes remain closed, but his hands begin to move me, his firm grip on my hips pushing me forward, then back. Forward, then back. It's enough to drive me crazy because each time my clit slides along his skin.

I bow my head and give in, just like he did. Sink my forehead into his chest as his lips find my neck now. He kisses me as I remain still. He rocks us back and forth as I breathe through the slow-building excitement inside me.

It's not hard and fast, like the other times we've fucked. It's something else. Something softer. Something natural. A lazy, easy motion that feels more like the rocking of a boat than the crashing of thunder.

He's relaxed. Maybe for the first time since we've become reacquainted. Totally at ease down here in this dark tunnel.

This is different. Something more than fucking. Something better than sex.

This is… maybe… *love*?

Maybe this is what it feels like?

If you'd have asked me if this slow motion would be enough to make me come before I met Tyler all those weeks ago, I'd have laughed. Sex was something physical. Something hard and fast. An act completed hastily in an alley or a hotel bedroom.

And even though we've done it that way, and those times were all great, this… *this* isn't *that.* This is more. And the climax I didn't think possible is building. Not because our bodies are merged, but because our emotions are.

"God. Dammit," Tyler whispers.

I know what he means. *Goddammit.* This is something new. Something unexpected. Something we both seem to need. And want, too.

He bites my ear, then my neck. One of his hands lets go of my hip to play with the fox tail, moving it in and out. Making me gasp and hold my breath as the feeling of both his cock and the plug rubbing against each other inside me take hold of all those slow, easy thoughts. Because… you know, sex is still sex. It makes you do things you don't have to think about. Becomes primal. Basic instinct. Just desire and…

"Maddie," he says, his chest moving up and down quickly, like there's not enough air to fuel him.

"Come," I whisper into his ear. "Just come. Inside me. Right now."

He moans out. Just a grunt. But it's a yes, and that's all I needed to know.

I let go of everything as he stiffens. I let go of the past, and the present. I think about nothing but us, together, in this moment. I don't care that it means something. It doesn't matter.

I. Just. Let. Go.

I feel him release inside me. Slick heat as his cock throbs against the walls of my pussy.

And that's it. I am there. With him. Waves of pleasure shiver up my body, making the hair stand up on the back of my neck.

And I feel… I feel like somehow… heaven has touched me.

Tyler Morgan has found my filthy soul and washed it clean.

He caught me, mid-fall, and lifted me back up with him.

Yes. That's exactly how I feel.

TYLER

With her sitting in my lap, staring at me, flooded in our shared desire, I see my whole, rotten life reflected in her eyes. In her knowledge of me. In who I was. In who I am. In who I might one day be. Our connection with each other is as ancient as the sodden shelter that hosts us, as strong as the power it generates, and as beautiful and complicated as the machinery that keeps it all at bay.

In other words… Shit just got real as fuck.

"Thanks," I say.

She nods. "You're welcome. Thank—"

"Pleasure's mine." I cut her off.

Smiles are shared. Smiles turn into giggles. Giggles turn into laughs. And laughs turn into me saying, "Sorry, sorry, I need you to hop off, you're gonna break my nuts."

More laughing as she lifts herself up, goes to her backpack, and pulls out a towel.

"That's some Girl Scout shit right there," I say.

"Always prepared," she muses back, then says, "Umm…"

"What?"

"I gotta take this thing off. Out. Whatever."

"Oh, right. Yeah, I guess you do. You want… help?"

She gnaws at her lips, which is cute as hell. "I guess?"

She laughs. I laugh. We're a regular basket of fuckin' giggles all of a sudden.

I love it.

I stand, cross over to her, turn her around, and take hold of the tail.

"You good?" I ask.

"We'll see."

I bend over, kiss her on both ass cheeks, and as I do…

"Oh, shit!" she gasps, as I withdraw the metal plug, kissing and massaging her as it goes. I toss the tail to the side, turn her to face me, and kiss her mouth while continuing to massage her sweet, sweet ass with both hands.

"So," I say into her kiss, "how was your first first date, Ms. Clayton?"

She snorts then says, "Considering I was expecting dinner and a movie, not bad."

I love this girl. So much so that I almost say it. Almost. But it feels like I'm doing things right so far, and so I'm gonna just play it safe.

It does occur to me that I don't play it safe when I have something sarcastic to say, but when there's something deeply sincere I could share, I hold back. But now's not the time to jump into that psychological fox hole (pun one hundred percent intended), that's what I pay Dr. Eldridge for.

"What?" That's me. Maddie's stroking some of my tangled mess of hair out of my face, wearing a look that's not quite sadness, not quite concern, but is definitely their second cousin.

"Nothing," she says, "Just… I dunno how I didn't recognize you. You're so… you."

"I didn't recognize you either."

"Dude, I was thirteen and I barely had tits when you last actually saw me. And when you saw me again I was wearing a wig. And dancing in a strip club."

"Valid points."

"But you… you're the same guy I remember. Except just more… hirsute, obviously."

I nod at her, thoughtfully. Then ask, "Hirsute means hairy, right?"

"Yes, Tyler." She sighs.

"Right. That's like a whole fetish category on my favorite porn website."

She rolls her eyes, pushes away from me, and starts toweling herself off.

"I dunno," I say, "For whatever it's worth, I don't feel the same."

"You don't?"

"No. Maybe? Yes and no. I mean nobody really changes after the age of, like ten, they just get taller. But after you hit double digits, you're pretty much locked, personality-wise. That's my theory, anyway."

"That's an insane theory."

"Um, yeah. Have we met? Of course it's insane. Duh. But I stand by it."

She smirks and shakes her head.

"That said," I go on, "spending every day almost literally dying for a few years will give you a whole new perspective on shit. I mean, really, everybody's always right on the edge of dying all the time anyway so there's nothing special about it, but when you're in war, you just become more aware of it, I guess."

She's done toweling off and is pulling on her jeans now. She offers me the towel, but I wave it off. I want what we made to dry into my skin and become part of me. I want to smell like us for pretty much the rest of my life.

I start pulling on my jeans too, stopping just before fastening the top button.

"How did Scotty die?" I ask.

She's bending down to pick up her bra, and pauses for a second.

I continue, "In my apartment—old apartment—you asked me if I knew how Scotty died. I thought I did. I obviously don't. How did he? You don't have to tell me if you don't want."

If shit hadn't gotten real before, it's sure as hell real now. But I needed to ask. Because… fuck it. She and I both know why.

She exhales, then keeps getting dressed, putting on her bra and t-shirt while she tells me.

"The stuff that you know happened. It did. He, uh, was fighting that fire in Colorado, and, um, y'know, went to push the other guy out of the way of some timber he saw coming down, like I think you must've heard about…"

She glances at me. I nod. She goes on.

"So, yeah, all that happened, but uh, yeah, that's… that's not how he died."

She doesn't look my way and I don't say anything. She sits down on the ground, putting on her shoes now.

"Uh, all that did was, like, um, crush his spine, but it didn't kill him. But the other guys couldn't drag him out right away because there was so much fire and shit raining down around them that every time they'd get close, they'd have to back away. So, y'know, the whole time he's trapped under this burning, like, fucking, whatever. So y'know, he's just stuck there, inhaling smoke, fire burning through his turnout gear. Through the moisture barrier and down to the thermal layer, so basically he's just being baked like a potato in tin foil—I know all this stuff because the doctors and everybody explained it to me."

She's tying her shoes.

"And so finally they got to him and somehow, like, somehow, he was still alive, and they got him out of there, and actually got him to the hospital, and got him into surgery right away, and... Oh, and so we got there like the next morning, and uh, and we were there for… ten days? I guess? Two weeks almost? Whatever. And so..."

She's standing now. Putting on her jacket.

"So he had a couple skin grafts, and like there was some discussion about how to repair his spine and if it could even be repaired, and how traumatic it would all be given the severity of his burns, and of course the whole time his lungs are filling with fluid and having to be drained and filling again, and…"

She pauses for a breath.

"...And, uh, so... So, yeah, so on like day ten or twelve or whatever it was, after watching this all happen, mom and dad were out of the room, and I was sitting alone with him, and watching him on the oxygen, and unconscious, and all of it, and it just seemed like fuck, y'know? Like even if he comes out of this there would still be this, like, insane, impossible mountain to climb. And it just seemed...

fuckin'... cruel to ask him to do that. And selfish. I mean the doctors wanted to save him because that's their job, and the other firefighters wanted to save him because that's their job, and like me and mom and dad wanted to save him because… Because of US. Right? Like WE wanted to keep him. But, shit, even if he *could* make it… What kind of life is that? And look, I dunno. I dunno what Scotty would've wanted if it was the other way around and it was me, or mom, or dad, or... You... Laying there. But I figured I'd just let him know that... Just give him the chance to decide what he wanted to do for himself. Because, you know. Scotty… If Scotty thought he was doing something for other people he'd just keep doing it, and I wanted him to know that he didn't have to. So... When it was just me and him, I leaned in, and I told him, 'It's OK. You don't have to keep going. It's OK. You can stop climbing now, Scotty..."

She's facing me. I'm shirtless. Pants unbuttoned. Stone faced. Stoic. Unblinking. With tears rolling down my cheeks and getting lost in my beard.

"...And so, y'know... He did. He stopped. His lungs collapsed right at almost that very moment, and he flat-lined, and I stood in the corner while they rushed in and tried to revive him, and failed, and called the time of death, and that was it."

She pulls the back of her hair from inside the collar of her jacket and flops it out so that it spills over her shoulders, and drops her hands to her sides.

"That's how Scotty died."

She says it with a shrug in her voice, its casual nonchalance a punch to my chest. And the look on my face must say everything because she follows up with…

"You asked."

MADDIE

I now know what it looks like to rip Tyler Morgan's world out from under him.

A couple weeks ago I was planning this moment—I mean, if he was gonna stick around making my life hell, make me think about those last few days I spent in the hospital with my brother every time I looked at his handsome, bearded face, then I was gonna make him relive it with me.

But now, after getting it all out, and not in any of the overly dramatic ways I'd planned—like punching him in the teeth when I had to say the part where they dragged Scotty out of that forest alive, or kicking him in the stomach when I had to say the part about Scotty being in the hospital—and I even left out the fact that he looked… well, there's no word to describe what Scotty looked like in the end. Not a word that's supposed to describe a human, anyway. So now, after getting it all out in the most calm, unaffected, unemotional way possible, it occurs to me that this might've been worse.

I think I just kicked Tyler in the balls and stomped on his face as I walked away.

No, my angel says. *Stomped on his heart.*

"I'm sorry," I say.

Tyler shakes his head, his face wet with tears, then swallows hard and says, "Why?"

"I'm… I should've been more careful in my delivery. I know you didn't know. And it's not something that should be said so casually, but—"

"No, why didn't you tell me this in the letters?" His eyes are searching mine. Like there's some elusive answer inside me that will explain everything.

Would it have made a difference? I almost say. But I don't.

I shrug.

He's still searching for that answer in my eyes.

It's not there.

So I sigh and consider his question. Because he probably deserves an answer. And maybe I should stop trying to punish him. I mean, I'm not over the fact that he just bailed out when I needed him. But is staying angry about it helping?

It's not helping *me*, that's for damn sure.

"Well," I say, stalling for time so I can pull my thoughts together. "I didn't want you to come home…" *Shit.*

Tyler raises an eyebrow.

"I mean, I *did* want you to come home. But I didn't want to you to come home for…"

The other eyebrow goes up. "Maddie, just say it already."

I let out a long breath and the truth comes with it. "I didn't want you to come home just for Scotty. OK?" I stare at him. Hard. Then soften. Swallow. "I wanted you to come home for *me*."

"Oh," he says.

"And maybe I felt a little selfish for that?" I shrug. "For wanting you, when Scotty was the one who was dying. And… well—"

Tyler has me wrapped up in his arms before I can even finish that sentence. He hugs me tight, his chest warm and hard. His embrace is everything I wanted seven years ago when I was standing in the corner of Scotty's hospital room watching him die.

And then I'm there. In that spot. Stuck in the corner. Just watching the whole thing play out. The beeping of the machines, and the shouting, and my parents…

Stuck.

Then it's gone. As fast as it came, it fades. The beeping stops. The chaotic voices wither away with the passing seconds and I'm right where I am. Wrapped up in Tyler's arms, just the way I wished I was on that day.

Does it matter that it's seven years late?

Does it really matter?

I decide no. It doesn't. Because he's here now. And late is always better than never.

"I'm sorry," he says.

I wipe the tears off my face. Look up, then wipe his tears away too. Our eyes lock and this time I think he finds the answers he was looking for. I know I do.

"You know, sometimes things just happen." I shrug. "You stayed away because you needed to at the time—"

"It was a mistake," he says.

But I put up a hand. "No. No. Maybe it wasn't. Maybe this turned out exactly the way it was supposed to."

"You stripping and me crazy?" He laughs that off because… yeah. Truth.

I huff out a breath of air, kinda loving this—hating the topic, but loving this all the same. Because at least it's real. At least we're being honest. At least I'm not angry anymore.

I don't know why I suddenly seem so Zen about things, but there it is.

Relief.

"I'm not angry at you," I say. Because I feel the need to say this out loud. "I'm not angry at anyone. Anymore," I clarify. Because clearly anger *was* my problem. Even Other Guy Ricky called that one. "I guess… I guess it's just over now."

"I get it." He sighs. There's a lot of hidden meaning in those three words. Things he's done, regretted, gotten past somehow. And now it's my turn.

I lean up on my tiptoes to kiss him. Enjoy the way he slips his tongue into my mouth. The little twisting motion he makes. The way our lips fit together.

It's a soft kiss.

A touching kiss.

A forgiving kiss.

And when we break apart, we are more together than ever.

Outside the night air is cool. And there's a little bit of wind, which makes the drone weave and dip.

I'm watching Tyler control it. My head tilts left with the drone when he barely misses the dirt hill surrounding the parking lot, then bobs right as he skims past a light pole.

"Tyler!" I say.

"I got it," he says, thumbs busy pressing on the touchscreen. But then the drone does some move out of a World War II dogfight where they aim straight for the ground. Maybe I made that up. That cannot be a real move because—

"Jesus!" I say, grabbing my hair. My twelve-thousand-dollar drone is gonna—

"It's cool," Tyler says. The drone pulls out of the nosedive and resumes flying, very low to the ground. But now it's all wobbly and shit. Off balance or—

He pulls it up just before it smashes into the concrete barrier in the empty parking lot.

"I thought you said you know how to fly this thing!"

He says nothing. Like he's concentrating really hard on flying. It goes high—very high. "There we go," he says. "Let's start the cameras—"

But then Tyler's whole body weaves right, like he's the drone, which also dipped right, because it barely missed one of those huge towers electrical plants tend to have scattered all over the place.

"OK, I think we have enough," I say, biting my nails. "Let's bring it home."

He sucks at drone flying. Which kinda makes me feel, you know. Proud.

Tyler's chewing on his lip. Which is goddamned adorable. Most of the time. Just not now, because it means he's trying really hard not to crash.

I ease my hands over his, my thumbs finding the controls on the touchscreen. "Here," I say. "I got this."

I expect a fight, but he just lets me have it.

"You're really good at drone flying," I say.

"Fuck you." He laughs.

"Seriously. That dogfight you were having out there with the wind was impressive." I wink at him as I steady the drone and bring it in for a landing in the middle of the parking lot then drive it over to us and make it stop a few feet away.

"Showoff," he says. "But it's sexy as fuck, Mads. Makes me hard when you do cool, kick-ass shit."

I swell a little with that compliment. "It's nice to know that I can do something better than you."

"Hell," he says, pulling me in to his chest. He's been like that ever since we came up from the tunnels. All touchy-feely. I love it. Makes me think we're like... a couple. "I'd put my money on you versus me every day of the fuckin' year."

He kisses me on the head, then breaks away to walk over to the drone.

Yeah, I think I love him.

Wait. Did I just—

Yup. Fuck it. "Tyler Hudson Morgan..." I say. "I think you might be that one special guy a girl meets and wants to keep forever."

He's bending down to pick up the drone when that comes out. He stands up, his back to me. Pauses. Takes a deep breath.

For a second I feel like that person who wrecks a new relationship by saying the L-word too soon.

He lets that breath out and turns to face me, looks at his feet and shakes his head.

My heart beats fast. Like it knows I really just fucked this all up.

"Madison Clayton... I... it... we..." He walks over to me, puts each of his hands on my cheeks, holds my gaze for what seems like forever, and says, "There's no one else it could've been."

CHAPTER NINETEEN

TYLER

"Shit," says Maddie, looking through her purse.

"What's up?"

"Can't find my house keys. Diane and Caroline are gonna be about done with me, I think. We already had to change the locks once after all my shit got taken with my car." She looks at me pointedly.

"I—What? It's not my fault!"

"*You* picked me up and left my car there."

"*I* did. Got it. OK. Sorry that your free will was malfunctioning that night."

She smirks and says, "Suck a dick."

"Is that what you're into?" I smile at her and bounce my eyebrows.

"Dork," she says.

Holy shit, this is great! I feel so… Normal. I can't believe it. I mean, if I step back and try to look at everything, I can't believe all that's happening.

Mostly because it feels…good. I've been pretty much on the run for the last dozen years, trying to find I dunno what. This. This feeling. And then, suddenly, here it is. I found it back where I started.

Shit. That's so hilariously cliché that it's cliché to even point out that it's so cliché. But fuck it. It is what's happening. And I don't feel like running now. So I'm just gonna sit back, enjoy it, and not examine it too closely. In my hard-learned experience, when things aren't all FUBAR, it's best not to think about them too much and just let 'em be.

I'm shit at doing that, of course. Letting things be. But I'm going to try. Because right now everything is… nice. Which is a word I've never used to describe anything ever before.

Which is also nice.

Fingers snap in my face.

"Where'd you go there, buddy?" Maddie asks. I must've been rambling. But I can tell I'm smiling, so I don't care.

"Nowhere. Sorry. What's up?"

"The club. We have to swing by Pete's. I need to see if I left them there."

"You wanna just come stay at my place and we'll find 'em later?"

"You mean stay at *Evan and Robert's* place?"

"You say tomato, I say my place."

She smiles. "Nah, I should go home. But you go out and get your own place and I will be there every night. I'm sure it'll be nicer than where I live."

"Well, that is very much incentivizing me to buy sooner than later. Damn, girl. You *ARE* really good at real estate shit!"

She shakes her head and rolls her eyes.

I'm an absolute scamp.

Everybody says so.

At this hour of the morning and at the speed I'm driving, it only takes about twenty-five minutes to get back to Vegas, but Maddie's already dozing off next to me. Of course she's exhausted.

It's been a long life for her so far.

I so much love looking at her sweet face with her eyes closed like that that I have to be careful not to drive us off the damn road.

"Mads." I reach over and nudge her. She stirs and opens her eyes.

"Shit, I fell asleep," she says.

"Wakey, wakey, eggs and bakey," I chime. Which makes me realize I'm hungry. I'm gonna get some eggs, I think. Possibly also bakey. We'll see.

"Wow." She yawns, looking at the sky through the windshield. "The sunrise is amazing."

"Yeah?" I ask. I hadn't noticed. I glance ahead to see what she's seeing.

Except I don't.

I don't see the sunrise.

What I see is early morning sky beginning to lighten from darkness, rousing itself from sleep, but the orange hue being cast onto the canvas of dawn isn't coming from an emerging sun. It's coming from something else. Something familiar.

"We're headed west," I mumble to myself.

"What?"

"We're headed west," I say louder. "That's not the sunrise."

"Whatayou—?" She doesn't get out the word 'mean' because she can now see clearly what I'm talking about.

It's Pete's. Pete's Strip Club. Pete's Strip Club in Las Vegas, Nevada. The place that brought me and Maddie together and back into each other's lives. Pete's Strip Club, owned and operated by one Pete Flanagan.

Pete's Strip Club that is, at present, being swallowed whole by what looks like a raging tornado of flame.

Oh, my God.

The inferno ahead that's gobbling up the building belches fire and smoke into the air. It is not the dawn, but the way the fire colors the dissipating blackness of the night in a surreal red haze offers a beautiful, ghastly imitation of it.

"What the fuck?" she whispers.

I don't say anything, just press down on the accelerator and propel us faster in the direction of the roaring conflagration.

As we approach, the swirling lights of fire engines come into view. There are four of them. All have their hoses out and aimed at the searing structure that just a few hours ago was a place called Pete's. But not anymore.

We pull up as close as we can get before the cops also in attendance stop us. Maddie throws open the passenger door, jumps out while the car is still rolling to a stop, and is past the police and skittering by the camera crews from the local news stations before anyone can even attempt to stop her.

I throw the Defender in park, jump out, and have to push my way past a policeman who tries to hold me back. I hope he doesn't think he's gonna shoot me or arrest me or anything. That would totally suck. The night's been going so well. Well, until now.

I don't recognize the firemen I see. Looks like they're from a different engine company than Evan's. But then, from behind, I spy a guy in full turnout gear who apart from wearing fifty pounds of shit and walking towards death itself otherwise looks like he's out for a stroll in the park. Not like he doesn't care—everything he's doing has an urgency and efficiency to it—but there's no panic or anxiety coming off him at all. His composed stillness in the midst of the roiling mayhem all around makes him stand out like a blue marble in red sand.

"Dean!" I yell in his direction. He turns in time to see Maddie streaking toward the blaze. (What she thinks she's going to do when she gets there, I have no idea.)

Dean steps to intercept her and stops her before she can melt her face off.

She's shouting almost incomprehensibly.

I can't hear what he's saying to her from where I am, but in my mind it's something like, "Hey, now. Relax, baby. Dean's got it. Everything's gonna be allllll right." (Apparently, in my mind, Dean has become Barry White.)

As I land where they're standing, I see that New-Guy Brandon and Baby-Face Jeff are also here. The guys at their station rotate shifts, so the fellas with them are unfamiliar to me. Faces I've maybe seen, but names I don't know.

"What the fuck, man?" I ask of Dean over the cacophony going on around us all.

Maddie's incomprehensible shouting continues.

"Dunno," he says. "Call came in. The cleaning crew showed up to do their thing and I guess shit was already burning when they got here."

"Thank God," I say. "At least nobody's inside."

And that's when it finally becomes clear what Maddie's been trying to sound out. "Pete!" she screams.

Her shout draws the attention of Jeff, who trots over to hear what's up.

"What?" asks Dean.

"Pete," I say. "He's the owner." I turn back to Maddie. "What about him?" I ask her.

"He basically lives here! I know he supervises what the cleaning crew does! Where is he?"

Oh, shit.

"Fuck," I mutter. "Did you clear it?" I ask Dean.

He shakes his head. "Nah, man. When we got here there was another crew on the scene. They said the cleaners told 'em the place was closed and that they didn't know if anyone was in there but they didn't think so."

"And they didn't fucking check?" I ask in astonishment.

"Shit was already lit up when they got here, man. They just got right to trying to contain it."

Maddie's still yelling and waving her arms. It's hard to make out the words, but not at all hard to understand what she's saying.

And then…

All of the sudden—and fuck, you can goddamn see it fucking coming…

"I got it!" shouts Jeff.

He slaps his visor down and goes tearing inside, through the wall of fire.

Doesn't put on his tank, doesn't even *consider* the best way to breach, just goes racing inside. I guess because, in his mind, he has to.

"Yo!" Dean calls after him.

And then…

Without a word, Brandon throws his oxygen tank on and rips off inside too. After Jeff. Heavy 44. That's where Brandon came from. The ones who rescue the rescuers.

Maddie turns to face me and buries her head in my chest. I don't know what else to do, so I stroke her hair as she cries all over my shirt.

The cop I blew past to get here rolls up, but Dean pulls him aside and seems to be explaining the situation. He's persuasive.

The hoses all around us are blasting full tilt, four crews of firefighters all working diligently to bring things back under some version of control. But the hoses seem to be doing almost nothing. It strikes me that we were just, not a half hour ago, embedded within more than enough water all around us to snuff this candle out in about ten seconds flat, and what a shitty irony that is, but whatever. It makes no difference now.

And then…

Without warning, there is an explosion.

I have no idea where it comes from, apart from somewhere within the building that is no longer a building, not in any meaningful sense. Upon hearing and seeing it, I flinch. Thankfully, Maddie flat-out jumps and shrieks so that she can't see me react the way I did. I don't give a shit because of my dumb fucking ego or whatever, but because it's clear in a real vivid way that I'm gonna need to be here for her, and I can't afford to allow my *feelings* to get in the fucking way right now. Even if they're authentic.

"What was that?" she screams.

"I dunno," I tell her in as soothing a voice as I can find. "Could be a lot of things."

And while that's true, I honestly can't imagine what could have caused a fireball like that to erupt from in there. It's a fucking strip club, not a chemical plant.

And then…

The roof collapses.

"No!" Maddie's wail rips through me.

"It's OK, it's OK," I assure her.

It's not OK. Not even a little bit.

And then…

As the fire swoops around on itself and swallows its tail, like some kind of cannibalistic swan of flame, Brandon emerges.

Carrying a limp Jeff over his shoulder.

The curtain of fire sweltering all around them makes it look like he's stepping out of the River Styx. I imagine.

"Crash!" shouts Brandon with an urgency I couldn't imagine his voice having.

Someone comes wheeling a crash cart over and Brandon tosses Jeff's ragdoll frame onto it as a paramedic cuts open his gear and starts warming up the paddles.

(Jesus. Is this what it was like when they had to come for me? I feel like an asshole. And then I feel like an asshole for thinking about myself right now.)

"What happened?" yells Maddie. "What happened to him?"

Brandon pulls his helmet off. Bends over. He's drenched with sweat. He takes a hit of oxygen. Then, gulping breaths, he says, "Smoke. And a… Dunno… Beam… Or something… Hit him in the head. He…" He stops saying the most words I've ever heard him speak, takes up more oxygen, and the sweat around his eyes creates the illusion that he's crying. I think it's an illusion.

And as I look over and see them pull off Jeff's helmet, I observe the blood that has baked itself onto his baby face.

Maddie is barely holding together. Given everything I just found out this evening, so am I. The parallels are impossible to ignore.

"Pete?" she now coughs out. "What about Pete?"

Brandon shakes his head.

"What does that mean?" she bellows. "He wasn't there?"

Brandon raises his eyes to meet hers, stands up straight, and shakes his head again. "No… He was."

And then…

Paroxysms of tears from Maddie. Only word to describe it. Shaking, convulsive paroxysms of tears as she collapses to the ground in a heap.

I start to go to her but I first ask Brandon, "What—?"

But once again, he just shakes his head and eyes me. *You don't want to know,* the eyes say.

Fuck. Fuck! FUCK! And he's right. No. I don't wanna know.

Time slows in combat. Everybody knows that, even if they've never been in combat. It's the same thing that happens in, say, a car accident. There's always that moment when shit gets preposterously slow for no good reason, the brain dialing it all down a notch because it can't hold onto the events in real-time.

As I look toward the smoldering heap that they're just starting to get under control now that the roof has collapsed, everything about it washes over me in half-time. The people running, the lights flashing, the world burning. It's kind of… beautiful.

That's a real oxymoron about fires and explosions and stuff. They're so destructive, but that destruction brings with it its own kind of poetic beauty. The same way a rose bursting into full bloom just means it's that much closer to wilting and dying.

The combustible force of life is a wonderful, amazing thing. But it comes at a cost. The comforting thing about that, to me, has always been that then, finally, after the price is paid, and the fire that drives us all forward is extinguished, we finally get to rest.

And, as I watch the cinders rising, turning all that was there into ash, I think of Pete.

Pete Flanagan. My friend. Thanks for everything, man. Go. Go be with her

again. Rest now.

Or maybe it's what I *have* to think to put enough of a spin on it to keep from having the glue that's barely holding me together melted clean away by the heat of everything happening at the moment.

And then…

"Clear!" someone shouts as they put the defibrillator against Jeff's bare chest.

I glance over at him again and see that his chest is stronger than I would've thought. Just because he seems small, I suppose. Even though I suddenly realize he's not really. But his chest is smooth. Young. I remember the smoothness of his hand when I gave it a shake a few weeks back.

I don't know why I think of that now.

"Clear!" whoever shouts again.

Doesn't matter.

I know death when I see it.

I've observed enough of it.

They can keep trying to shock him back to life all they want.

Jeff's gone.

He's gone.

Goddamn it, kid.

Part of me wants to just go make them stop, but they're already loading him in the EMT truck to, I suppose, keep giving it their best.

I've said it before… People fighting the inevitable always gives me the hardest time. But if it makes them feel better to try, who the fuck am I to stop them? They need to believe, so let 'em believe, I guess.

And there's absolutely no fucking time to even begin thinking about all the shit I'm starting to think about. Maddie's coming undone and I need to be there for her.

I pat Brandon on the shoulder and he nods at me like, *Go.* And so I do. I go to Maddie, who's still crumpled on the ground in the parking lot.

"Hey—" I start, but she waves me off. That's fine. I get it. I mean, damn, I really just wanna try to fix it. But I can't. So I'll stand here and see if I can not get in the way.

And then…

Like out of fucking nowhere—and this is probably the last thing in the world I'm expecting—her phone dings.

This is not something I should be able to hear. There's so much going on that the dinging of a cell phone shouldn't even register. But it does. I dunno why. But it does.

She has an odd look on her face. I can't describe it. Not in words. But if I had to try I'd say it looks pained, defeated… knowing, I guess.

She pulls her phone out of her jacket pocket and, sure enough, the screen is lit.

She looks down at it, slowly.

And then…

She throws it to the ground, balls her hands into fists at her sides, looks up at the dawn-breaking sky being kissed by tendrils of hot orange and sooty black…

And she lets loose a guttural, primal scream that begins in the center of the earth, rips its way through her body, past her breaking heart, out of her mouth, and up into whatever bullshit heaven sits in the sky, where a bullshit God looks down laughing, having broken his promise to me that I was being given the chance to repair the damage I created.

That was never the deal.

I get it now.

I am back here to be forced to watch Maddie suffer.

Because I missed it all the first time.

Fuck you, God, you lying cunt.

I pick her phone up off the ground to see what it was that affected her so.

It's a text.

It says…

"U got 3 weeks. Nowhere left to hide, bitch."

CHAPTER TWENTY

MADDIE

I don't see the fire. I don't see the men trying to put it out, or the trucks, or the hoses, or the ambulance, or the police.

I don't even see Tyler. Or Evan, once he gets here.

I see the text.

Tyler has my phone, so I'm not looking at it. But it's burned into my mind like a brand.

This was Logan.

We wait there, just watching the responders do their jobs, Tyler and me together. He's devastated, his arms around me in a constant hug—a need for support just as much as it is supportive.

New partners. Everything was so great and now…

Now Pete and Jeff are dead. Burned alive. In a fire I—

I stop myself there. I was gonna say *caused.*

But fuck that. I didn't do this. I didn't kill Scotty, I didn't kill Pete, and I didn't kill Jeff. I don't owe Carlos Castillo shit. Tyler will not pay that motherfucker back. I will not pay that motherfucker back—

But then things slow down. Stop, maybe. Everything around me goes still. Sounds recede with my vision. I no longer hear the deafening roar of water spraying onto the flaming building. The sinister crackling of things burning goes silent. The shouts of men go unheard as…

An idea forms in my head.

That's right, Devil says. *That's what you need.*

That's all I hear.

Him.

Me. That part of me that fell.

But not the sad part. Not the defeated part. Not the part that always loses, no matter how hard I try.

You have a bad temper. Ricky Ramirez said in that car the day he drove me home from Carlos Castillo's compound. My temper is my problem. That's what he said.

No. It's not. My temper isn't my problem. My problem is Carlos Castillo and his stupid henchman, Logan. My problem is that I let him believe I owed him. My *problem* is that I *didn't* lose my temper with him, I went along. Let him lead me down a path that resulted in this outcome.

Two people dead.

I wait for her. That angel inside me. So she can pop up and make her case. It's a long wait, I think. Time has stopped, so I'm not really sure, but it feels long. Like she's wrestling with her options. Her feelings. Her rage.

Revenge, my devil says. *That's what you need. Revenge.*

He's been wrong before.

This is probably a very bad idea.

But I am the reigning queen of very bad ideas these days.

So I pull myself back from the edge. I rein in the rage, the fear, the desperation and the sadness. Sounds of fire, and water, and men return. I see the building, collapsed into a pile of charred beams and broken walls. I see the flashing red lights of trucks. I see Evan, standing in front of us, talking with Tyler. I look at them. Each of them. See the truth written on their faces. Both of them overfull with miserable reality.

And I make a decision.

I do owe Carlos Castillo something after all.

Payback.

End Of Book Shit

You've been here before… you know the drill. The EOBS is the part of the book where Johnathan and I get to say anything we want about it. Process, themes, where it came from… shit like that.

Well, this time we're doing it a little different. We decided to ask each other three questions about the process and just go from there.

Johnathan is up first! My questions to him were:

1. Since this is now your second novel, did you notice it felt different to write book two, versus book one?
2. What did you learn about yourself as a writer? Like… did you notice your style evolved?
3. What is your favorite thing about writing Tyler's character?

And so, without further ado, here's Johnathan…

1. Since this is now your second novel, did you notice it felt different to write book two, versus book one?

It doesn't really feel like a second novel because it's the same world, same characters, and a continuation of the story. It feels rather more like I'm writing a massive novel spread over four major acts (as in playwriting – what we're doing is kind of like a big four-act play).

I think what feels different is that *Sin With Me* was an introduction of characters to the reader – the book was very much constructed to be that – so in *Angels Fall*, we now have to deliver on the promise of book one. So it's almost like writing *SWM* felt like a really great and successful freshman year, and the last thing you want to fall into is a sophomore slump, so I suppose my expectation of and approach to the work was maybe a little more rapacious.

Insofar as there was an urgency present that didn't feel as palpable in the first book. Because the first book was almost like an experiment, right? Like, "Let's try this and see how it goes." And when it felt like it went well, there's that self-imposed responsibility to replicate that successful experience.

Now, as I write this, *Sin With Me* has yet to be released, and so who knows how it will be received. But that's not what I mean when I say "successful." I mean it felt like a successful artistic endeavor, and so that's the only measuring stick I'm using. And honesty, it's the only one I really care about.

Which is, of course, bullshit.

I very much care about how readers respond. It is for readers that I am doing this. But when all is said and done, I'm the one in the mirror when I brush my teeth, so I'm the one I have to live with ALL the time, and I'm the one who has to feel proud about what I've made. And if I feel that I've done the best possible work I can, in whatever the medium is I'm working, that's what lets me sleep at night.

There's a great TED talk by Elizabeth Gilbert, the author of *Eat Pray Love*. It's on YouTube. Check it out if you haven't. It's all about "genius." The idea of it. The premise of it. The burden of it. And she discusses the onus an artist puts on him or herself when they feel an obligation to replicate an achievement. At the end of the day, she concludes that success or even "good work" is not the creator's to own. Because the creator isn't really. Not really the "creator," I mean. I am not the source. The universe is the source. And if I get lucky and the special gift from the universe (in this case the story, the book) lands in my brain, then I'm fortunate. But it's not mine to claim.

Now, let's be clear, this is also an easy way to divert responsibility if you make something shitty. ("Wasn't me. The universe made the shitty thing and I just handed it over.") But if, in the striving to create, one can free oneself from the responsibility of *having* to make something perfect, then you actually liberate your mind to find the specialness hidden inside of what you're doing. The work can breathe. And that's true for just about all of life.

So, I'm not sure that answers the question, but that's how it felt.

2. What did you learn about yourself as a writer? Like… did you notice your style evolved?

Although I'm an actor first and these are my first proper novels, I've been writing for a long, long time, so my style/my voice is pretty firmly established. But the thing about writing in the first person is that the voice is the voice of the character you're writing. So stylistically, I suppose there's something about Tyler and Maddie's voices that steer me and not the other way around. Y'know, I'm eager to see how the tone of the next books we have planned after the *Original Sin* series emerge and change.

I can say that I have learned, quite frankly, I can write much more quickly than I ever thought possible. Writing a series of books to be released in the tight time frame we have for this series has been a real test of my ability to do fifty things at once, if nothing else. Because I'm also still working on my other two careers (acting and producing/writing television), I have every moment of every day filled with something active. Which I'm not complaining about. It's amazing.

I have never been good with downtime. Someone asked me recently what my hobbies are, and I was like, "what's that now?" I'm lucky enough to practice my hobbies for a living, so with the addition of novel writing to my résumé, I get to wake up every day with something creative to focus on.

That said, MAN WE'RE WRITING A LOT OF BOOKS QUICKLY.

So I suppose this entire experience is teaching me to be patient and at the same time urgent. Which sound like contrary skills, I suppose. But when melded together become something akin to efficiency.

Y'know, truth be told, I'm learning something about myself as a writer that I always knew, but is being reinforced: I'm willing to die for an idea I believe in. You learn very quickly in television to pick your battles carefully. Not everything is precious and not everything is worth saving. In the parlance of TV writing (and probably other writing too) it's known as "killing your babies." Which is macabre as fuck, but ideas do feel like babies. Things that have been birthed from your brain and that feel precious. So picking and choosing what to stomp your feet about and what to roll over on is a talent you have to cultivate.

All that said, if there's an idea or plot point or character attribute that I believe in strongly, I will burn down the whole fucking village if I have to in order to defend it. And I hope that I do that sparingly enough that it doesn't become white noise. I value my writing partnership with Julie exceedingly much and honoring and respecting that partnership while at the same time standing fast behind my passionate opinions is something I think I'm maybe learning how to balance even more than I already knew.

Because working with Julie is something that I think I'm going to be doing for a long time. And like any long-lasting relationship you need to grow together. Not as one.

That's fucking stupid. I hate it when people say dumb shit like that. Because forfeiture of your own personality and sense of individual passion isn't collaboration, it's co-dependence. But growing as individuals on parallel tracks is crucial for longevity and what I aspire to in all the relationships I have that are worth keeping.

I guess I also learned that I can be honest with someone I'm working with and that vulnerability strengthens the working relationship. Laura, my wife, is the only person on earth who knows me almost as well as I do. I am completely and unabashedly myself with her at all times. I owe her that. I said vows and shit to that effect. (Actually... Truth be told... We had a Conservative Jewish wedding ceremony, so the whole thing was in Hebrew. Laura and I joke all the time that neither one of us are completely sure what the fuck we vowed to do. Or if we're even really married. The rabbi could've just been fucking with us. Anyway.)

But after Laura, Julie knows more about me and sees more about the person I am than probably anyone else on the planet. And that shit has happened quickly. And that's fucking intense. But we're making work together that's intense, so the relationship has to be brazen.

And I guess that even though I'm a cold-blooded motherfucker who doesn't trust anybody... I trust her. And that's something I've learned about myself as a writer, and a partner, and a person. I can trust more than just one other person on this planet. I can trust two. So, good. Quota's all full. Now I can stop trusting people again. Phew.

3. What is your favorite thing about writing Tyler's character?

I don't have one thing about Tyler that I like. Or Maddie either for that matter.

I love everything about both of them.

Years and years ago, I was acting in a play at Lincoln Center in NYC. I was in rehearsal one day, figuring out the character, and the director gave me a simple note that changed my entire life. He said: "Don't judge him."

That was it. Probably one of a dozen notes he handed out that day, but for me it was just about the most important thing I had ever heard. Because what that note actually meant was "don't *think* about what the character is doing, just *do* it."

And that translates into writing, big time. Write your characters. Don't judge them.

So when I'm writing inside the minds of Tyler or Maddie, I'm just going on the journey with them. They're leading me. Sometimes they'll do shit that I'm totally not expecting. At the end of the third book in this series, Tyler does something that I was not expecting at all. I was just writing and the next thing I know this thing was on my computer screen that I hadn't planned. The structure of the journey and the scene stayed the same, but Tyler's behavior in it was totally unanticipated by me. And shit, if I'm surprised, the readers most likely will be too.

I can tell you a moment that happened in this book that's like that: Way back in book one, *Sin With Me*, in the chapter where Tyler and Maddie connect up for the first time, there's a bartender who calls Tyler "chief." Tyler goes off on a mental rant about how he hates it when people call him "chief." He says he's not sure why, it just rubs him the wrong way. And I didn't have a specific reason for writing that back then, it just felt right and I knew that it made sense.

Then in this book, in the chapter after Maddie and Tyler have sex in The Four Seasons on Thanksgiving, they run into Tyler's estranged father in the lobby. And even though that's a Maddie chapter, I was tasked with writing that portion of this book because Julie had her hands full with other work and in order to keep our deadlines, I had to take the first pass at it. Which we can do with each other because for the most part, everything's been plotted and outlined, and Julie and I know what's going to happen in each chapter. But the tiny details, the nuance, that's found in the moment. So while I knew that we were about to meet Tyler's dad, I didn't know exactly how that interaction would go.

So when Tyler's father didn't recognize his son and then leaned into him and said, "Didn't catch your name, *chief...?*" I actually gasped. I remember it vividly. I was writing on an airplane, and I leaned back in my seat, put my fist up to my mouth, and gasped. Because I discovered WHY Tyler feels a way about something that I knew he did but didn't know where the origins of his feelings came from. Until that moment.

So that's my favorite thing. That magical discovery. And it's not just restricted to Tyler. It's every moment of everything that happens. There's a bunch of moments like the one I just described in this book (and all of them), but I won't inundate you with them. I'll just say that as Julie and I are writing this series, thus far, nothing feels forced and there are many magical moments that are causing us to feel, like the Elizabeth Gilbert TED talk, that we are just the conduits. We are not the controllers of this saga.

It is simply passing through us on its way to you. And we hope you love reading it as much as we have loved writing it.

Because without you, there would be no need for us.

My thanks, my love, and my unceasing gratitude to you all.

-JM
11 February 2018

And now it's my turn. :) Johnathan's three questions to me are:

1. Now that you're several books into this partnership process, has working together been harder, easier, or about what you expected?

2. You're working simultaneously on jointly written books and solo work. Can you keep all the stories in your head at once, or do you have to parse out time for each?

3. At this point in the Huss-McClain adventure, the TV series version of THE COMPANY is getting closer to happening every day. Does it feel exciting? Nerve wracking? Still too far from being real to feel like anything yet?

JULIE

1. Now that you're several books into this partnership process, has working together been harder, easier, or about what you expected?

I think it's both easier and harder at times. Like… when it's easy, it's VERY easy. And when it's hard, it's VERY hard. I don't know if that makes sense, but so many things we've done together just come naturally. Like writing the TV pilot was incredibly easy. And Sin With Me was incredibly easy as well.

Since I'd never written a screenplay before (and no idea how to even start to do that) Johnathan took lead on that. And it was all very satisfying for me because I'd already written the story. The world was mine, the characters were mine, all the dynamics between the characters were mine. And Johnathan didn't try to change that at all. I mean, I'm gonna be honest and tell you that the STORY is different. Certain things that happened in the book have been changed, but never once did I hesitate about it. It all felt right. Throughout the entire script-writing process I felt that Johnathan and I were one hundred percent making The Company a BETTER story.

And the best part of writing The Company was filling in the details of scenes I only hinted at (like when Harper kills everyone on her birthday) and expanding that into a real scene. Because I never wrote that scene in the books and it turns out, when we were finally "done" with the pilot, it ended up being the first scene. We had started the writing process thinking the scene with James and Sasha out on the prairie was the first scene, but it got bumped because the Nick and Harper on that super yacht was so just… EVERYTHING. So fantastic!

So when we started writing Sin With Me I took lead because, let's be honest, I've done this a shitload of times. Just like he was the expert script-writer, I was the expert romance novel writer. And it went pretty easy. At least FOR ME. Lol Because Johnathan let me take lead and adapted his style to mine. Which I was grateful for.

But when it came time to write Angels Fall, I could see that he was maybe struggling a little to adapt to my "easy-going" style. Like when I write, if I fuck something up, I let it go until I'm done. Because I'm me, I know what I did wrong, I know how it needs to be fixed, and when I'm writing alone, the most important thing is to just… KEEP WRITING!

Writing with a partner changed all that. I mean, he can't read my mind. I wish he could, but he can't. And I knew it was kinda driving him crazy that I would just fuck shit up in the story and tell him to worry about it later, ya know, like I usually do when I write alone. So we agreed to try his style for book two.

Johnathan is kind of a perfectionist. And I don't mean that in a bad way, but he doesn't like to make mistakes. He likes to get it right. So for this book when I'd fuck something up he didn't let me say, "Later." He wanted it fixed. Which was a hard adjustment for me. So when things got hard, they got REALLY HARD. It's like… we have no middle, we're either cruising along and everything is perfect, or we're at full stop because we're having issues.

I'd be lying if I said it's been perfect, but I'm not lying when I say I wouldn't change a thing. Not one thing about how we write, or what it took to come to an understanding, or anything. Things worth doing require effort and we are a thousand times better because of our disagreements because we're honest about working things out. But all relationships require WORK. And all the work we did on our writing relationship (and friendship too) paid off in the end. We're more committed now than we were yesterday. We're better writing partners today than we were last month. And we're better friends too.

I think Angels Fall is a GREAT book. I love it so much. It might be my favorite of the series, although I love them all. I think Maddie came into her own in Angels Fall this is the book that made me fall in love with her.

2. You're working simultaneously on jointly written books and solo work. Can you keep all the stories in your head at once, or do you have to parse out time for each?

It's pretty easy for me to keep the stories straight once I'm actually writing. Because I write in first person I AM the character I'm writing. So, for example, right now I'm writing The Pleasure of Panic as my solo book. And when I'm Issy Grey or Finn Murphy, I'm THEM. I know how they are, what they're doing, and where they need to go. And when I'm writing Maddie and Tyler, I'm THEM. And so it's pretty easy for me to switch between stories because what I'm really doing is switching between characters.

The one thing that IS very difficult is finding TIME to write all these people. :) But Johnathan has been a champ about this part. He has been really great about it. So thank you, Johnathan. I appreciate that more than you know.

3. At this point in the Huss-McClain adventure, the TV series version of THE COMPANY is getting closer to happening every day. Does it feel exciting? Nerve wracking? Still too far from being real to feel like anything yet?

It's still kinda unreal to me. I mean, I was in London a couple weeks ago and I had to have a call with the entertainment lawyers about the book rights for the TV series deal and just listening to them explain things to me was both exciting and scary. (I'm in good hands, so don't worry about the scary part!) So it's starting to "become" more real as time goes on, the negotiations get further along, and the reality of what it will really mean if we make it to the finish line sinks in. And at the end of the call my lawyer says, "So, do you feel good about this"?" My answer was, "I have no clue what I'm doing." And he replied, "You're in London to sign books for fans who love you, so you know exactly what you're doing."

And I appreciated that little reality check. Like… it's OK. I'm doing fine. We're gonna figure this out together. So… yeah, I'm a little excited. And once we hammer out this initial deal and sign those papers I'm gonna be very excited because that's when I get to TALK to people—important people—about what I created. About what Johnathan and I BOTH created when we took on this new project. And yeah, if it all goes through I'm probably gonna cry with happiness. Because these characters in The

Company are REAL to me. And being able to see them come to life on TV, and follow them, and fall in love with them all over again—I have no emotion to really describe how that will feel, I just know it will be amazing.

THANK YOU, ALL OF YOU, for being a part of my life and going on all these journeys with me. I started this new Huss/McClain partnership with YOU GUYS in mind. So I hope you're loving this new period of my writing career as much as I am.

--JH
March, 6, 2018

Johnathan and I would like to thank all of you for reading our second book together. We hope you enjoy it just as much as all the books I wrote alone. Actually, we hope you like this better. :)

And if you've got a minute, and you liked the world we created, and the story we told, and the characters we gave life to… then please consider leaving us a review online where you purchased the book.

We are not traditionally published – WE ARE INDIE.

And we rely on reviews and word-of-mouth buzz to get our books out there. So tell a friend about it if you have a chance. We'd really appreciate that.

Much love,

Julie & Johnathan
www.HussMcClain.com

About the *Authors*

Johnathan McClain's career as a writer and actor spans 25 years and covers the worlds of theatre, film, and television. At the age of 21, Johnathan moved to Chicago where he wrote and began performing his critically acclaimed one-man show, Like It Is. The Chicago Reader proclaimed, "If we're ever to return to a day when theatre matters, we'll need a few hundred more artists with McClain's vision and courage." On the heels of its critical and commercial success, the show subsequently moved to New York where Johnathan was compared favorably to solo performance visionaries such as Eric Bogosian, John Leguizamo, and Anna Deavere Smith.

Johnathan lived for many years in New York, and his work there includes appearing Off-Broadway in the original cast of Jonathan Tolins' The Last Sunday In June at The Century Center, as well as at Lincoln Center Theatre and with the Lincoln Center Director's Lab. Around the country, he has been seen on stage at South Coast Repertory, The American Conservatory Theatre, Florida Stage, Paper Mill Playhouse, and the National Jewish Theatre. Los Angeles stage credits are numerous and include the LA Weekly Award nominated world premiere of Cold/Tender at The Theatre @ Boston Court and the LA Times' Critic's Choice production of The

Glass Menagerie at The Colony Theatre for which Johnathan received a Garland Award for his portrayal of Jim O'Connor.

On television, he appeared in a notable turn as Megan Draper's LA agent, Alan Silver, on the final season of AMC's critically acclaimed drama Mad Men, and as the lead of the TV Land comedy series, Retired at 35, starring alongside Hollywood icons George Segal and Jessica Walter. He has also had Series Regular roles on The Bad Girl's Guide starring Jenny McCarthy and Jessica Simpson's sitcom pilot for ABC. His additional television work includes recurring roles on the CBS drama SEAL TEAM and Fox's long-running 24, as well as appearances on Grey's Anatomy, NCIS: Los Angeles, Trial and Error, The Exorcist, Major Crimes, The Glades, Scoundrels, Medium, CSI, Law & Order: SVU, Without a Trace, CSI: Miami, and Happy Family with John Larroquette and Christine Baranski, amongst others. On film, he appeared in the Academy Award nominated Far from Heaven and several independent features.

As an audiobook narrator, he has recorded almost 100 titles. Favorites include the Audie Award winning Illuminae by Amie Kaufman and Jay Kristoff and The Last Days of Night, by Academy Winning Screenwriter Graham Moore (who is also Johnathan's close friend and occasional collaborator). As well as multiple titles by his dear friend and writing partner, JA Huss, with whom he is hard at work making the world a little more romantic.

He lives in Los Angeles with his wife Laura.

JA Huss never wanted to be a writer and she still dreams of that elusive career as an astronaut. She originally went to school to become an equine veterinarian but soon figured out they keep horrible hours and decided to go to grad school instead. That Ph.D wasn't all it was cracked up to be (and she really sucked at the whole scientist thing), so she dropped out and got a M.S. in forensic toxicology just to get the whole thing over with as soon as possible.

After graduation she got a job with the state of Colorado as their one and only hog farm inspector and spent her days wandering the Eastern Plains shooting the shit with farmers.

After a few years of that, she got bored. And since she was a homeschool mom and actually does love science, she decided to write science textbooks and make online classes for other homeschool moms.

She wrote more than two hundred of those workbooks and was the number one publisher at the online homeschool store many times, but eventually she covered every science topic she could think of and ran out of shit to say.

So in 2012 she decided to write fiction instead. That year she released her first three books and started a career that would make her a New York Times bestseller and land her on the USA Today Bestseller's List eighteen times in the next three years.

Her books have sold millions of copies all over the world, the audio version of her semi-autobiographical book, Eighteen, was nominated for an Audie award in 2016, and her audiobook Mr. Perfect was nominated for a Voice Arts Award in 2017.

Johnathan McClain is her first (and only) writing

partner and even though they are worlds apart in just about every way imaginable, it works.

She lives on a ranch in Central Colorado with her family.

85032696R00171

Made in the USA
Lexington, KY
27 March 2018